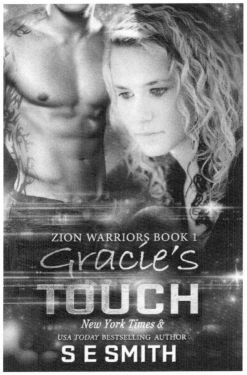

By S. E. Smith

Acknowledgments

I would like to thank my husband Steve for believing in me and being proud enough of me to give me the courage to follow my dream. I would also like to give a special thank you to my sister and best friend Linda, who not only encouraged me to write, but who also read the manuscript.

—S. E. Smith

Science Fiction Romance
GRACIE'S TOUCH: Zion Warriors Book 1
Copyright © 2012 by Susan E. Smith
First E-Book Published July 2012
Cover Design by Melody Simmons

Synopsis

Gracie Jones was little more than a child when the Earth was invaded by an alien species. Escaping into the subway tunnels of New York City, she hid in fear of being captured. Discovered by four men who became her protectors, she fought alongside them, and they became known as the Freedom Five. At seventeen, she made a decision that turned the tide in the war between Earth and the Alluthans, but in exchange, she gave up all that she knew.

Kordon Jefe is a Zion Warrior and the commanding officer in charge of the Confederation of Planets' military. When an unknown species begins attacking some of their outer settlements, he is assigned to discover who they are and stop them—at any cost.

Gracie finds herself stranded millions of light years and hundreds of years in the future in a distant galaxy on an undeveloped moon. When an old enemy threatens once more, she does not hesitate to use her knowledge to try to stop them once again. Only this time, it is not just Earth she will be saving, but the Confederation itself.

When their two worlds are thrown together, Kordon is unsure what to do with the strange, delicate creature who fights and behaves unlike anyone he has ever encountered before. One thing he does know—he plans to keep her.

Contents

Chapter 1

"Good morning, good afternoon, and good evening to all the citizens of the world. This is Gracie, reaching out to touch each and every one of you with love and hope. The Freedom Five, along with groups from around the world, are pushing back against the Alluthans. Forces around the world have freed thousands of captives over the past several weeks. Over two hundred Alluthan fighters have been destroyed in the past week. Our fight for freedom is heating up, and we expect a breakthrough soon, so don't give up!"

Gracie Jones leaned into the microphone attached to the bank of computers and continued sending out news, stories, and hope to the millions of listeners in fifteen different languages. She spent at least three hours a day during different times, sending the messages out. Adam worried it would open them up to attacks if the Alluthans traced the signal, but Gracie was a master at bouncing signals off the satellites the Alluthans hadn't destroyed.

She was just ending her broadcast when Chance came in. One look at his face and she knew he was furious. She also knew what the cause was, Adam or Adrian had finally told him about her plan. She winced when she looked at his face again. The confrontation about to come was not going to be a pleasant experience.

"This is Gracie's Touch signing off," Gracie said in a husky voice filled with emotion.

* * *

Fifteen minutes later she was ready to scream. She'd known it was going to be difficult, but she'd never expected it to be this difficult! She turned to Adam, pleading silently for his help.

"It's the only way! I'm the only one who can do it," Gracie said again, looking intently at the four men standing around her. "There is no other way."

"Like hell there isn't!" Chance said fiercely. He jerked away from Adam, who grabbed at him.

"Chance..." Gracie began.

"He's right, Gracie. There is no way in hell we are going to let you do this," Mark said.

Gracie sighed again in frustration. "Adam, you talk to them. You know I'm right."

Adam watched as Gracie rose gracefully from the chair in front of the row of computers. He shut his eyes briefly in an effort to get control of the rage burning inside him. He knew she was right, but he didn't want to be the one to admit it. Adam opened his eyes and looked at his younger brother, Adrian, who hadn't said a word throughout the whole argument. He had the same look of resignation in his eyes.

"Gracie is right. She is the only one who can do this." Adam spoke quietly but with authority. As the leader of one small group of New York rebels known as the Freedom Five, it was up to him to make the tough decisions. He wasn't sure he would be able to live with some of those decisions if they survived the fight for their freedom.

Five years before, Earth had been invaded by a group of ugly-ass aliens. There had been no warning, no promises of peace, nothing. The half-organic/half-robotic aliens had simply begun gathering up as many humans as possible and placing them in huge holding camps protected by a shield of some kind.

Millions perished from lack of food and medical care. It was later learned, thanks to the work of computer hackers—or geeks as Gracie liked to be called—that the aliens were planning on using the humans as renewable parts for their own deteriorating forms. The Alluthans were experimenting on the captive humans to test their limitations and compatibility.

Gracie lost her parents and an older sister when the aliens first attacked New York. Adam, his brother Adrian, and two other survivors, Chance and Mark, found her hiding in the old subway system six months later.

She had escaped with her laptop and some external hard drives, and had managed to tap into one of the maintenance room's access points to monitor what was happening. The governments of the world finally banded together to fight the threat, but not before a devastating number of humans had died or were lost in the large alien holding camps.

Gracie was the youngest daughter of two university professors at NYU. Her ability to understand computer languages, and languages in general, was unbelievable. By fifteen, she had mastered eight different languages fluently and another seven on a conversational level.

She also used her skills at deciphering computer-generated languages to stay one step ahead of the Alluthans. For the past two years, she'd focused on studying the language and computer applications of the Alluthans so she could find a way to defeat them.

Adrian looked at his brother with a tense frown on his face. "You know it is suicide. She'll never make it out."

"That's not true!" Gracie said, turning to frown at the four men towering over her petite five-foot-four frame. "I have an excellent chance of escaping."

"And how, pray tell, do you figure that?" Chance growled, folding his arms across his massive chest.

"Chance, I can speak, read, and write their language. I've been studying it extensively, as well as their computer applications. Team Two has one of their supply ships in the old warehouse down by the river thanks to me. All I have to do is program it to autopilot to the mother ship.

"Once on board, I'll upload the programs I've developed to bring down the shields protecting all their bases and prisoner camps around the world. Once it has downloaded, I'll reprogram the ship to bring me back to Earth," Gracie said with a plea for understanding in her voice. "I know I can do this!"

* * *

Chance walked over and drew her against him, holding her close. She was the closest thing to family he had left besides the other guys standing with them.

He had lost his family also and had vowed to protect Gracie from the first time he saw her emerald-green eyes staring fearfully back at him in the dark tunnel five years ago.

He didn't want to admit for a long time that as she matured, his feelings for her grew beyond a brotherly love. At seventeen, Gracie was still too young. Chance was waiting as long as he could before he claimed her as his own, but he feared he would never get the chance to tell her how he felt about her.

"What if they find you? What if it doesn't work and you get trapped there?" Chance asked huskily as he held her against his hard length.

"They won't. It will work. I've double and triple-checked the programs to make sure they would work. You saw for yourself how the shield collapsed, and I was able to take control of the ship and bring it down. The alien didn't have a clue about what was happening," Gracie said as she wrapped her arms around Chance. She wanted to give him reassurance, but she also needed it herself.

"When do we do this?" Adrian asked.

"Tomorrow morning," Adam replied. "We've received confirmation from around the world that everyone will be ready."

Mark nodded. "You better come back, little britches, or I'm going to be mighty pissed at you."

Gracie smiled softly before replying. "I will, Mark. I will."

* * *

Gracie slowly walked into the bathroom and stared at her reflection. She tried to calm the trembling in her hands as she pushed her short, thick strawberry blonde hair away from her face so she could wash without getting it wet. Gracie wouldn't say she was beautiful—more like cute.

Her hair was cut in a bob that came to her chin; her eyes were too big and a deep, dark green. She had a short, button nose and lips just a little on the full side. She was very pale from having spent most of her time underground in the subway tunnels of New York. She was also very petite for her age, but that was mostly due to not having very much food for too many years.

The guys had finally set up grow lights in one tunnel, and they grew what they could. Mark had been the farmer of the group, having come from the Midwest in search of survivors. Chance knew a little, but that was mostly because of the pot plants he used to grow when he was a teenager.

Adam and Adrian were native New Yorkers used to the mean streets. They were the fighters of the group and had been instrumental in saving the lives of each of them on more than one occasion.

Gracie watched as her hair swished around her face as she leaned forward and drew in a deep breath. She tried to sound confident about what she was about to do, but in reality she was scared to death. She wasn't sure it was going to work, and she knew if it did, there was an excellent possibility she wouldn't survive.

She figured it would be a one-way ticket, but she also knew that if the guys knew that, they would never let her go. If there was a chance they could turn the tide of this war and defeat the aliens, she was going to take it.

The only reason she was the best candidate for this mission was because if the aliens figured out what she was doing and tried to stop her, she had a chance of counteracting their programming.

So, scared or not, she was it. She washed her face and brushed her teeth before pulling on a comfortable pair of worn jeans, an oversized T-shirt with a picture of New York on the front, and slipped into her running shoes. She grabbed some personal items and shoved them into her oversize leather bag along with an extra shirt and her hoodie.

Last, she grabbed her tablet PC and chargers. Looking around for the last time at the little bed set up against the stone wall, Gracie pulled aside the blanket she used as a door and walked down to the main staging area.

Chapter 2

Adam, Adrian, Chance, and Mark were waiting for her by the time she got to the center area they used as a main living quarter. Chance helped Gracie up onto the platform, then stood back as the other six men who made up Team Two looked her over.

"Not much to you," one of the men said before he spit on the floor. "Maybe if they catch you they won't think there is enough of you to eat. You sure as hell aren't big enough for parts."

Adrian, who was standing slightly to the left of the man, turned in a blur of motion and struck the man in the jaw, sending him to the floor on his ass. "Shut your mouth!" he snarled, clenching his fists tightly. "She is risking her life to do something no one else can, you piece of shit. Give her the respect she deserves."

"And don't spit on the floor. This is our living area," Gracie said as calmly as she could.

The man's words had sent a shiver down her spine. They frequently received reports that the aliens were using humans for parts to repair the damage to their own organic bodies. Gracie didn't want to think of her family ending up that way.

Chance could sense how the words of the man upset Gracie, and it took everything in him to not just kill the bastard right then and there. He walked over and pulled Gracie close to his body, trying to give her what little protection and support he could.

* * *

"Gracie," Chance called out quietly a few hours later.

Gracie and the guys had gone over the plans again with Team Two before calling it a night. They looked over every aspect of what they were about to do. It was essentially Gracie's plan.

When she'd first worked out the programming to not only disarm the shields protecting the Alluthan spaceships, but also to override their system and bring it down using a simulator, she had been ecstatic. If a worldwide, systematic coordination of attacks could be organized, then it was possible to turn the tide of the war and possibly even bring it to an end.

It took over two months for Gracie to finally convince the four guys it was a possibility, and that only happened when she took over the supply ship now down in the old warehouse. The Alluthan on board had had no idea that it was not following a direct order from the mother ship.

Once Gracie proved she could override, control, and operate one of the spaceships, Adam began communicating with other rebel forces around the world through the ham radio and low-frequency signal setup.

Gracie knew she would never be able to sleep after the other team left. Crocker, from Team Two, said he would have the things she would need on the supply ship for her arrival at five the next morning. Everything was ready. Now she sat listening to the communications going on back and forth between the different bases of the Alluthans on the ground and the mother ship.

That is where their downfall will be, Gracie thought. *They put all their eggs in one basket, or in this case, one ship.*

The Alluthans believed the humans too primitive to attack them in space. Everything was run from the mother ship—all communications, orders, even power was distributed from there. If it was destroyed, then all their resources were gone.

Gracie started when she heard Chance's voice call out to her. Turning, she watched as he came into the small computer room the guys had set up for her. She couldn't help but smile as she watched him. She loved him so much. She had since the first time she saw him five years ago. His gentle touch had drawn her out of the alcove she was hiding in, and his strong arms made her feel safe.

She knew he loved her too. She'd tried to act upon their love six months ago, but Chance had said it was not the time. He had made a promise to Adam to wait until she was eighteen before he claimed her as his. She had argued, but Chance remained firm. Adam was the father figure to them all, and they respected him.

Adam wanted to make sure she was old enough to understand her decision. Gracie did understand. She also understood life could be short. With considerable reluctance, both she and Chance agreed they would wait until she was eighteen to act upon their physical desires.

Now, it looked like their love would become another tragedy in history—for she knew deep down she was never coming back. In a way, she was glad they had never made the final commitment to each other. Perhaps it would be easier for Chance to move on.

Gracie knew she would always regret not forcing the issue for her own selfish reasons, as she would have loved to have that memory to take with her when she died.

Gracie forced a smile on her face and rubbed the tears away as she looked at Chance's worried face. "Hey, Chance," she said in a husky voice filled with emotion.

Chance heard the tears she was fighting so hard to push back. Rushing forward, he wrapped his strong arms around her tightly. He pulled her close, holding her like he would never let her go.

"Let me go with you," he whispered against her forehead. "Let me go with you, and we can both come back. I'll tell Adam that you need me."

Gracie squeezed Chance close to her and closed her eyes. "You can't. I'm good, but not that good. The Alluthans scan each ship for heat signatures. If they pick up two signatures in a supply ship designed for one, then they will destroy it before it ever gets near them.

"Besides, Adam needs you here to help with the attacks. You are supposed to take out the camp holding my parents and sister. You promised to see if they survived," Gracie said, looking up into Chance's eyes, pleading with him not to argue with her.

Chance slid his arms up and gently cupped Gracie's face between his large palms. He pressed a kiss to her lips, groaning when she opened to him. Tonight could very well be their last night together, forever. Chance briefly thought of his promise to Adam, then thought, *To hell with it*. Gracie was his.

"Come with me to my room. Let me love you, Gracie," Chance murmured against her lips.

Gracie was torn between wanting to push Chance away from the hurt she knew he was going to feel when she was gone, and her own selfish desire to grab what little life she had left. The feel of Chance's hand on her breast made the decision for her. She would be selfish and take what little happiness she could with her.

* * *

Chance squeezed Gracie's hand as he pulled her after him out of the alcove set up as a computer room. He hated that he could not give Gracie a real bed for her first time or even the promise of a full night. Instead, all he could give her was a small pallet on a cold stone floor and a few hours at best. He resolved to make it the most beautiful experience that he could for her. She deserved that and more.

They had almost reached the area he claimed as his own when Adrian came running up to them. He was breathing hard and looked pissed as hell. Chance instinctively pulled Gracie closer as his stomach knotted. Something had happened, and it wasn't going to be good.

"Fighters are headed this way," Adrian blurted out. "Word is they are going to level this part of the city, including the holding camps."

Gracie gasped. Her parents and sister, if they were still alive, were in the holding camp. If the Alluthans took out the warehouse down by the river, then their chance of bringing down the mother ship would take much longer and more lives would be lost.

"I have to leave... now," Gracie said. "When are the fighters expected?" she asked as she pulled away from Chance.

"A couple hours at most," Adrian responded grimly.

Gracie nodded and looked back at Chance one last time before turning to follow Adrian. "Gracie," Chance said hoarsely knowing his time with her was coming to an end.

"I love you, Chance," Gracie said, letting one of her hands run up and over his cheek as a single tear coursed down hers. "I always will."

* * *

The next hour was a blur as the teams worked together to get everything in place. All those who could be evacuated were in areas outside of the attack zone. Gracie reviewed the instrument panel of the supply ship and hooked up her laptop to the control panel. The software program she developed quickly uploaded. She designed a type of dump upload, so the program uploaded immediately, then unpackaged. This made it easier to get all the files on the system as fast as possible.

Gracie nodded to the men from Team Two as they began filing out of the supply ship. Crocker looked at Gracie for a long moment before saying anything. Gracie waited patiently for him to say what he had to say.

"You know, if you succeed you'll be a hero. If your program does what it is supposed to do, you'll have saved the Earth and millions of lives," Crocker said gruffly.

Gracie smiled at the big man with the gruff voice. "I don't want to be known as a hero. Just as another human who refused to give up or give in. I couldn't have done this alone. It took everyone..." Gracie's voice faltered as her throat thickened with tears at the thought of all the senseless deaths, "... everyone who has lived and died over the past five years to get to this point. I just hope it works. I'm tired of being afraid," Gracie ended softly.

Crocker leaned down and brushed a kiss across Gracie's forehead. "It is Gracie's Touch that has given all of us the hope of seeing that day. Take care, little girl, and come back home."

Gracie nodded as she watched the big, gruff man walked off the ship. She turned all the way around and watched as the four guys who she considered her closest family walked onto the ship. Adam was first, followed by Adrian and Mark, with Chance coming up in the rear.

"You stick with the plan. If you have any problems, if you get even the weirdest feeling, you abort and get your ass back planet side, do you understand?" Adam said sternly.

Gracie smiled as she watched his Adam's apple move up and down. It was the only way to tell when Adam was upset about anything. "I understand. I will, I promise."

Adam hugged Gracie tightly to him and kissed the top of her head. The thought of never seeing her again and being the one to give the order for her to complete this mission was killing him inside. His arms tightened for just a moment before he released her and walked out without a backward glance.

Adrian cleared his throat. He was the quietest one of the group and held his emotions close to his heart, never letting on he felt anything. He stared down at her for a moment before saying anything.

"Come back," he ground out before brushing a kiss across her cheek and turning to follow his brother.

Mark looked down into Gracie's eyes and smiled. "Come home to us, little britches," Mark said gently as he pulled Gracie into his arms and rocked her gently back and forth for a moment before kissing her on the lips. "Come home for Chance."

Gracie's eyes filled with tears as she felt Chance's arms come around her and pull her away from Mark. She turned and buried her face in his strong chest. She wanted to remember what he felt like, what he smelled like, everything about him. She wanted...

needed… this memory to give her the strength to turn away from him and leave. Gracie bit back a sob that threatened to escape. It wasn't fair! She should be looking forward to having a future with Chance, not leaving him. She loved him so much.

"Gracie…" Chance choked out. "I… Don't do this. Stay. We can find another way to defeat them." Gracie was about to respond when the ground shook from an explosion several miles away. The attack had begun. She forced herself to pull away from Chance and looked up into his eyes one last time.

"I have to do this. Go on, go, while I still can. Go, Chance, please," Gracie begged.

"Chance…" Adam called out from the platform. "Let her go. We need to move now."

Chance growled out his frustration as he crushed his lips to Gracie's in a brief, hard, passionate kiss filled with love, anger, and pain. "Come back to me, Gracie. You fucking come back to me," Chance bit out harshly before he turned and walked down the platform.

Gracie pushed the control to close the platform door, watching as Chance slowly disappeared from her sight. She blew one last kiss to all the guys and smiled before the door closed, sealing her fate forever.

Chapter 3

Gracie moved into the pilot's seat and strapped herself in. She could feel the vibrations from explosions, but ignored them as she set the supply ship's course for the mother ship. She opened the front view screen panel so she could watch what was happening as she left the Earth's atmosphere. The supply ship lifted off smoothly and moved rapidly upward following Gracie's pre-programmed coordinates.

Gracie looked in dismay at all the destruction to New York. She could see the fighters in the northwest highlighted against the fires burning from their attack. She prayed everyone was able to evacuate in time. In moments, she was thrust back against the seat as the supply ship went through the Earth's atmosphere.

As the blackness of space engulfed the small ship, Gracie got her first look at the mother ship. She stared at it in a combination of awe and despair as she saw how enormous it was. It had to cover at least the size of Manhattan alone!

Gracie knew if larger ships were coming, the Earth would never stand a chance. She needed to destroy this one. If she could take down the mother ship, it would not send for additional ones.

From what she was able to learn from the files she had accessed, these ships traveled great distances alone, one mother ship and its "offspring"—meaning the fighters, supply ships, and ground forces. If a planet was found to contain an abundant amount of resources, then the mother ship would send for more. If not, it would use what it needed before destroying the planet and moving on to the next one. Gracie needed to destroy it before it decided on either option.

* * *

She listened as the supply ship gave the needed code for admittance to the mother ship for refueling. As soon as the large panel doors opened on the outer edge of the ship, Gracie patched into the computer system through a backdoor she'd discovered a couple of months ago. The Alluthans were getting better at closing the doors, but they were still arrogant enough to think the humans too primitive to learn their language, much less their computer codes.

Gracie left a digital copy of her notes on deciphering both for Adam. She wanted to make sure all her work over the last five years was not wasted. That was one nice thing about having parents who were researchers, they believed in taking notes and showed their children how to do it also.

Gracie smiled as the virus she uploaded finished. It was a simple one that grew every time it was uploaded to another system, changing its signature to make it more difficult to detect. It would wipe their system clean once finished. The Alluthans would lose control of everything.

Gracie watched as the supply ship connected to a docking port, and an arm extended, recharging the fuel cells. She monitored the activity, frowning when she heard a disembodied voice on one channel, giving directions for the attack on specific sites around the world. They were pinpointing some of the major areas where the rebels were.

Patching into the channel, she watched as the programmed instructions flooded her screen. She frowned again as she focused on the rush of data scrolling down it. Her breath caught as she picked out keywords.

Typing quickly, she began redirecting the fighters to other areas away from the original commands. Most of the areas were over open water and shouldn't pose a threat to humans.

A warning flashed at the bottom showing a probe flash as the intrusion was detected. Gracie glanced at her other screen. The program to disarm the Alluthans defense systems was almost complete. It was spreading, but not as quickly as she wished. Gracie quickly typed in a few commands and watched as the warning faded.

She continued uploading one code after another, determined that if the Alluthans found and stopped one virus, they would not be able to stop them all. She uploaded the last one and looked at the power-cell indicator. Refueling was done, and it was time to leave before they opened the platform to begin loading and found her.

Gracie punched in the release code and waited anxiously until she heard the sound of the fuel arm disengaging. She hit the program that would take her home with a sigh of relief.

Maybe, just maybe, I will get to be with Chance, she thought as a wave of hope swept through her.

She felt the thrusters kick in as she started to return the same way she had come, and was almost to the open panel doors leading out into space when a voice came on over her audio com. She listened as it gave a command for her ship to return to the docking port.

Gracie punched in a command to override the auto-command when the operator tried to take over her controls. She listened as the voice came over again.

"Supply ship 100982 return to docking port 2-225."

Gracie smiled as she saw her programs kick in. She had an ace up her sleeve if she needed it, but she needed to be far enough away when she dealt it not to get caught in it.

Gracie flipped the audio and gave her announcement to the millions of resistance fighters on the Earth far below. Gracie's eyes gleamed with tears as she gave the command that would hopefully bring this war to an end.

"Good morning, good afternoon, and good evening. This is Gracie reaching out to touch you with love and hope. Today the people of Earth are ending the siege of the Alluthans. Rise up and fight, for freedom is ours. This is Gracie's Touch saying, *Freedom for all!*" Gracie's husky voice called out to all the millions on the beautiful blue-and-white ball below her.

She watched as lights flared all over the globe as the united governments and rebel forces joined together and made a decisive assault against the aliens who thought them too weak to win.

Gracie was about to hit the button that would speed her way home when the supply ship shuddered violently, throwing her to the side. Gracie's eyes frantically flew to find the cause. She punched in the command to silence the alarms as she fought for control.

No fighters followed her as they were unresponsive due to the command to shut everything down. Gracie could see multiple failures occurring on the mother ship, but it would take longer for each system to completely shut down. The mother ship was turning to follow her. It sent out several bursts from its pulse cannons.

Her shields immediately came online, but the bursts took a toll on them, and they read eighty-five percent. Gracie felt dread seep through her. If the mother ship followed her and the self-destruct program activated, Earth would be in peril from the fallout. The only way to ensure the mother ship did not endanger the Earth was to lead them away.

Gracie quickly programmed a new route into the navigation system. Tears blurred her vision as she sent the command and felt the supply ship turning. She increased her speed, knowing it would not be long before the mother ship lost all power and the self-destruct initiated.

She braced her palms against the front console as another jarring jolt hit the supply ship. She was moving as fast as the supply ship could go without sending it into hyperdrive. The navigation panel said they were nearing Mars.

She didn't know if the signal she sent would make it to Earth or not, but she had to try to send one last message. She had to tell them she was sorry and say good-bye. Gracie opened the communications program and typed in the password for one of the satellites she used to send her transmissions.

"This... this is Gracie," Gracie waited a moment. She trembled as she continued. "Chance, this is Gracie saying I'm so sorry. I won't be coming home after all." Gracie drew in a shaky breath and forced herself to continue.

"I hope you get this message. I wanted to tell you I love you. I want... need... to thank all of you for saving me so long ago. Chance, you and Adam, Adrian, and Mark will always be with me. Please keep up the fight for freedom, knowing I'll always be with you every time you think of me. Th-this is Gracie, saying goodnight and good-bye, my love," Gracie ended the transmission as tears choked her and her vision blurred so badly she couldn't see anything.

Impatiently, she brushed the tears away. If she was going to die, she was going to take those pissant aliens with her. Gracie programmed the supply ship to enter hyperdrive and set the mother ship's navigation system to follow. She also set the self-destruct to half the time. Both ships would explode during the light jump making sure nothing else was damaged.

Gracie watched out of the front view as the stars seemed to blur together. Within seconds, she was pushed back against her seat. She closed her eyes and waited for the end. Everything seemed to slow as she felt the push from the mother ship as it exploded. The shockwave threw the ship forward with such force, the shoulder strap on the harness broke, throwing her forward. As darkness descended, Gracie drew a picture in her mind of Chance holding her in his arms and smiled.

* * *

Grand Admiral Kordon Jefe strode into the conference room in a dark mood, but his grim thoughts didn't show on his face. He'd just finished reading the report sent in on the latest attack by a new alien species on one of their remote mining planets. Everyone was dead and the planet stripped of most of its resources.

The last message received from the mining colony was sent two weeks before. Some imbecile captain on the remote station of Atphlon didn't think it important enough to investigate the emergency signals being sent out until two days ago. That captain was now washing floors on Atphlon as a private. Kordon didn't tolerate idiots under his command.

He didn't bother to nod to the other officers standing around the table waiting for him to sit first.

He moved to the chair at the head of the conference table and sat, pulling the data grid closer to review the information the frigate sent to the site looking for survivors. He already knew every detail in the report; now he wanted answers.

"What have you to report?" Kordon looked at his head of security.

Chief Bran Markus cleared his throat before answering calmly. "Two hundred and fifty-eight colonists dead or missing, any resource worth having gone, the colony destroyed. The source appears to be the same as before. We were able to get a brief glimpse of some of the attackers and one of their vehicles before communications were terminated." Bran nodded to a center screen displaying the mining foreman as he sent the distress signal.

"We are under attack by an unknown force. They... they have captured most of the men as they came out of the mines. All women and children have been killed." The man wiped his face as sweat dripped down it. "Those bastards have some type of shield we can't get through. We need immediate assistance." A loud explosion could be heard in the background. "Th-they've breached the complex headquarters. Th—" The transmission ended as screams filled the air.

Captain Leila Toolas, his chief medical officer, responded. "From the details I've been able to retrieve from the bodies left, whoever was there killed any female not able to reproduce and the young children immediately. From the list there were fifteen females within a breeding range unaccounted for. The men..." Captain Toolas paled as she continued. "The remains of the men show body parts missing. Limbs and internal organs were removed with surgical precision."

* * *

Kordon kept his expression blank as he took each report. He finally came to his communications officer, a Ta'nee. The Ta'nee were known for their language and communication skills. The rich red hair down the center of Lieutenant Mohan's head flared with different colors as she spoke.

"I have never encountered the language or signals recorded by the mining foreman. It was very perceptive of him to record the communications being transmitted. It will take time to decipher it as there is no known database to compare it to," Mohan said. The fur along her cheeks changing to a slightly darker color as all eyes turned toward her.

Kordon nodded, ignoring the changes. He knew the Ta'nee were very shy and did not like being the center of attention. He looked at each officer intently so they would understand what he was about to say. He had worked with all of them for the past twenty years with the exception of Mohan, whom he brought on board almost a year ago.

"I want answers. Find out if there are any signature marks from their ship. I want to know every ripple in space that has occurred in that region within the past month. Mohan, monitor all frequencies. Let me know if you hear anything out the ordinary.

"Toolas, get me a detailed report on the bodies. I want to know exactly what you know and what you think in the report. Bran, get me a report on the types of weapons that could have been used to cause that amount of destruction. I also want information on what types of shields they could have used. Report back in four hours."

Everyone stood immediately as Kordon stood and strode back out of the conference room. He walked over to the commander's chair on the bridge and gave the order to the helmsmen to proceed to the mining colony. He wanted to look at the destruction first hand.

* * *

Three years after crash landing

Gracie moved quietly, stalking her prey. It was a small creature not much bigger than a squirrel. She didn't know the names of any of the creatures on the moon she had crashed on—in truth, she didn't care... at least, not at first.

Gracie had woken up three years ago to the alarms sounding and a terrible headache. She finally managed to shut off the alarms resounding through the supply ship. She was amazed she was still alive.

When the computer indicated the supply ship had crashed on the surface of an unknown moon it took Gracie a minute to realize that something strange—besides not being dead—had occurred. It didn't matter how hard she tried, the response from the computer system came up the same—unknown. Gracie shut everything down except life support, even though the system verified the atmosphere was suitable for her life form.

A week after she landed she was finally so sick of being confined to the small supply ship she would have fought a bear to get out of it. Her first step onto an alien world should have been filled with trepidation, but Gracie was beyond that.

She was alone. She no longer feared death, but welcomed the possibility. A part of her knew she was grieving the loss of Chance. It took almost six months for her to finally talk herself into moving forward, and to begin stretching out of her comfort zone.

The first six months she stayed close to the supply ship. She focused on finding enough food to supplement the MREs Crocker had stowed aboard the ship. It was strange, but it was almost like he'd expected her to need them. Gracie didn't need much. She had gotten used to living on very little during the years they'd lived in the subway system.

As the months turned to years, she'd learned to hunt, gather, and forage for most of her food supplies. She often wondered if this was what early humans must have done and felt when they fought for survival. The moon had a few predators, but Gracie learned to avoid them. For the most part, they were primarily just small mammal-type creatures like the one she was hunting now. She made sure to only seek them out a couple of times a month so she would not reduce the population, although they seemed to be plentiful.

Gracie aimed the bow she'd made and let the arrow fly. It had taken her over a year to get any good with one. Gracie grimaced as she approached the dead creature. She still got queasy when it came time to kill and clean them though. It was only because she had no other choice that she did it. It was that or starve to death, which she'd come very close to doing.

She swung the bow over her shoulder and walked over to pick up the dead "squirrel." She would have protein tonight. Working her way back to the supply ship, she marveled at how fast the plants on the moon grew.

In the three years she had been on it, there'd never really been a winter. The coldest it seemed to get was in the thirties, if she had to guess. *Not near as cold as a New York winter,* Gracie thought before she could stop herself. She fought against the wave of sadness that flooded her. *This is why you shouldn't think about it,* she scolded herself.

Quickly, she pulled away some of the vines that threatened to cover the platform door before she walked down to a nearby stream. The water was good as long as she boiled it for at least five minutes first. She neatly and efficiently cleaned her supper and set it in a large container she used as a pot, to cook over the open coals of the fire she kept burning. Laser guns were good for starting fires, she'd discovered after several failed attempts to do it the Girl Scout way and in a fit of temper.

Several hours and one full stomach later, Gracie turned the supply ship's power on. She did a systems check at least twice a month to make sure the fuel cells were not leaking and to check for any communications in the area.

She felt comfortable that the moon was uninhabited except for her and the few creatures she saw. In three years, not a single space ship nor communication had been seen or heard. She figured she must have traveled at least a fifty-mile radius from the ship, and there was also no sign of additional life.

Turning on the power, Gracie set a random pattern for the computer to scan for any type of signal. She leaned back and carefully pulled the last picture of her with the guys out of the protective sleeve she kept it in. Gracie smiled and gently touched the tip of her finger to Chance's cheek. She wondered if they were all okay. She liked to dream Chance had found her parents and sister and moved on.

Perhaps the Earth was now free, and Chance had married someone else. He could have a child by now … one that looked like him. She imagined sitting with the guys, her and Chance's son or daughter on her lap, while the other guys cooked barbeque and drank beer. She remembered her parents having friends over and she and her sister playing with the other kids. Gracie was so focused on her daydream it took a moment for the sounds coming through the communication systems to register.

Gracie sat up straight in shock as the voices came over the system again. She didn't understand them, but she might be able to figure it out eventually. It sounded just like the chatter she used to listen to between the ham-radio operators. Her fingers trembled as she set the computer to record.

Gracie listened to the traffic for almost an hour before she made a decision. She could hear the different cadences and even laughter. Laughter was good, she kept telling herself. Looking around the small supply ship, she figured she had two choices— die alone on this small moon or try to find a way off it and back home. Either way, she would eventually end up dead.

Pushing the transmission button before she could talk herself out of it, Gracie leaned forward and began talking softly, hesitantly at first. "This is Gracie's Touch reaching out to anyone who can hear this. I am currently stranded on an unknown planet or moon. If you can understand this, please respond. I repeat... this is Gracie reaching out to touch any friendly ship who could offer assistance. If you receive this message and can respond, I need assistance."

Gracie repeated the message over and over before she felt she needed to power down for a while. The solar cells could power the supply ship's systems for a short period, and she wanted to conserve the power as much as possible. She would listen and try again tomorrow once the sun was up.

"This is Gracie's Touch saying goodnight," Gracie said before she shut down the system.

Her heart was pounding as she realized she had either done the smartest thing she would ever do or the dumbest. Only time would tell. Looking out through the front view screen at the dark forests slowly devouring her little home, she knew there was no going back.

Chapter 4

"Sir," Mohan said as she approached Kordon.

She forced herself not to twist her soft fur-covered hands together as she waited for him to acknowledge her presence. She fought back her reservations about approaching him with the information she had, but he had ordered any unusual communications be reported to him immediately. That was the only reason she broke protocol and made her way down to the engineering room.

Mohan flushed as another male crewman gave her an appraising look. The Ta'nee were known to be very sensual creatures. Mohan was only half Ta'nee, though. Her father was a human male from a distant planet called Earth.

Her mother and father met when he was doing research on the Ta'nee at their invitation. Her mother, one of the younger daughters of the chief, met and fell in love with him. Their union was a good one, producing many offspring. Most of her sisters and brothers preferred to remain on Ta'NeeWak, but Mohan wanted to explore more after learning about her father's history and the history of his world.

That information was what gave her the reservations she was having about approaching the admiral. Her father taught her the old language of his planet. Earth Standard was based on many of the words, but the message she listened to earlier was from the old ancient language no longer taught except to those who studied Earth's history. She did not know anyone else who spoke it except her father and her.

Kordon finished listening to his chief engineer before turning to Mohan. He knew she would never have ventured down to engineering if she could have avoided it. He let his gaze flicker over her. No one, including Mohan, would know what he was thinking. His face remained carved in a blank mask. He learned long ago not to reveal his emotions or thoughts to anyone unless he wanted them to think they knew what he was thinking. It was a good way to end up dead.

"Walk with me," Kordon said, moving without checking to see if Mohan followed. He waited until they were in the lift before he nodded for her to explain her presence.

"Sir, you asked to be notified immediately if I heard any unusual signals or conversations," Mohan began.

"I am assuming from your presence in engineering you found something," Kordon responded.

"Yes, sir. Over the past several hours there has been some routine communications between several long-range freighters. There was nothing unusual about their transmissions, signals, or any indication they were having difficulty from a foreign source," Mohan stated as she watched the numbers flash as they went up.

She tried desperately to ignore the scent of the man standing next to her. It was becoming more difficult the higher they went. She fought the shiver of desire that rippled through her as she remembered the feel of his strong hands against her fur-coated breasts.

They'd had one brief, incredible night of passion on a spaceport in the Cumin system before she transferred onto his warship, the *Conqueror*. At the time, Mohan didn't even know his name. They met in one of the local bars, and before she knew it, they were in her bed. Kordon was the best lover Mohan had ever had, and she was devastated the next morning when she woke alone.

Eight months later, she found herself commissioned to his ship. Kordon calmly explained he chose her because she was the best communications officer in the fleet. He also made sure she knew he did not fraternize with crew members.

Mohan was forced to bury her embarrassment and her desire for him. Unfortunately, she still seemed to have problems with her fur changing colors around him. He knew it meant she desired him and was trying to entice him. Fortunately, other crew members just thought it was natural for all Ta'nee as it seemed every one of them did it.

"What is unusual then that would force you to interrupt me?" Kordon asked impatiently. He had things to do. He still needed to review the reports from Toolas.

"There was another message being broadcast in the background using the same signal signature as the species that attacked the colony," Mohan said hesitantly.

Kordon's eyes swung around at that, narrowing. "Could you decipher it?"

Mohan nodded reluctantly. "Yes, sir, but it was strange. It was a call for help. I've translated it and sent both the translated version and the original version to your office."

The doors to the lift opened, and Mohan gave a sigh of relief. She waited as Kordon strode out of the lift heading for the admiral's office off the bridge. Kordon ignored the men standing at attention as he made his way to his office. Perhaps they finally had a lead.

* * *

Kordon sat down in his chair and swung around to his console. Pushing in a series of passwords, he accessed the files Mohan sent him. Within seconds, he heard the soft, lilting voice in the message. A shiver went down his spine as her voice seemed to touch something deep inside him. He ordered the program to restart and increase volume. Sitting back, he closed his eyes, trying to imagine the face behind the voice.

"This is Gracie's Touch reaching out to anyone who can hear this. I am currently stranded on an unknown planet or moon. If you can understand this, please respond. I repeat... this is Gracie reaching out to touch any friendly ship who could offer assistance. If you receive this message and can respond, I need assistance."

The voice was soft, hesitant at first, but gained in strength as the female repeated her request for help. Kordon frowned as he listened to the slight tremble in it, as if she was afraid. The voice sounded young, and the cadence was strange. He didn't understand what she was saying, though some of the sounds were familiar. It was her last words that held him transfixed to his seat.

"This is Gracie's Touch saying goodnight," the soft voice said before it faded away.

She sounded sad and something else. Kordon gritted his teeth. He didn't like that sound in her voice. A voice like that should never be sad or... heartbroken. That was it. She sounded like her heart was broken.

Kordon swung around and stood up. Walking over to the windows overlooking the darkness that surrounded them, he stood stiffly with his legs slightly parted. His mind played the message over and over.

The sound of the female's voice seemed to call to him, beg him to find her, protect her... love her. Kordon started as that thought passed through him. Love? He had heard of it. He supposed he had even seen it before in others. That emotion was as foreign to him as feeling fear.

As a Zion warrior and commanding officer in charge of the Confederation of Planets military, he did not allow emotions to be a part of his life. Zion warriors were bred to be fierce in battle, in control at all times, and nearly indestructible with an ability to heal rapidly and withstand great amounts of pain. That was why they were the officers of the Confederation of Planets.

While many of his crew came from other star systems, his fighting force all came from the Zion star system. Those were the only members of his crew he trusted implicitly.

"Have Lieutenant Mohan report to my office immediately," Kordon said to the computer without turning around.

Within moments Mohan was back in front of the only man who could truly scare her. "Yes, sir?"

"Explain the language the female is speaking. It is somewhat familiar. What history do you have on it?" Kordon asked, turning to face Mohan.

Mohan cleared her throat flushing as it came out as a purr. "The female is speaking an ancient dialect from a planet called Earth. It is on the outer regions of the Confederation and is rather isolated. It did not come to the Confederation's attention until one of their spaceships ventured into the path of one of the long-distance freighters back in 2198, Earth-year calendar.

"The language is taught only to those in charge of studying Earth history or those who want to listen to the old recordings from the Great Battle against an unknown species called the Alluthans," Mohan paused. She was hesitant to tell Kordon what her search came up with using her private archives.

Kordon kept his expression blank, but he could tell Mohan was holding something back. "Continue."

Mohan flushed again. "The name the female kept repeating sounded familiar, as well as the words she kept saying. I knew I had heard them before, but was unsure of where. I... have my personal archives with me. My father was very passionate about his home world and its history. I went through the copies and cross-referenced the name and keywords. But..." Mohan looked at Kordon, confused for a moment. "... it doesn't make any sense. There must be some mistake, but even the computer is giving me an incorrect reading."

Kordon fought to keep from reaching out and shaking Mohan. Why couldn't she just give him the facts he asked for without him having to drag it out of her? Breathing deeply through his nose, he waited as she worked out what she was hesitant to tell him.

"Earth history tells of the rebel forces that fought against the Alluthans. One group, called the Freedom Five, was made up of four males and one female. The female was called Gracie Jones. For several hours each day over the course of five years, Gracie would broadcast to the millions of humans fighting. She called it Gracie's Touch. She always ended her broadcasts the same way... except for her very last one which was received several days after the Alluthans were destroyed." Mohan said, wringing her furred hands together nervously.

"Why do you think the computer is giving you incorrect readings?" Kordon said as his gut tightened.

Mohan looked unsure for a moment as she responded. "I did a crossmatch of voice, rhythm, pronunciation, everything. It all came back with the same results," Mohan said in puzzlement.

"What were the results?" Kordon bit out impatiently.

Mohan's head jerked up at the change in tone. She couldn't remember Kordon ever speaking in anything but a cold, calm voice. Even when he'd made love to her, he spoke the same as he did if he was giving a speech or talking during one of their meetings.

"They came back as being Gracie Jones, the female member of the Freedom Five," Mohan responded.

Kordon felt the muscle in his jaw tighten as he forced his next question out. "What happened to the female?"

Mohan smiled sadly. "She was killed, but not before she saved millions of lives on Earth and brought about the end of the Alluthan invasion. She is credited with bringing down their shields. It is thought she was killed when the mother ship exploded."

Kordon nodded tensely. "Send me a copy of the files you have on her, including any images," Mohan nodded and turned. Kordon stopped her before she left to ask her one more question that was bothering him. "Mohan?"

"Yes, sir?" Mohan asked, turning at the opened door.

"You said her last transmission was different. What was different about it?" Kordon asked.

Mohan's eyes grew sad as she spoke the words that she memorized as a young cub. "She said, 'This is

Gracie saying goodnight and good-bye, my love,'"
Mohan waited a moment to see if there were any
more questions, but Kordon had already turned his
back on her. She turned and left, wondering if he
even realized she was gone.

Kordon stood gazing out the window again,
letting Gracie's final words echo through his mind.
He would know her voice anywhere if he heard it.
Her haunting last words shook him. He did not want
to think of the female with the voice he'd heard as
being dead.

He frowned as the waves of foreign emotion
washed through him, and hoped the image of this
long-dead female would lay them to rest. Kordon
unclenched his fists as his computer sounded, letting
him know he had new information available.

Moving almost with a sense of dread to his
console, he touched the screen and immediately the
file opened to reveal a young female with eyes the
color of rarest gems and a smile that knocked the
breath out of him.

Kordon gripped the armrest of his chair and sank
down slowly. His eyes absorbed every minute detail
of the female. His fists clenched in rage that
something so beautiful, so delicate should be
destroyed. Reaching out to touch the soft curve of her
cheek, Kordon was amazed to find his hand was
actually trembling as he gently stroked it.

* * *

Gracie was tired. She hadn't slept much the night before. She was worried about whether she should have sent out the message.

She spent the daylight hours working hard, hoping it would allow her to fall into an exhausted sleep. She hunted for fruit several miles away, gathered enough firewood for a couple of weeks, and cleaned the supply ship until she was sure it was shiny enough to be seen from outer space. Throughout it all, she forced herself to stay away from the control console.

By late afternoon, a storm developed, forcing Gracie back inside. She kept glancing at the communications console before finally giving up and switching it on. She let it rotate through the pre-set sequence, feeling dejected when she didn't hear anything.

Maybe last night was a fluke. Maybe no one was really out there, and it was all just her wishful thinking. Gracie fought a dozen battles with herself before deciding she needed to try to send a signal again. If no one heard it or responded, then she was in no worse shape than she already was.

Gracie leaned forward and began transmitting. "This is Gracie's Touch reaching out to anyone who can hear me. I am stranded on an unknown planet or moon. If you receive this message and can understand me, please respond."

Gracie repeated it several times before she let her forehead rest on the console. With a tired sigh, she pushed up to end the transmission. "This is Gracie saying goodnight to all."

"This is the *Conqueror*. I have received your message. Waiting for a response," a soft, accented voice responded just as Gracie was about to switch off the console. "I repeat. This is the *Conqueror*. I have received your message. Waiting for a response."

Gracie giggled as the first words she'd heard in three years came over the communication console. Her hands trembled so badly she had to shake them before pressing the transmit button. "This is Gracie. Who am I speaking to?"

Mohan turned and quickly told one of the men working next to her to get Kordon. "This is Lieutenant Mohan Ta'nee from the warship *Conqueror*. Please identify yourself."

Kordon came to stand behind Mohan. He picked up one of the headsets and nodded to her to continue. Mohan nodded as she waited for a reply.

"Oh, this is Gracie. Gracie Jones... from New York," Gracie said with a nervous giggle. "I don't suppose you know where that is, do you?" Gracie asked hesitantly.

Mohan sat back in shock as she listened to the reply. Kordon growled impatiently for her to continue. Mohan jerked forward. "Yes, Gracie Jones. My father taught me of the place you call New York." Mohan looked frantically up at Kordon, not sure how much information she should give.

Kordon leaned down and growled quietly into Mohan's ear. "Lock on her location. Ask her where she is and who is with her."

Mohan nodded again. "Gracie Jones, can you specify your location and number of beings with you?"

Gracie bit her lip as she looked out over the dark surface. "I'm alone. I'm not sure where I am. The computer keeps coming up with unknown. I think the navigation system was fried when I crashed," Gracie replied.

"How long ago did you crash, Gracie Jones?" Mohan responded.

"According to my calculations it's been three years, eighteen days," Gracie responded. "Do... do you know if the Earth is okay? You said your father told you about it. How does he know? Did he tell you if the humans were able to defeat the Alluthans? Did your people come to help ours?"

Mohan gasped as she listened to Gracie's question. She was asking as if the battle was still being fought. Mohan looked to Kordon, who nodded for her to answer. "Yes, Gracie Jones. The humans defeated the Alluthans, and everyone is doing well."

Gracie couldn't hold back the tears as the news swept through her. "Mohan?" Gracie whispered.

"Yes, Gracie Jones," Mohan responded.

"Did your father... did your father ever hear of a group called the Freedom Five? I wanted to know if Chance... if the guys were okay," Gracie choked out.

Mohan heard the tears in Gracie's voice and looked up in desperation to Kordon for guidance. Something strange was happening, and she didn't know what to do. "Answer her," Kordon said.

"Yes, Gracie Jones, my father not only heard about them, but he told me tales of their great fight," Mohan said. "All four of the men survived, although the ones called Adam and Mark were wounded badly. The other two were also wounded, but not as severely."

Gracie was silent as she let the words Mohan told her sink in. They'd all survived. Chance was alive. If Mohan's father knew about them, then there must be a way to get home. Gracie jumped when the warning light indicating low power came on. The solar cells were not holding power the way they used to.

"Gracie Jones, are you there?" Mohan asked.

"Yes. I have to go. The solar cells are not holding power very long any more. I'll try to transmit again tomorrow if possible. This is Gracie reaching out to say goodnight," Gracie said as the power failed and the lights on the console went out.

The only light was the lightning streaking across the dark sky. Gracie moved over to the seats she used as a bed and curled up. Chance was alive.

She closed her eyes as exhaustion caused by lack of sleep and stress overwhelmed her. A smile curved her lips at the knowledge that she might be able to make it home after all. She went to sleep and dreamed she was in Chance's arms again. It was a dream that she never thought she would have again.

Chapter 5

Kordon rubbed his hand over his eyes. He was working on less than two hours sleep in almost thirty-six hours. He pored over the archives Mohan sent him.

Late last night, he held a meeting with his officers. Bran was skeptical of Mohan's explanation. He was more concerned with the fact the signal came from the same signature code as the attackers of the mining company.

The heated discussion that followed tried his limited patience. Bran insisted it must be a trap to lure unsuspecting travelers. Kordon couldn't discount his concerns.

Three days had passed since the last transmission. Mohan was able to get a general lock on the signal, but there was still a vast amount of space and almost a half-dozen or more planets and moons capable of sustaining life in the region. It would take weeks, if not longer, to search each one.

"Admiral," Mohan's voice called out through the com system. "I am picking up a transmission from Gracie Jones."

Kordon sat back. "Patch it through to my office and make sure you lock onto the signal this time."

"Yes, sir," Mohan replied.

"Gracie Jones, this is the *Conqueror*. Please respond," Mohan's voice came over the com system.

Kordon leaned back listening intently. He didn't realize he was holding his breath until it whooshed out as Gracie's soft voice echoed throughout his office.

"Oh, Mohan, I'm so glad to hear your voice. I was afraid I had dreamed you up," Gracie said in her husky voice.

Mohan chuckled at the excitement in Gracie's voice. "I was afraid of the same thing. Where have you been, Gracie Jones?"

"It has been storming here. The solar cells were dead, so there was no power unless I fired up the fuel cells to power the supply ship. I try not to do that very often since I might need it later on," Gracie said. She was so excited to have someone to talk to after so long it was hard to contain her enthusiasm.

Kordon punched in the information Gracie unknowingly gave. A storm on any of the planets or moons would show up on their sensors. He triangulated the information with the signal signature.

Within moments, a small moon registered on his screen. Kordon pulled up the specifications and found it matched an atmosphere suitable for sustaining life forms. Kordon sent a command and the coordinates to the helmsman. The *Conqueror* could be there in two days' time.

Satisfied, Kordon sat back and listened to the soft cadence of Gracie's voice as she talked about the moon she was on and listened to the questions she asked. He had informed Mohan to give just vague details and answers to her questions. *Soon,* he thought, *soon I will know if the voice matches the image I have.* If it did, there would be even more questions than answers. If Gracie Jones turned out to be the female of the Freedom Five, then she'd not only come back from the dead, but she'd somehow managed to survive over eight hundred and fifty-two Earth years after the Great Battle.

* * *

Two days later the *Conqueror* was in orbit around the small moon in the Glasis system. Kordon looked down on the moon from the conference room viewports. White clouds covered a good portion of the moon.

Mohan was trying to raise Gracie Jones. If they could make a connection, it would save time and resources in pinpointing her location.

Kordon was surprised at the aggressive energy flowing through his body. Normally, Zion warriors only felt this type of adrenaline rush before battle—*or life mating,* a small voice whispered in the back of his mind.

Kordon bit back an oath as the thought slammed into him. Zion warriors became very aggressive when confronted with their life mates. The need to possess and protect their females was a part of their genetics from the days when they would invade other worlds, capturing the females and taking them back to their home world.

Kordon turned as several of his fellow Zion warriors came into the conference room. Bran nodded in greeting. He had elevated the warship's alert status to high. Kordon looked at the other four men who stood beside Bran. He knew all of them well. Nodding to Bran, Kordon took a seat at the head of the table.

"Has Mohan heard anything yet?" Kordon asked even as he already knew the answer.

"Nothing. I don't like this," Bran said with a small frown. "It could be a trap."

"Have your sensors picked anything up out of the ordinary?" Kordon asked, leaning back in his chair.

"No," Bran said, shaking his head in frustration.

"We still don't know anything about the species that attacked the mining camp. They could have some type of shield. The mining foreman mentioned a shield of some type," Quan commented. "They could be using this female's voice to trick us. Perhaps have us think she is defenseless."

Kordon looked at one of his best fighters. Quan might be over six and a half feet tall like all Zion males, but he could move like a shadow. He had a long scar along his left cheek from a battle a few years ago. He had saved Kordon's life that day and earned the mark for it.

Kordon studied the image of the female from the files Mohan sent him. He stared into the sparkling green eyes and felt his gut twist again. Growling, he pushed himself up out of his chair and turned toward the viewport windows. His fists clenched and unclenched as he fought for control. He snarled when he felt a hand on his shoulder.

Cooraan looked at him in concern. "What is it?"

Kordon shook off the hand and stared out at the darkness. "I'm not sure," he replied in a hushed tone. "There is something about the female's voice…"

Quan looked at the other three men. Out of the five Zion warriors, he was the oldest. "Perhaps it is a trap. We will soon find out and be ready for anything. If it appears the female is part of a trap, then we will deal with her as we have any of our other enemies," he said calmly.

Kordon was about to respond when Mohan requested permission to enter. "Sir—" Mohan flushed several shades as she saw all the warriors standing together.

Quan growled when Mohan let her gaze brush over him. She flushed even more, her fur changing several different shades. Mohan stood frozen for a moment before she turned her eyes back to Kordon.

"Sir, you requested to know when a contact was made with Gracie Jones. I was unable to keep the connection for more than a few moments, but I was able to triangulate the signal and have a lock on it," Mohan said, letting her gaze flicker over Quan again before she looked at Kordon once more.

Quan let out a low snarl at Mohan. Kordon threw him a heated look. "Send the information to my com immediately along with the recordings of the transmission."

Mohan bowed and backed out of the room quickly without looking back. Kordon put his hand on Quan's arm to stop him from following. Quan looked down at the hand and back up before taking a deep breath and letting it out.

"She's mine," he said quietly letting his gaze turn to the closed door.

Kordon nodded. On a warship with a crew of almost five hundred, it was not surprising this was the first time Quan had encountered Mohan, especially since Mohan was very shy around most males on board. Before this incident she'd rarely left the communications room. Kordon recognized the feelings of aggression and possessiveness Quan was demonstrating.

Kordon turned to Bran. "Prepare the shuttles. I want to see who this Gracie Jones is and why she is using a signal pattern from a ship known for attacking planets under the protection of the Confederation."

* * *

Gracie groaned in frustration. *Why did the stupid solar cells have to die now? What was Murphy's Law? If anything can go wrong, it will?* Gracie banged her fists on the console again, but nothing happened. It seemed the solar cells and the fuel cells had decided to quit working at the same time.

She didn't know anything about mechanics or machines. If she couldn't program it or hit it with a wrench, she was hopeless. The guys always fixed everything. Gracie sat down suddenly in the chair and pulled her knees up to her chest, wrapping her arms around them. At first it was just her lip that trembled, then she hiccuped. By the third breath she was bawling like a baby, with her head buried against her knees.

Her whole body shook as the despair at being alone again crushed what little spirit she had left. She was going to die on this miserable moon all alone. Why couldn't she have just died like she was supposed to when the mother ship exploded? Why was she being punished?

Gracie was determined she was going to throw the mother of all pity parties, and she wasn't inviting anyone else to come! She had the right to be upset, dammit. Gracie cried and cried and cried before she wiped her nose and eyes against her pant leg.

"Fine! If this is what I have to look forward to, then FUCK YOU!" Gracie screamed as she jumped to her feet. "I will fucking die the way I fucking want to, and no one can tell me I fucking can't!" Gracie yelled out as the platform door descended. "And I can say fuck all I want to, and no one can tell me it is a bad word, so there!" Gracie added at the top of her lungs for good measure before she froze in horror.

"Oh, fuck!" she whispered as she stared at the group of huge-ass men standing outside the supply ship, staring at her like she was some kind of banshee from an Irish fairy tale.

Gracie stumbled backward trying to hit the button to close the platform door but kept missing it. She screamed out when one of the men broke away from the group and charged at her.

Turning, she scrambled over some boxes of supplies, knocking them over trying to get to the front of the supply ship. She had no idea what she would do when she got there, but she hoped by then her brain would figure something out. She continued throwing things behind her, ignoring the loud curses as the man following her collided with them.

Sliding into the area she normally used for sleeping, she spied her bow. Gracie grabbed it with one hand while grabbing her arrows with the other. She turned just as the huge male reached the open doorway. Gracie fitted the arrow into the notch and swung around, pointing it at his chest.

"Stop!" Gracie called out frantically as she pulled the string back. "Please... stop," she whispered.

Kordon froze as he stared into the dark green eyes of the female who moments ago was screaming as if she were being tortured. He could hear the others coming up behind him, but he did not move.

In truth, he felt almost frozen as he stared at the breathing image of the female who had haunted his every waking and sleeping moment since he'd first heard her voice. He straightened until he was standing at his full height. He held back a smile as he watched her eyes grow larger as he towered over her petite form. He growled in a low, deep voice his displeasure at her thinness. He would see she was fed properly from now on.

"Please don't make me hurt you. Please just go away," Gracie was saying over and over in a pleading voice. *I really don't want company if they are big enough to squish me. Being alone is nice. Really, it is,* Gracie thought desperately. *I never had to worry about being crushed like a bug by creatures bigger than me when I was alone.* Gracie had no idea she was still speaking out loud.

Gracie gasped when she heard a feminine chuckle behind the huge male staring at her like she was breakfast, lunch, and dinner all rolled into one. Her arm was beginning to shake from holding the bowstring back, and her nose was beginning to itch from all the crying. *Oh, hell.* Gracie thought, just as a sneeze overcame her. *Damn Murphy's Law.*

The sneeze caught her by surprise so fast she accidentally let go of the bowstring, firing the arrow. Gracie sneezed loudly again, then gasped as she saw what she had done. With a cry, she dropped her bow and moved forward without thinking.

Kordon saw the moment the female's hand released the arrow at him. He moved, turning as the arrow approached. His swift reflex was instinctive, developed through years of training and battle. He ignored the slight pain in his arm as the arrow sliced through the sleeve of his uniform. The arrow quivered as it embedded in the metal framing next to him.

Kordon vaguely heard Mohan's cry and Bran and Cooraan's roars of rage, but none of them could get through the doorway with him blocking it. Kordon turned briefly to command the men to stand down. He jerked back around when he felt delicate hands running over his chest and arm where blood was beginning to seep from the cut the arrow had sliced.

Kordon stared in shock as the female who called herself Gracie Jones babbled and patted on him. "I'm so sorry. I had to sneeze, and I didn't mean to sneeze, but I had to because I was crying, and I was crying because the stupid solar and fuel cells died, and then I decided to throw a temper tantrum, but then you guys showed up and..."

Gracie stopped when she felt a set of huge hands slide up her arms to circle her throat. She wondered why they felt so gentle when she knew he was about to break her neck for trying to kill him.

"You're going to squish me now, aren't you?" Gracie whispered as she stared up into the darkest blue eyes she'd ever seen.

The feminine voice said something to the man, and he chuckled softly, surprising all of them, including himself. Mohan had explained what Gracie was saying from the time she begged him to leave her alone until she asked if he was going to squish her.

Kordon looked down into the brilliant green eyes looking up at him in a combination of guilt, fear, and resignation and decided he didn't like any of those emotions. He wanted to see something else in her eyes when she looked at him. He wasn't sure what, but fear was not it.

His hold tightened around Gracie Jones's neck, drawing her closer. He watched as she closed her eyes and tilted her head back, giving him better access to it. Her shoulders slumped for the briefest of moments before she jerked them back so she stood ramrod straight.

Kordon drew in a breath, marveling at how beautiful the petite female standing in front of him looked. Her face was pale against the rosy-colored highlights in her disheveled hair, which was longer than in the images Mohan sent to him. Her lips were slightly parted, and she was drawing in short little breaths of air as she struggled to remain still. Kordon's eyes jerked up when he saw her open her eyes again. They shimmered brightly, but no tears fell.

"It's okay. I'm ready. I'm not afraid to die," Gracie whispered, more to convince herself than the man holding her by the neck.

Mohan repeated what Gracie had just said to Kordon. Kordon frowned as he looked down into the brilliant eyes. It was not "okay" as she said. He was not ready for her to die. He would never be ready for her to die.

Kordon lowered his head as he gently pressed his hands under her quivering chin to raise it to him before he brushed a light kiss over them. The moment his lips touched hers, he knew without a doubt she was his. He would claim her, take her, and never let her go.

Gracie jerked as she felt the warm lips against hers. She hadn't been kissed in over three years. Gracie frowned. She hadn't been held in over three years either, and it felt pretty damn good! But... she was confused. She didn't understand why the huge man was kissing her when she'd almost killed him.

Of course, it was by accident, but he didn't know that, did he?

The man said something under his breath, and Gracie heard a soft reply. She tried to pull back away from the warm, masculine scent of the man holding her, but he tightened his grip, forcing her to remain still. Gracie was about to try pulling away again when the soft, feminine voice spoke again.

"Gracie Jones, Admiral Jefe says he has no plans to squish you today, and you will not be dying," Mohan said, peeking around the huge shoulders of Kordon.

"Mohan?" Gracie's voice broke as she whispered.

Mohan's delicate furred face peeked around Kordon, and she smiled, showing off her small sharp teeth. Gracie's eyes widened as she stared into a face that sort of resembled a human's, but seemed to also resemble that of a beautiful feline.

Mohan had a strip of dark red hair flowing down the center of her head, but her face was covered in a light coating of soft fur. Her ears were small and pointed at the ends and flicked back and forth as if she was listening to something behind her. She was wearing a form fitting black uniform with a symbol over her left breast in the shape of a space ship with multiple circles around it. Gracie giggled when Mohan wiggled her tiny nose at her.

"Yes, Gracie Jones. I am Lieutenant Mohan Ta'nee, communications officer aboard the Confederation warship *Conqueror*. The male you almost killed is Grand Admiral Kordon Jefe, Commander of the Confederation military. The others behind me are

Zion officers, also from the *Conqueror*. I will introduce them to you later, if you would like," Mohan said with another friendly smile.

She pushed against the chest of the man called Kordon, ignoring his low grunt of displeasure. Mohan said he wasn't going to crush her, and Gracie wanted to hug the only friendly voice she'd known and heard for the last three years. Gracie frowned up at Kordon when he still didn't let her go.

Glancing back at Mohan, Gracie asked in puzzled confusion. "What is his problem? Why won't he let me go? You said he wasn't going to squish me or kill me, didn't you? I'm not going to try anything. I promise," Gracie added as she felt the huge man's hands slide down to her wrists.

* * *

Mohan bit back a sigh. She recognized the protective stance Kordon took to block the other warriors' view of Gracie. She was having the same problem with Quan trying to pull her back behind him. He and Kordon had actually gotten into the first heated argument she'd ever seen between two Zion warriors over whether she should be allowed to come with them or not.

Mohan flushed when she felt a pair of hands grip her hips from behind. She knew the fur on her face was changing colors rapidly as she hissed back at the huge Zion warrior glaring at her and snapped her sharp teeth at him.

"Are they always like this?" Gracie giggled as she saw Mohan was having the same problem as she was.

Mohan snapped at the man towering above her again. Gracie watched in amazement as the man reluctantly let her go. Gracie looked up and snapped her teeth at Kordon, but all he did was look amused. *Maybe I need sharper teeth,* Gracie thought.

* * *

Kordon barely contained the laugh that threatened to escape him when the petite female he was holding looked at him with such a serious expression and snapped her teeth at him, then looked confusedly at Mohan when he didn't respond. He heard Mohan's hiss of frustration at Quan and was able to interpret Gracie's imitation in trying to get him to release her.

Kordon let his hands circle her wrists, amazed at how small they were. He reluctantly stepped back a step to let Mohan enter. He wanted to know more about Gracie Jones, why she was screaming when they arrived, and how she'd ended up being on a moon, millions of light years and over eight hundred years from her planet.

Chapter 6

Gracie looked on silently as men from another shuttle disembarked. Mohan had questioned her for over two hours non-stop. Gracie was confused at first when Mohan kept asking question after question about Earth and what happened leading to her being on the moon. It seemed Mohan already knew the answers, because she often just nodded as if what Gracie was telling her was old news. It couldn't be that old! Gracie didn't know where this Glasis system was or how far it was to get back to Earth when Mohan asked how she made it to the moon.

Gracie kept pressing for answers of her own. She asked about the news of the war against the Alluthans and how Mohan knew what happened, but the Ta'nee—Gracie was still trying to wrap her head around the fact so many different alien species existed—never gave her a straight answer. Gracie decided Mohan would make an excellent politician back on Earth.

If that wasn't bad enough, the whole time Gracie had to deal with the Admiral shooting out a question in his language to Mohan, who would then translate it while he kept touching Gracie.

Gracie tried to ignore it at first when he sat next to her on the row of seats she used as her bed and played with a strand of her hair. She kept pulling it away from him at first and tucking it back behind her ear. A minute later he would pull another strand out and begin playing with it. When Gracie slapped at his hand, he had the nerve to tug on her hair, forcing her closer to him.

Gracie finally got fed up with the distraction and pulled her hair up into a ponytail. That, unfortunately, seemed to amuse him more! Gracie flushed as she remembered having to ask Mohan to repeat a question or answer several times.

The Admiral decided if she wouldn't let him touch her hair, he would run his fingers along the back of the neckline of her T-shirt. Gracie kept slapping his hands away and they kept coming back, until she finally turned and gave him her toughest "knock it off" look. The jerk just raised his eyebrow at her and smirked.

Gracie finally had enough and tried to move, to sit on the floor next to Mohan and the giant standing over her, but the Admiral grabbed her as she stood, pulling her onto his lap. Gracie's gasp was almost as loud as Mohan's. Gracie was never as happy as when the first shuttle arrived and the inquisition ended.

* * *

Turning a dark look toward the man currently directing orders to the men disembarking off the new shuttle. She flushed a bright pink when he seemed to sense her glaring at his back and turned to look her in the eye.

Gracie was determined not to let the pompous jerk intimidate her, so she just stared back, refusing to give in first. She had dealt with four macho guys for too many years and had learned a long time ago that if she gave in, she would never be able to stand up to them. His vivid blue eyes told her he knew what she was doing before he turned to answer a question from one of the men.

"The Admiral desires you," Mohan said as she came to sit next to where Gracie was told to sit and not move.

Gracie rolled her eyes. "Well, he's just going to have to get over it. I have a guy, and I'm not looking for anyone else," Gracie said stubbornly.

She refused to focus on the huge dark warrior issuing command after command. No matter how he made her insides quiver and warm up. She had her own warrior back home on Earth.

"You have a male?" Mohan said in surprise, looking around. "But I thought you said you were alone," Mohan added in confusion.

"I am here but not back home on Earth. If your father is from there, then I can go home. I have to go. I promised Chance I would come back," Gracie said anxiously.

"Chance?" Mohan asked faintly. "This is the male Chance from the Freedom Five?"

Gracie was nodding with a soft smile on her lips. "Yes. I love him so much. It almost killed both of us when I left. He probably thinks I'm dead, but once I get back, I can be with him again. Oh, Mohan, he makes me feel like..." Gracie turned away as tears choked her at the thought of seeing all of the guys again. "I can't wait to see him again."

Mohan felt a horrible sense of dread as she watched a tear drop onto Gracie's hand as she sat with her head bowed. Mohan glanced at Kordon, then back to Gracie. Placing her hand over Gracie's, Mohan squeezed it gently.

"Gracie Jones," Mohan began gently. "You cannot return to your male."

Gracie's head shot up at Mohan's words. "What do you mean I cannot return to him? Of course, I can. If your dad could..." Gracie was saying, but stopped when she saw the sadness in Mohan's eyes.

"Your male is no longer alive, Gracie Jones," Mohan said quietly.

"What... but you said..." Gracie fought for control as she wrung her hands together and looked around frantically. "You told me they lived. You told me Chance lived. You said... you lied?" Gracie asked in a strangled tone.

"I did not lie to you, Gracie Jones. The males lived ... over eight hundred of your Earth years ago. It is the calendar year 2851 in your Earth time. I believe..." Mohan said quietly, gripping Gracie's hands tightly between her own. "I believe the explosion in hyperspace created a rip sending you forward in time."

Gracie sat frozen for a moment as Mohan's words slowly sank in. Everything she knew, everyone she knew no longer existed. They had not existed for a very, very long time.

Gracie let her gaze travel over the supply ship that had been her home for the past three years before letting it move to the thick forest. The sounds of another shuttle approaching drew her attention to the sky. She was seeing everything as if for the first time.

Everything was gone. Chance was gone. There was nothing to go back to, no one to go home to. All the strength that had kept her going from the moment she entered the dark tunnels of the subways to her subconscious hope that she would find a way home suddenly deserted her as overwhelming grief flooded her.

She had lost everything! Her parents, her sister, her world, and the one man she loved. She should have died when the explosion happened. It would have been a more humane death than what she was feeling right now.

Gracie pulled away from Mohan without saying a word. She moved slowly around the stack of containers they were sitting on, moving toward the thick edge of the forest. She looked down, startled at Mohan's hand on her arm as she took another step away.

"Where are you going, Gracie Jones?" Mohan asked in concern as she took in the pale complexion of Gracie's face and the blank look of shock on it.

Gracie looked up at Mohan for just a moment, and a small, sad smile curved her lips. "Where I should have gone three years ago, Mohan. I'm going home," Gracie said. "I'm going home."

Gracie pulled away suddenly and took off for the thick forest. She knew where she was going. She had been there hundreds of times during the first six months. Back then, she thought she had a reason to fight to stay alive. Now she knew differently and would not hesitate.

Gracie vaguely heard Mohan's cry of alarm, but it did not slow her down. In fact, it helped her increase her speed. She ran with experience through the thick growth. She knew the path by heart and the quickest way to get there.

There was a deep ravine dropping into a river almost a mile from the supply ship. Gracie had discovered it the second week she was on the moon. She had visited it many times when she was deeply lonely and depressed. It was only her promise to come home that drew her away from the edge time after time.

But that promise no longer held her. Gracie knew that in death she would finally be with her family, with Chance, because the pain in living was too much for her young heart to bear any longer.

Mohan's questions and answers played through Gracie's mind as she ran. It explained so many of her questions. Mohan already knew everything about what happened because it was history. That was why her father was from Earth.

Space travel and aliens were now a daily part of Earth living. There was no fighting for your life, no camps with millions of human prisoners, and no living in subways. Hell, there probably weren't even any subways anymore.

A sob tore through Gracie as pain speared through her. She ignored the branches cutting her face and arms and the burning in her lungs from not enough oxygen. She focused only on ending the overwhelming pain searing her alive.

* * *

Kordon was directing the engineering team on repairing the supply ship so it could be transported back to the *Conqueror*. The technology and computer systems would need to be analyzed to see what could be learned about the Alluthans. Kordon had no doubt they were responsible for the destruction of the mining camp.

He was discussing what he wanted done with Bran and Cooraan when he heard Mohan cry out. Kordon turned quickly, catching a glimpse of Quan as he was entering the forest. Mohan ran over to them, pointing in the direction Quan had run.

"Gracie Jones!" Mohan called out urgently.

Kordon took off, following Quan. Bran and Cooraan were right behind him. He heard Quan yell out up ahead and picked up speed, catching him as Quan turned in a circle.

"What happened?" Kordon growled out.

"I don't know. I heard Mohan cry out and saw the human female running for the forest. I tried to catch her, but she was too far ahead. I am not sure which way she went," Quan ground out in frustration.

Cooraan was looking at the ground while Bran was moving along the path studying the foliage. Cooraan called out suddenly and began moving through the undergrowth. Kordon could see a small, narrow path.

"This way," Cooraan said. He took off at a slow run keeping his eyes on the ground.

"There!" Kordon growled out, pointing to a piece of torn clothing from Gracie.

Confident they were heading in the right direction, the men picked up the pace with Kordon taking the lead. They'd covered almost a mile when Kordon caught the sound of Gracie's choking sobs. Pushing ahead, he burst out of the forest into a small rocky clearing.

Gracie stood looking down over the edge of a deep ravine. Her shoulders shook with the force of her sobs, and she had her arms wrapped tightly around her waist. She never turned around, but her quietly spoken words stopped him.

"Don't come any closer, please," Gracie whispered, keeping her back to him.

Kordon growled in frustration. He didn't understand her. He needed Mohan, *now*!

As if just his will was enough to make it happen, Mohan burst out with Quan holding her by the arm. She was breathing heavily and had a small cut along one cheek. She impatiently pushed Quan away when he tried to wipe it.

"Gracie Jones," Mohan called out. "Come away with me, Gracie Jones. Things will not seem so bad."

Gracie turned slowly, and the look on her face tore at Kordon. He remembered the look on his mother's face when their village was attacked one night by slavers when he was younger. It was not until she saw his father and her sons safe that the look disappeared.

"Ask her what is wrong," Kordon said, taking a step closer—only to stop when Gracie moved backward. "Tell her I will fix whatever has upset her."

Mohan looked at Gracie for a moment before moving slowly toward her. "I am so sorry, Gracie Jones. I should never have told you. Please forgive me," Mohan whispered as she moved a step closer. "Please, Gracie Jones. Come to me."

Gracie shook her head. "I would have found out sooner or later. I think I must have always known I would never see them again." Gracie's voice caught on a sob. "It's not your fault, Mohan. I was stupid to believe in the hope. I shouldn't be here, Mohan. I shouldn't exist. I belong with them," Gracie said, taking another step back and closing her eyes briefly as she pulled a picture of her parents and sister into her mind.

The look in Gracie's eyes when she opened them froze Mohan for a moment. There was a sense of calm acceptance that made Mohan realize that nothing she could say would stop Gracie from completing her next decision. Mohan wondered vaguely if this was the same strength and resolve that gave Gracie the courage to board the Alluthan mother ship so many years ago before leading it away, knowing she would not live.

"Admiral, she means to end her life. She knows everything... everyone she ever knew is dead,"

Mohan murmured as she watched a small serene smile curve Gracie's lips.

Gracie felt a sense of peace come over her as she took the last step bringing her to the edge of the ravine. She didn't look down at it.

Instead, she thought of her new friend and was thankful she had met her and found out the truth. She thought of Mark, Adam, and Adrian and the way they used to tease her and call her "little britches." And she thought of Chance and wished she could have spent that one night in his arms.

Gracie smiled at Mohan. "Good-bye," Gracie whispered in a low voice. "This is Gracie's Touch signing off one last time. I'm coming home at last, guys," Gracie closed her eyes and took the step that would take her home.

Chapter 7

Kordon cursed under his breath as he heard Mohan's softly spoken words. He flicked a glance at Bran and Cooraan who were coming up on each side of Gracie. Mohan was between him and Gracie. Quan gave a sharp nod. He would take care of Mohan.

Everything seemed to happen in slow motion as Gracie said good-bye. Kordon rushed forward as Quan grabbed Mohan, who let out a sharp cry of denial as Gracie stepped backward into open space. Cooraan and Bran each grabbed for Kordon's ankles as he flung himself over the edge after Gracie.

Kordon closed his hands around Gracie's slender wrists, wincing when he heard her cry out in pain at the crushing force of his grip. He trusted Cooraan and Bran to make sure he did not fall any further. Each of the warriors held his ankles.

Kordon felt his breath leave him as his upper body slammed into the rocky surface of the ravine wall. For a moment, his grip loosened, and he felt one of Gracie's hands slip from his grasp.

"Mohan!" Kordon yelled out furiously. He would not lose his life mate.

"Yes, Admiral?" Mohan called out above him.

"Tell her to give me her hand," Kordon yelled through gritted teeth.

He knew he was crushing the bones in the delicate wrist he was holding, but he couldn't loosen it without fear of her falling. Gracie wasn't looking at him, but down instead. She wasn't moving or making any noise, so he didn't know if she was conscious or not.

"Gracie Jones!" Mohan called down. "Gracie … Gracie … please!" Mohan begged.

Gracie looked up slowly first at Mohan, then at Kordon. "Let me go," she said.

Kordon tightened his grip, regretting the flash of pain in Gracie's eyes at it. "Mohan, how do you say 'I will never let you go' in her language?" Mohan told him.

Kordon looked deeply into Gracie's eyes and repeated it to her. "Gracie, I will never let you go. Never," Kordon said.

Gracie's eyes flashed with confusion as she listened to the accented words the huge warrior was saying in her language. "But… why?" she whispered.

"Mohan, how do you say 'I claim you as mine'?" Kordon called out again.

"Kordon, is there no way you can have this conversation later?" Bran yelled down as he dug his feet into a crack in some rocks. "You are heavy as a *baskleen*."

"Mohan!" Kordon roared out as he felt Gracie's wrist begin to slip. Mohan quickly repeated it in English.

Gracie's eyes widened as she heard what Mohan said. Her eyes locked onto Kordon's deep blue ones. "I claim you as mine, Gracie," Kordon said quietly.

Gracie shook her head and closed her eyes. It was too much. She didn't want to think any more. She didn't want to hurt. But most of all, she didn't want to be alone.

"Please, Gracie. Listen to him. He would not say this if it was not true. Zion warriors do not offer claim unless they mean it," Mohan begged. "Please, give him your other hand. Give life a chance again... for yourself and your friends from long ago. They lived a good life. I will tell you about it. Your Chance had a mate and children."

Gracie's head jerked up at that. "He married? He had kids?" Gracie whispered.

"Yes," Mohan said. "It was with your sister, Violet."

Gracie's eyes filled with tears at the mention of her older sister. Mohan would not have known her name if she hadn't survived. Gracie looked back into the deep blue eyes staring so determinedly down at her.

Gracie swung her other arm up, gasping as he gripped it tightly in his other hand. "Pull us up!" Kordon yelled out.

"I thought he would never ask!" Cooraan growled.

Quan and Mohan helped pull Kordon back up slowly. Once Gracie was within reach, Quan reached down and lifted her up over the edge, holding her in his arms when her legs gave out. As soon as Kordon was back on solid rock, he rose to his feet and took Gracie into his arms, holding her close as she turned away from everyone and buried her face in his chest with her eyes closed. He needed to get her aboard the *Conqueror* as soon as possible.

"Bran, you and Cooraan take care of getting the supply ship back to the *Conqueror*. Quan, you and Mohan will come with me," Kordon said.

Kordon knew, as much as he would like to have Gracie to himself, until she learned their language, he would be dependent on Mohan to help them both. He never wanted to come so close to losing her again, he thought fiercely, pulling her even tighter against him.

He glanced down and noticed she was holding her wrist gingerly. He would not be surprised if it was broken. Kordon brushed a kiss against Gracie's soft hair as another new feeling he had never experienced slowly began to fade—fear.

* * *

Gracie lay quietly in the darkened room, waiting. She wasn't sure what she was waiting for, but she was waiting. It had been a week since the incident at the ravine when she'd tried to take her life. At times, Gracie felt ashamed of her weakness.

She spent the first three days in the medical center on the *Conqueror*. The medical officer, another new alien species for Gracie, insisted on doing a complete examination on her. Gracie's wrist had been broken in two places. She also had numerous cuts and abrasions from her run through the forest and the impact against the rock face of the ravine, in addition to being malnourished.

The doctor insisted that Gracie remain under observation to make sure nothing else was wrong. Her wrist was braced, and she was given bone accelerator treatments twice a day to increase the healing. Her cuts were sealed, and she was placed on a strict diet to boost her weight gain and give her additional nutrients. Gracie remained in a daze through it all.

She actually remembered very little of her trip from the ravine to the medical center on the warship. It seemed like her body and mind couldn't take any more and just seemed to go into shutdown mode.

She remembered vaguely waking up in a warm set of arms that made her feel very protected. She thought she was dreaming of Chance again and even murmured, his name, which caused the arms around her to tighten, followed by a low growl and the name Kordon. Gracie simply closed her eyes again and drifted.

She remembered Mohan coming to see her several times a day. She talked about what she was doing and how Quan was getting on her nerves by growling and snarling at any male who looked her way. She admitted she liked not having to deal with other males looking at her, but that didn't mean she needed Quan.

She even talked a little about Earth history. She told Gracie that after the mother ship exploded the remaining Alluthans were quickly destroyed with their power, shields, and resources gone. She told Gracie how Mark and Adam were injured. Mark lost a leg during the battle due to wounds he received. Adam was blinded in one eye and was known for the black patch he wore over it.

Chance and Adrian were able to free the prisoners in the New York camp where Gracie's parents and sister were. Gracie's parents did not survive, but her sister, Violet, did. Violet was actually leading a rebel group inside the compound. Chance was wounded during the initial battle, but it was not life threatening. He and Violet married six years after the battle and had three children, two boys and a girl. They named their little girl Gracie.

"… After her aunt," Mohan said quietly as she brushed Gracie's hair. "You are considered the Mother of Freedom for Earth and are still revered today for your skills and your sacrifice to your planet. The term Gracie's Touch is considered to be a blessing. Billions return to Earth once each year to celebrate you and the messages of love and hope you gave."

"I don't want them to know about me," Gracie said in a small voice. "It is better if I remain dead."

Mohan paused as she ran the brush through Gracie's glossy hair. She looked up at Kordon as he stood in the doorway watching. He had her record all their conversations and translate them for him. He'd monitored every moment of Gracie's life since she was brought aboard the *Conqueror*. He knew it would take time for her to heal.

He thought about the look on his mother's face so many years ago when she thought she had lost all of them. He finally understood what that look meant. A Zion warrior might not show emotion to others or acknowledge pain, but that did not mean they did not feel, Kordon realized.

Kordon watched as Gracie slowly slid down under the covers of the bed and closed her eyes. He stood watch over her until her breathing deepened. Nodding to Mohan, he quietly left the room, but he never left Gracie.

* * *

Now, she awoke to a new room. She looked around for a moment before forcing herself to sit up. The lights came on automatically and softly lit the room. It was surprisingly large. She frowned as she looked around. She didn't remember coming here.

She vaguely remembered falling asleep as Mohan talked to her some more about what happened to Earth after the battle. Gracie swung her feet over the edge of the bed and gasped as she looked down at the beautiful nightgown she was wearing. It was a deep emerald green and shimmered in the low lighting. She didn't remember changing into it, either!

Gracie frowned in frustration. She didn't like this feeling of detachment. She was tired of feeling sorry for herself. What was that saying her parents were always telling her? *Oh, yeah,* Gracie thought. *Change the things you can, accept the things you can't, and be wise enough to know the difference. Well, I can't change what happened three years, or even eight hundred years ago. I can change how I deal with it. If this is the hand fate is dealing I better try to learn how to play.*

The first thing was getting rid of the pity-party attitude. Next, she needed to learn the language. She loved Mohan, but she needed to learn what everyone else was saying too. Third, well, third she would figure out later when she got through with one and two.

Gracie stood up and swayed as the effects of being in a horizontal position versus a vertical one for so long shook her. She closed her eyes and put a hand to her head to steady the dizziness. She hadn't taken more than a step when she felt a warm arm wrap itself around her waist. Gracie opened her eyes to thank Mohan, but the words died on her lips as she met the dark blue eyes of Kordon.

"You are dizzy?" he asked slowly.

Gracie started as she realized he was speaking English. "I... yes... you?" she stammered.

Kordon smiled. "I learn your speech," he said proudly.

Gracie giggled quietly. "Yes, I can see that. You are learning to speak my language very well."

Kordon frowned as he tried to keep up with the words Gracie was saying. His arm tightened around her as she swayed again. He looked down with concern as she closed her eyes again.

"You sleep... lay down," Kordon commanded, trying to find the right words.

Gracie shook her head gently. "No, I would like to sit down for a moment. I think I have been lying down too long. I think if I sit for a few moments I will be okay," Gracie said slowly, knowing Kordon was trying to follow along with her.

Gracie blushed as she felt the heat of Kordon's hand through the thin material of her nightgown. His fingers were splayed out and dipped down slightly as he guided her to a chair near the bed. Gracie breathed a sigh of relief when he gently lowered her down and stepped back to sit on the bed so they were almost eye level.

Gracie looked around the room. It was larger than she expected for a room on a warship. She could see the bedroom contained a huge bed and off to the side was a large bathroom. Her eyes flickered over to a dresser of some type before moving to glance through the doorway into what appeared to be a living room.

"This is a very nice room. I hope I'm not taking it away from anyone," Gracie said hesitantly.

Kordon watched as Gracie nervously straightened the skirt of her nightgown over her legs. His eyes darkened as he remembered dressing her in it last night. Kordon talked to Toolas, the Baskten healer in charge of medical. Toolas told Kordon it was not unusual for Gracie to be so tired. Between her injuries and being malnourished, it was to be expected, but she should make a complete recovery with proper medical care and proper nutrition.

Toolas was more concerned with the depression Gracie was experiencing. Toolas explained Gracie would need a good support system in place to help her adjust to the new world she found herself in and time to accept what happened to her old one.

Besides Kordon and Mohan, only a few select officers and Toolas knew about Gracie's history.

Kordon wanted to keep it that way for a while. He decided to withhold the information from his reports to the Confederation Council until he knew more.

"You are not. This is my rooms. You stay here," Kordon said slowly, thankful he could communicate with Gracie.

Gracie's eyes widened at Kordon's softly spoken statement. "But where will you be staying?" Gracie asked, puzzled.

"Here," Kordon responded with a grin.

Gracie's hands shook as she looked everywhere but at the man sitting on the bed across from her. "I don't think that would be a very good idea. Perhaps … perhaps I could ask Mohan if I could stay with her," Gracie said quietly, glancing under her eyelashes at the huge man looking at her with a frown.

Gracie felt a shiver go down her spine as she looked at Kordon. He really was breathtakingly handsome in a huge sort of way. He towered over her petite five-foot-four frame by at least a foot or more. His black hair was cut short, except for one long piece in the very back, which was braided with silver and blue beads threaded through it.

Gracie remembered seeing the other men who were getting off the shuttle having the same thing, only with different colored beads. His face was a dark tan color with markings across his forehead and down along one side of his face ending below his right eye. She noticed the same markings running down the right side of his neck before disappearing under the collar of his shirt. Gracie vaguely wondered how far the markings went.

He was bigger than any man she'd ever seen before. Not even Adam was as big as Kordon. Gracie didn't understand why she got so nervous around him. Except for the light kiss he gave her when she'd accidentally almost killed him, he really hadn't done anything else but play with her hair and her neck and make her sit in his lap.

Okay, maybe she could understand why she was nervous. Whenever he touched her, she got all warm and quivery inside. It wasn't the calm warmth she got when Chance touched her. No, this was a hot, achy warmth that confused and scared her. The thought of Chance caused tears to fill her eyes again.

Gracie started when she felt Kordon's warm hand under her chin. "What is makes you sad?" he asked as he brushed his thumb against her chin.

"I was thinking of how different you are from Chance," Gracie said, looking into Kordon's eyes, confused.

Kordon bit back a curse at the mention of the other man's name. Mohan told him of Gracie's love for the male. He'd read all the archives she had sent to him, and it mentioned there was speculation on a relationship between the two, but nothing in the archives showed the male ever claimed the female like he later did her sister.

Kordon refused to let Gracie dwell on the other male. He was gone, and Kordon was here. He did not like that Gracie would compare them. If Gracie had been his, he never would have let her go alone.

Kordon tilted Gracie's head back, refusing to let her look away from him. He wanted her to know it was him there. He would not allow her to compare him to the other male. He would not allow her to pretend he was that male. She would know it was Kordon who claimed her as his life mate.

"The only difference is I am here now, and I have claimed you as mine, Gracie Jones," Kordon said before crushed his lips down over hers in a kiss that left no doubt as to who he was.

Gracie stiffened at first, but the same hot, achy warmth that caused her insides to melt and her pussy to clench seemed to have a different idea of how she should react. Gracie melted into the sweet hunger that seemed to build since she had first touched the huge Zion admiral.

She leaned forward into Kordon and slowly let her hands move over his wide shoulders before wrapping them around his neck. Her fingers twisted in the long thin braid down his back, holding him to her as she opened her mouth.

The first touch of his tongue against hers had her groaning in need. She never even noticed when he picked her up in his arms, turning back toward the bed, and gently laid her back down. Gracie pulled away and cried out as she felt his hand on her breast, pulling at her distended nipple through the thin satin.

"Oh!" Gracie moaned as she arched closer to Kordon's warm hand.

Kordon looked down at Gracie's flushed face and passion-dazed eyes. "Look at me, Gracie Jones," Kordon commanded. "Look at me and say *my* name. Tell me *who* you see."

"Kordon," Gracie whispered huskily, looking into his dark blue eyes. "I see Kordon."

Kordon growled in triumph as he pulled back enough to slide the straps off of Gracie's shoulders. "I claim you, Gracie. You are mine. I not allow anyone to take you from me … not you nor a man who no longer lives. You are mine. Tell me," Kordon said in a voice that said there would be no arguing, no going back.

Even in his stilted English, Gracie understood what Kordon was saying and what was about to happen. He was telling her she would become his. Gracie knew deep down she could fight it, but the outcome would remain the same.

Kordon had claimed her. Gracie's mind fluttered briefly to the saying "… be wise enough to know the difference." Did she really want to change this? There was something going on between her and Kordon. She might not understand it, but did she really want to not see where it took her?

She didn't fight for it before and look what happened. Gracie knew she could survive alone. She'd spent three years doing that and almost six months when she was a child in the dark tunnels before the guys found her. No, if she did this it was because she was ready to belong to someone.

"I'm yours, Kordon," Gracie said huskily. "I'm yours."

Kordon pulled back and slowly began undressing, never taking his eyes off Gracie. From the first moment he'd heard her husky voice, he knew she was his. He remembered his father and his father's father talking about when they had first met their life mates. They told him just the sound of their life mate's voice gave them a sense of peace, of serenity.

They also told him he would become very protective and possessive of his female. They laughingly told how their mates fought them every step of the way whenever they became too possessive or protective, but they added it was well worth the making up. While Zion Warriors were ruthless and cold toward any others, Kordon's father and father's father admitted their life mates had them wrapped around their delicate little fingers. Kordon could finally appreciate what they were trying to tell him.

Gracie sat up, ignoring how the satin of her nightgown pooled around her hips, leaving her breasts bared. Her eyes were glued to Kordon's broad chest. He had removed his shirt and was unfastening the pants of his uniform.

Gracie ran her fingers over the pattern of marks running down the right side of his body. The marks continued to his hip as he pushed his pants down revealing his huge, swollen cock, which jerked when Gracie's reached around to touch it.

"What do they mean?" Gracie asked as she let her fingers trace the symbols.

Kordon stood rigid as he fought for control. "They tell which clan I come from, who my family is, and the battles I have won," Kordon said through gritted teeth.

His cock jerked upward at each delicate trace and was beginning to throb painfully. He was not used to having to deny his desire. Normally when he was with a female, he took what he wanted while giving the female extreme satisfaction before leaving.

Now it was as if he knew instinctively Gracie needed this time to explore him. He would give her the time, even if it killed him. As her touch moved lower, a light sweat broke out over Kordon. He decided he probably was going to die if she didn't satisfy her curiosity soon.

"Gracie," Kordon choked out as her fingers ran over his hip bone.

Gracie bit her lip to hold back the smile threatening to break free. It was empowering to know she had this type of effect over someone as powerful as Kordon. Gracie leaned forward and pressed a kiss to the mark on his hip, listening as Kordon drew in a deep breath before letting it out in a long hiss.

Gracie glanced up and noticed Kordon had his eyes closed, and his mouth was pressed into a straight line. A muscle ticked in his jaw. Gracie turned her head slightly and looked at Kordon's cock as it jerked up toward his stomach. The tip was different from the few glimpses she'd caught during the times when she accidentally stumbled across the guys and from magazines they tried to hide from her.

His cock was rounded at the end like a human's but there were a series of small ridges circling it as well. He was long and very thick. At the junction between his legs, he had no testicles; instead at the base of his cock was a series of thicker bands.

Gracie opened her mouth and let the tip of her tongue flick over one set of ridges around the tip of his cock, curious as to how he would taste. Kordon's eyes snapped open at the touch of Gracie's tongue on his cock.

His breath exploded out of him, and he could not hold back any longer. Kordon stepped back away from Gracie. Kicking his boots off, he quickly finished undressing.

Gracie watched his every move in fascination. Somewhere inside her, she knew she should be scared or worried. She had, on more than one occasion, stumbled across the guys, including Chance, having sex with a female from another rebel group.

She remembered hiding and watching as they made love, curious about it. She didn't remember any of the guys being as big as Kordon, but she'd never really got that good a look. Both the guys and the women they were with seemed to be enjoying the experience from the muffled cries she heard. It was one of the reasons she hadn't been afraid to press Chance to make love to her.

It was only Adam's insistence she was too young that prevented it from happening. *Well*, Gracie thought as Kordon came toward her, *I'm not too young anymore.*

Gracie gasped when Kordon gripped her by her hips and lifted her so he could pull the rest of the nightgown off of her. When Gracie would have pulled her legs up, Kordon growled out a warning for her to remain still.

"Open for me, Gracie. Let me taste your sweetness," Kordon whispered harshly.

Gracie looked deeply into the dark blue eyes that became darker as his desire flared. Slowly relaxing her legs, they fell open for Kordon. She reached her arms over her head and gave herself to him totally. She wanted to do this. She wanted to know him as a woman knows a man.

A man... Gracie's breath caught... *a man she cares about.* She wouldn't say she loved Kordon. She didn't know him well enough to say that. *But,* she realized in shock, *there was something there.*

It was the way her body reacted when he touched her. It was the way a warm, soft feeling grew when he came into the room or Mohan spoke of him. It was in the craving to hear his voice even if she couldn't understand what he was saying. It was also in the way he made her feel when he looked at her, like she was the only one there... the only one who mattered.

"Kordon," Gracie moaned out as her fingers sought to grip the headboard of the bed desperately.

Kordon's face was buried between Gracie's legs, which he pulled over his large shoulders, forcing her to open wide for him. He gently stroked her at first, letting the moisture from her arousal coat his fingers.

She was so wet he bit back the urge to just take her. Kordon moaned as Gracie's sweet taste flowed over his tongue. He buried his mouth in her, nipping and stroking her as his fingers slowly invaded her body—searching out all her secrets and claiming them as she cried out hoarsely.

Kordon pushed his tongue between her swollen lips, seeking entrance to follow his fingers which moved in and out of her in a rhythm as old as time itself. When he plunged his fingers in as far as they would go, he felt the barrier blocking her womb and heard her gasp of pain.

Kordon pulled back slightly with a frown that quickly turned to a sigh of satisfaction. The male, Chance, may have been the first to claim Gracie's heart, but Kordon would be the first to claim her body, and if he had his way, the last one to claim her heart.

Murmuring soothingly to Gracie, he pulled back enough to brush a kiss along the inside of her thigh. "You are mine, Gracie," Kordon whispered before he thrust his fingers up through the barrier, breaking it.

He knew he was larger than human males and thicker. He did not want her first time to be any more painful than necessary. A Zion male was also built differently from human males in that the bands around their cocks swelled during sex, locking the female to the male. The ridges at the top moved during this time, massaging the female's sensitive channel and increasing each partner's pleasure.

That was one reason many women sought out a Zion male for sexual encounters. Kordon had heard more than once that once a female tested the lovemaking skills of a Zion male they were never satisfied with anything less.

Gracie gasped as pain swept through her. She could feel Kordon's thick fingers deep inside her. He held them still as her body adjusted to his forceful intrusion. Gracie blinked back the tears as the stinging began to fade. She tried to pull away, but stopped when Kordon nipped the inside of her thigh when she tried to pull her leg off his shoulder.

"It will not be as painful now," Kordon murmured as he pressed a kiss to the red mark from his teeth. "My cock is too thick for you to take without first breaking the barrier protecting your womb. It may still be uncomfortable at first, but your body will accept mine. I am sorry I had to hurt you."

Gracie only understood part of his words as he spoke in a combination of her language and his, but she understood enough to know what he was trying to tell her. He wanted to minimize her discomfort. Gracie knew it would hurt since it was her first time. In a way, she was glad Kordon knew what to do.

Gracie's hips began moving on their own as her body began heating up again, and Kordon moved his fingers inside of her. She moaned loudly when she felt him spreading them to stretch her. She felt a slight burning, but more than that she felt a desire to feel *him* buried inside her, not his fingers.

"Please, Kordon. I want you. I want to feel you," Gracie moaned again as he put three fingers inside her and spread them apart.

Kordon chuckled as he ran his tongue over the swollen nub of Gracie's womanhood. She was soaking his fingers as he worked her, and he could feel her clenching at them.

He moved up slowly, kissing her soft skin as he covered her body with his own. Gracie looked up at him with a dazed smile and lifted her arms to his shoulders, running her hands lightly over him before placing them around his neck to pull him down over her. She wrapped her legs around his waist, moaning as she felt the thick head of his cock rub against her.

"You are beautiful," Kordon said in his own language as he crushed his lips down on Gracie's.

He shuddered as he forced himself to take her slowly. He felt her stiffen for a moment as the thick, bulbous head of his cock fought for entrance into her swollen heat. He pulled back slightly and pushed forward again until he felt her body open, and he slowly sank into her heated core.

Gracie trembled as the ridges stroked her sensitive walls. She couldn't prevent her body from arching into Kordon, driving him deeper into her. The first band around his cock started to swell as Kordon felt the heat building toward his first climax. There were four bands in all, and each would swell before releasing his seed, giving him total satisfaction.

He wanted Gracie to climax each time with him. As he moved deeper into her, he could feel the tightness as he stretched her. Her body fought at first but soon recognized his claim. He focused on letting the ridges along the top of his cock stroke her until she squeezed down on him tightly as her first orgasm erupted from her in a hot flow.

"Oh, oh, oh..." Gracie cried out as her body stiffened with a powerful climax that left her breathless and shaking. "Kordon!" She whimpered as the waves of pleasure kept washing through her.

"This is just the beginning, my Gracie," Kordon whispered in broken English as his own body tightened as the first band released. Kordon groaned loudly as wave after wave pulsed from his body into Gracie's tight one.

"The beginning?" Gracie whispered, looking up at Kordon in shock. "I thought..." Her words faded as Kordon smiled wickedly.

"I told you Zion males are different from human males," Kordon said as he began pumping deeper into Gracie.

Gracie gasped as she felt the swollen band rub her at the same time as the ridges. Her body immediately reacted to the simulation, and Gracie let out a small scream as she writhed under Kordon.

Kordon grunted as he pulled Gracie even closer against his chest and began pumping hard and fast. The first band had locked them together. He would not be able to pull out of her without hurting her until he had come several more times.

Gracie's body stiffened as she felt the pressure building again inside her. She frantically dug her nails into Kordon's hair and bit down on his shoulder as the pressure exploded, sending out shockwaves of pleasure as she came again. Kordon's hoarse yell followed as another band on his cock released, sending waves of pleasure soaring through him.

He felt Gracie's small tongue licking at the bite mark on his shoulder, and he let his head fall forward until it rested in the curve of Gracie's shoulder. He pressed a kiss into the soft skin as he drew in deep breaths.

Never before had he reacted so strongly during sex. He had been lucky if he spent two bands during the course of a night. With Gracie, he could already feel the third band swelling and pushing him deeper into her. He shuddered as the soft, heated walls of Gracie's channel closed around his hard length.

"Gracie," Kordon moaned into her skin. "Gracie," he repeated as he began moving again.

Kordon thought about how it would feel to take Gracie from behind. He wanted to see her spread out under him, her ass in the air as he watched his cock disappear inside her. Just the vision of it was enough to cause his cock to swell.

Pulsing streams exploded into Gracie as he slammed as deep as he could go into her. Gracie screamed as she shattered. Kordon's loud roar blended with her cry as the last two bands swelled together in such an intense release Kordon collapsed on top of Gracie in disbelief.

Kordon was stunned. Never before had he experienced total release and satisfaction. His body pulsed with energy as the intense pleasure rocked him over and over. Kordon stiffened and pulled away slightly, afraid he might be crushing Gracie. Just the thought of it caused him to chuckle. The more he thought about it, his chuckle soon turned to laughter as for the first time in a long time he felt a sense of freedom.

Gracie looked up with a pout pushing her lower lip out and pinched the side of his neck. "What is so funny?"

Kordon looked down on Gracie's flushed face. He brushed a kiss across her little nose before replying. "You ask me when I first see you if I..." Kordon frowned as he tried to figure out the word she'd used. "... quish you. I quish you now."

Gracie's pout turned into a beautiful smile as she brushed a kiss across Kordon's lips. "Squish. I asked you if you were going to squish me." Gracie giggled.

"I say that. Quish," Kordon said arrogantly.

Gracie looked up intently at Kordon for a moment. "Kordon."

"Yes, my Gracie?" Kordon whispered.

"You can squish me anytime you want to," Gracie whispered back.

Chapter 8

Kordon stared down at Gracie's sleeping figure. He needed to go, but he wanted to stay. Running his hand over his face, he bit back an oath as for the first time he wished he was not the Grand Admiral but just a warrior whose most time-consuming activity was training. His com-link sounded again, letting him know he was late for the meeting he had scheduled.

"You better go," Gracie's sleepy voice said as she peeked up at him through thick lashes.

Kordon groaned again and leaned down to brush a kiss over Gracie's swollen mouth. It was amazing some of the things she could do with it. Kordon had been afraid she would be too sore to take him again, but Gracie showed how creative she could be. Kordon felt his cock beginning to swell again just thinking about it.

"I return later. Sleep," Kordon said quietly as he brushed Gracie's hair back from her face.

"'kay," Gracie murmured, closing her eyes again.

Kordon rose and forced himself out of his living quarters. He strode to the lift and gave the command for the bridge. He nodded in acknowledgement as the crewmen stood at attention.

Kordon walked into the commander's office, nodding at Quan, Cooraan, Toolas, and Bran. Mohan was not present. Kordon frowned but made no comment when he saw the small nod from Quan. She was probably in the same place as Gracie if the satisfied look on Quan's face was anything to judge by. He moved to a tray set on a side table and poured himself a hot mixture made from different dried plant leaves from his planet.

"You said another colony has been attacked," Kordon said as he sat down with the hot beverage and pulled up the latest report.

"Corasone Five. Over a thousand dead, three hundred injured," Bran said, displaying a holovid of the planet. "It is a remote colony in an isolated area. Not much there, but barren wasteland. The colonists were trying to cultivate it using a new technique a group of scientists discovered."

Toolas kicked in what she discovered. "The same pattern of destruction was found by the warship that responded to their distress call. Any females capable of reproducing were taken. All others, including children, were killed. The men who were not killed during the fighting were killed later by having their organs and limbs surgically removed."

"The three hundred injured were found primarily in sealed tunnels or thought to already be dead. The warship that responded reached Corasone Five within twelve hours of the first distress call. You can see from the images what they found," Cooraan said coldly.

"Were any other communications recorded? What about energy signatures from the attacking ship?" Kordon asked as he processed the information from the responding warship with what his team was telling him.

He looked at the location of the most recent attack and the attack on the mining facility. They were both on the outer edge of the Confederation's protection.

Pulling up a star chart, he touched the regions to bring up the statistics on them. He pulled up a second screen and compared the information. He drew a line from one to the other.

Pulling up a third screen, he filtered for any planet in the region with life forms on it. A small moon used for mining showed up. It was a self-contained domed city containing over five hundred miners and their families. Kordon overlaid the images and noticed it fell within the line of the other two planets that were attacked.

Quan spoke up. "Mohan recorded a series of unusual communications. She has been working on deciphering them, but has not been able to figure out the base pattern for the language."

"There were no energy signatures that we could detect. It would depend on how long the ship or ships departed as to whether we would have. They must have been gone for at least four hours before our warship arrived," Bran finished.

Kordon nodded, looking intently at the small moon. It would take them two and half, possibly three days at maximum speed to get there. It was off the normal grid for the warships to patrol.

Kordon looked at Bran. "Set a course for the New World Dome mining colony on Stratus Moor."

Bran frowned at Kordon, but nodded. If Kordon wanted to go there it was for a reason. "And, Bran,"

Kordon waited until Bran turned to look at him. "Prepare for battle."

Bran looked at Kordon with a cold grin. "With pleasure, Admiral," he said before turning and leaving.

Quan looked at Kordon with a grim expression. He was not worried about going into battle. He just didn't want to do it with his life mate on board. She was to be protected at all cost.

It took him half the night to finally get the little hellcat to quit fighting him. He finally ended up tying her up and taking her. Quan couldn't help the small smile that lifted the edge of his mouth. She was purring by the time he got done with her.

"Quan, see if Mohan can make any process on deciphering the language that was recorded. I want a report in twelve hours," Kordon said as he made the decision to contact the Confederation Council with his findings. As much as he wished he didn't have to, his report would include Gracie.

Quan rose with a sharp nod. That meant he would have to untie her from his bed. Quan flexed his shoulders, feeling the sting from the claw marks his life mate had inflicted when she fought him. They were almost healed. It looked like they were about to get some company.

Toolas looked at Kordon for a moment before she cleared her throat. She waited until the others left so she could present her suspicions to Kordon alone. She sat quietly as he finished giving his instructions to Cooraan.

"You have something to say, Toolas?" Kordon asked.

Toolas cleared her throat and blushed. "Yes, sir. I wanted to present my suspicions to you."

Kordon nodded.

Toolas sat up straighter before continuing. "I believe whoever is doing this has an agenda."

"Go on," Kordon said making a steeple of his fingers and looking intently at Toolas.

"I think the females are to be used for breeding. They only take those capable and within a certain age range—fourteen to thirty. All others are killed," Toolas said, pulling up the records and data she'd marked.

"Go on," Kordon repeated. "And the males?"

"I think they are parts," Toolas said, paling at the idea. "They take parts they can use... organs, especially but limbs as well. The victims are alive at the time with no wounds. Anyone with a wound or disease is discarded."

Kordon's face tightened at the idea that this was the type of creature Gracie had fought against. The archives stated she had actually boarded the mother ship alone so she could disable it. The thought of her being used as a breeding machine for them turned his stomach.

"Anything else?" Kordon asked.

Toolas shook her head before standing. "No. I will continue looking over the information that has been collected. If I find anything new, I will inform you immediately."

Kordon nodded. He turned to the reports and looked at the star charts again. If it was the Alluthans, the only one who really knew anything about them was the one person he didn't want anywhere near them. Gracie. Kordon's gut twisted at the thought of her having to once again deal with the creatures that had changed her life.

* * *

Quan entered his living quarters quietly and walked toward the bed where he had Mohan tied up. She turned her head as he approached and hissed at him. It would seem she was in no better mood than she had been last night. Her eyes widened as Quan pulled the shirt over his head.

"Oh no, you don't!" Mohan hissed out as she fought against the restraints holding her wrists above her head and the two holding her legs apart.

Quan growled low at her denial of him. "Yes!" he growled out as he climbed over her soft body.

Quan groaned as the soft fur coating her body ran along his heated flesh. He leaned over and blew a hot breath against her distended nipple.

Mohan cursed when a purr escaped her throat and her body arched. She hated the sensual nature of her Ta'nee half. She was rare among her kind, even among her own sisters and brothers, as she'd only had a handful of sexual encounters and only with males she was drawn to on a deeper level. Her only lapse into a one-night stand had been with Kordon, and that was after she had drunk far too much.

Mohan hissed as Quan bit down on her nipple, causing it to sting briefly before he rolled his tongue over it. She was frustrated; she wanted him again after he'd tricked her last night.

When he caught up with her in the lift on the pretense of asking her a question she didn't think anything of it. She had spent the last several days doing everything she could to avoid him. She might have been able to convince him she wasn't interested in him if her stupid fur had cooperated, but the moment the doors of the lift closed and his scent filled it, her fur started rippling in a mad rush of colors.

The next thing she knew she was in his living quarters. It wasn't until he made his outrageous claim that she was his that she tried to leave. When he tried to stop her, she bit him.

For a Ta'nee, that was a big no-no. A Ta'nee's bite was only given to her mate. Their saliva contained a chemical agent that increased their sexual stimulation, and on the right person, a bond. Mohan hadn't meant to bite Quan. She'd fought like the wildcat she was when she felt the taste of him. If he didn't feel the same for her, she would always be alone.

"Easy, kitten. Easy," Quan said as he slid his hand down over the soft, light coating of fur on her flat belly. "Easy," Quan whispered as he let his fingers test her readiness for him.

"Quan..." Mohan half moaned, half purred. She moved against his fingers, trying to force them inside her. "Please..." Mohan arched against his palm.

"Admit you are mine, Mohan. Admit you are mine, and I will release you and give you what you are begging me for," Quan said against her swollen mound.

"Yes," Mohan whispered, frightened.

Quan rose up over her again and looked down into her beautiful dark eyes. "Yes, what?" Quan asked harshly.

Mohan's eyes glittered with unshed tears. "Please don't hurt me," Mohan whispered. "Please."

Quan's eyes softened as he looked down on the most beautiful female he'd ever seen. "I could never hurt you, Mohan. You are my life mate... mine to love and mine to protect," Quan said gently.

Mohan bit her lip before she responded. "Then I am yours."

Quan growled in triumph as he sliced through the bonds holding Mohan's hands. "What about my legs?" Mohan asked as she ran her soft, fur-covered hands over Quan's cheeks.

Quan grinned wickedly before he slowly impaled his swollen cock deeply into her. "I like having you spread open and ready for me," he said with a groan as he began moving faster, letting the swollen bands on his cock lock him to Mohan.

"Mine, Mohan. Mine," Quan said as he felt his first release. Mohan just purred.

Chapter 9

Gracie sat next to Mohan in the communications room listening to the recordings the mining foreman made before he was killed and the few transmissions recorded from Corasone Five. The familiar sounds sent a shiver down her spine. She understood what they were saying because she had listened in on all their communications over a five-year period.

"Destroy unused portions. Return to mother ship," Gracie was saying softly as she listened to the voices coming through the headset. "All parts received. New breeders have been contained for implantation."

She forced the nausea down as she continued deciphering the mismatch of communications. There wasn't much really, just disjointed phrases. Gracie had been about to explore the ship when Mohan showed up earlier outside of Kordon's living space with Quan in tow.

Gracie smiled at the huge warrior who was practically standing over Mohan and growling at any male who walked by them. Mohan just rolled her eyes and whispered frantically for Quan to knock it off. At least that was what it sounded like to Gracie.

She had spent a good portion of the morning studying the language most commonly used on board the ship. It was called Confederation Standard. She was able to identify the main letters that made up its alphabet and most of the sounds, thanks to the computer console in the room. There were a few she was having a little bit of difficulty with and wanted to ask Mohan about, but overall, she felt confident it wouldn't take long for her to learn the language.

When she felt like her brain was about to explode, she'd decided a walk through the ship might help her relax. That was when she practically walked right into Mohan standing outside the doors.

Mohan asked if Gracie would like to accompany her to the communications room. She felt confident Gracie might be able to help her with the deciphering of the language.

Mohan became concerned when Gracie turned pale as she began playing the communications. Quan was about to call for Kordon when Gracie held up her hand for him to stay.

She listened through the communications once before she began speaking in a soft monotone, translating the Alluthans' communications into English. Mohan listened intently as she began speaking before translating it into Confederation Standard so the others could understand. Quan turned sharp eyes on Gracie before he quietly left the room.

"Kordon?" Quan called quietly into his comlink from outside the communications room.

"Kordon," the deep voice responded.

"Gracie Jones has translated the messages. It is the Alluthans. Mohan is translating for you now," Quan said calmly, looking on as his life mate's head bowed closer to that of Kordon's mate.

Quan listened as Kordon breathed in deeply before responding. "On my way."

Quan turned to watch as Gracie showed Mohan how to read the message in Alluthan. Mohan smiled gently at the small human sitting beside her, nodding in understanding. Quan felt his heart swell at his life mate's gentleness. He would give his life to protect both females from a fate such as that of the women who'd been captured.

..*

Gracie laid her head on Kordon's chest, feeling totally exhausted. She'd spent the day with Mohan in the communications room. Kordon came down briefly to talk to her about the transmissions.

Gracie explained the language was identical to that of the Alluthans who attacked Earth. She would need more information to tell if their programming or anything else had evolved over the past three or eight hundred years. If not, or if not by much, she knew the back doors into their systems.

She explained everything she knew about the Alluthans. How they were primarily solitary spaceships, rather like scavengers, except when there was an abundance of resources. She explained the infrastructure of the mother ship based on what she'd learned on Earth, and about the fighters, supply ships, and ground forces.

Afterward, Kordon simply touched her cheek and left, with a nod to Quan, who nodded grimly back at him. Mohan gently guided Gracie out, and they ended up in the dining hall where Mohan began giving Gracie intensive language lessons. Gracie surprised Mohan with her quick ability to catch on. It was during this conversation that Mohan asked Gracie how she was feeling now.

"I feel needed... useful," Gracie told Mohan hesitantly, glancing at Quan, who was seated a couple of feet away with a group of warriors.

He glanced over, but didn't move to join them. It was as if he knew Gracie needed time alone with another female. Gracie gave him a small, grateful smile before turning back to Mohan.

Gracie played with the cup in her hand. "I'm still scared and sad. It is hard to lose everything and everyone you ever loved one time. But to lose them a second time..." Gracie's voice faded as she stared into the gold-colored liquid.

"A second time...?" Mohan asked gently.

Gracie looked up into Mohan's dark eyes. "When you told me everyone was okay, that the Earth was fine, I thought I would be going home. I thought I would see Chance again. Maybe even see my parents and sister."

Gracie paused for a moment before continuing. "I felt hope again and a reason for still being alive." Gracie took a deep breath before finishing her thought.

"Then you told me it was all gone. Everyone, everything that was important to me. The things that made me fight so hard for survival when all I wanted to do some days was give up—were gone. I can't describe the pain, Mohan. I can't believe my heart didn't shatter into a million pieces from it."

Mohan looked at Gracie for a moment before she gently cupped one of Gracie's small hands in hers. "Perhaps it could not shatter because it was no longer yours to break. Perhaps your heart already knew it belonged to another. One who is in your world now and who will do everything he can to protect it."

Gracie stared at Mohan before a tentative smile curled her lips. "Maybe you are right."

Kordon knew about the conversation Gracie had earlier with Mohan. She was still under orders to record all of their discussions, even the private ones. It was not that he did not trust Gracie or wanted to infringe on her privacy. He simply wanted to learn everything he could about who she was now.

He'd read the archives and what history said about her. Her courage and intelligence were, without question, as were her loyalty and her compassion for others.

He was still frustrated with their language barrier, but he knew Mohan was teaching her Confederation Standard and he was learning her ancient English. It would take time, but each day it was getting better.

He knew part of his fear was the depression Toolas told him about. He still feared Gracie might try to end her life. He had argued that point with the Confederation Council when they heard about her being alive.

Since at least one human sat on the Council, the news was unbelievable. The Council had originally wanted Kordon to send Gracie to Paulus, the capital city, but he refused, citing a need for her knowledge on the Alluthans.

It took every ounce of his patience, not to order the Human Council member's residence to be destroyed when he had insisted Gracie be returned as soon as possible. It was only when the Council member's request was overridden by the other members that Kordon was able to breathe a sigh of relief.

He returned afterward to the communications room and practically dragged Gracie out. Between her conversation with Mohan where she admitted she missed the human male, Chance, and the slimy human councilman, Kordon needed to reassert his claim on Gracie. They had come together in an explosion of need.

When Gracie suggested she be on top, Kordon fought the idea. A Zion Warrior was always on top. It gave him the control. But one look at Gracie's pouting lips and twinkling eyes made Kordon give in with a disgruntled grunt.

Now, as she lay draped across his chest with him still locked to her, he wondered why he'd never tried this position before, as it allowed him to enjoy the view of her tantalizing breasts while giving him deeper access to her sweet channel. He found if he pushed up as she came down, he could easily touch her womb while sucking her pert nipples.

"Knock it off!" Gracie said sleepily in Confederation Standard.

Kordon's eyebrows rose as he chuckled. "Knock what off?"

"You're thinking about sex again," Gracie said, rubbing her cheek against his bare chest.

"Why do you think I'm thinking of sex?" Kordon asked with another chuckle.

Gracie rose up enough to look into Kordon's dark blue eyes. "I can feel you moving inside me," Gracie whispered. "I can feel the bands moving and stretching me, and the tip of your cock is like fine fingers rubbing deep inside me and turning me on again."

Kordon's eyes turned even darker the more Gracie described the feeling of having him deep inside her. With a deep groan, Kordon wrapped one hand around the back of Gracie's head, pulling her lips down to his while his other hand began massaging her ass.

"Ride me again, Gracie," Kordon said against her lips as he lightly ran his fingers along the inside curve of her ass. It caused Gracie's breath to catch and her back to bow. "Ride me."

"Oh, Kordon, you say the most wonderful things," Gracie said as she began riding her warrior.

* * *

Two days later, the *Conqueror* was in orbit around the small moon containing the New World Dome mining colony on Stratus Moor. The *Conqueror's* long-range sensors did not detect anything unusual, but Kordon's gut was telling him something entirely different.

Mohan opened communications with the mining colony and the director-elect welcomed them. A small welcoming party greeted them. Kordon and Quan both wanted to leave Gracie and Mohan on board the warship, but both were unable to let the women be that far from them.

Gracie smiled as a woman not much older than she, with a small girl on her hip, stepped forward to greet them. She was the foreman's wife. Kordon reluctantly agreed that the women could go with Delaira while the men talked. Kordon wanted to see what type of defense systems were in place.

"Your daughter is very beautiful," Gracie said as she followed Delaira through the tunnels of the domed city. "How old is she?"

"Lara will be a year old in a month," Delaira said with a smile.

Mohan giggled when the little girl waved her arm at her, trying to pat her fur. "She is adorable."

The women spent several hours exploring the small market some of the miners' wives set up to trade together and enjoying refreshments. Delaira shared the trials and tribulations of being the wife of a miner, but she also shared the joys of it being a close-knit community.

They were making their way back toward the mining offices when an explosion knocked them against the wall. The lights flickered for a moment, but stayed on. Delaira tightened her hold on Lara as the little girl started to cry.

"There must have been an accident in one of the mines. It doesn't happen often, but it does happen. I will take you to the offices, then I must see if there are any injuries," Delaira said quickly.

Mohan gripped Gracie as another explosion rocked the complex. Screams could be heard in the distance and small fires were beginning to pop up as cabling was knocked loose. Red emergency lights filtered through the smoke. Mohan froze as she heard static coming through the comlink from the *Conqueror*.

"We are under attack," Mohan said, holding the comlink against her ear. "An unknown ship has appeared. The *Conqueror* is taking heavy fire. It is returning fire, but the enemy ships have a shield protecting them."

Gracie paled as she heard Mohan's description. "I need a computer. I need a computer now!" Gracie said frantically.

Delaira held the sobbing infant against her and nodded. "This way."

Gracie, Mohan, Delaira, and her daughter struggled to climb over a crumbled rock wall blocking the corridor. Delaira coughed as dust filled the air and quickly wrapped her scarf around her and her daughter's heads. Mohan and Gracie were left with trying to stretch their shirts up high enough to cover their noses and mouths. All around them screams and shouts could be heard. Delaira pushed open a door and stepped inside.

"Go. There is a console with emergency power. I must go check on the others," Delaira said before she disappeared down the darkened corridor before Mohan or Gracie could stop her.

Gracie moved over quickly to the console and straightened the chair. She sat down at the console and began punching in a series of commands looking to see if she could tap into the Alluthans' computer system again. Sweat beaded and ran down her face, creating a dirty path, but she ignored it.

It took almost ten minutes, but she was finally able to find an open door. Thank God the Alluthans were solitary creatures. This might be the reason they had not evolved if their programming was anything to go by. It was slightly different from eight hundred years ago, but not by much.

She slipped inside and began typing a simple but effective virus that would take their systems offline for a little while. It wasn't her best virus or her most effective, but it replicated quickly.

She was breathing heavily from a combination of fear, adrenaline, and dust. Mohan sneezed several times. Gracie punched in the command and sighed. If it was going to work they would know in a few minutes.

"Gracie, we need to leave now," Mohan's fear-filled voice said. She was looking out of the doorway down the corridor. "I do not recognize those coming toward us. My instincts tell me to run."

"Go, Mohan. I have to disable this, or they can stop it. I didn't create a very complicated virus. Go and I will catch up with you," Gracie whispered as her fingers flew over the keyboard.

"No, we go together. I will not leave you, Gracie Jones," Mohan said, pulling a small laser pistol out of her holster.

Gracie worked as fast as she could before she felt confident it would take a while for anyone to unravel what she'd done. She pulled the power on the computer console and rose up, heading for the doorway where Mohan was standing lookout.

"Go now," Mohan whispered, pointing to a corridor across from them.

Gracie nodded and moved rapidly through the doorway, followed by Mohan. They climbed over the rocks hoping the sounds of falling rocks, distant screams, and popping electrical wires would cover them. Since neither of them knew their way around the maze of tunnels, they decided to find a good place to hide and wait for the warriors on the *Conqueror* to find them.

Neither one would admit to their fear for their life mates. Gracie couldn't imagine finally finding love again only to lose it a second time. She jerked to a stop as she realized she did love Kordon. Not in the same innocent way she'd loved Chance, but with the love of a woman for a man.

Mohan looked back with a question in her eyes when Gracie didn't follow her immediately. Gracie shook her head silently and motioned for Mohan to continue. She loved Kordon. Gracie trembled with fear at the thought of never seeing him again. What if he was trapped, hurt… or dead?

Mohan motioned for Gracie to move back as a group of Alluthan warriors went by, dragging several women behind them. Gracie recognized them from the marketplace. They were crying and begging for the creatures to release them.

A scream from behind the group made Mohan and Gracie jump. It was Delaira. She was holding the limp body of her infant daughter against her. Two of the creatures were working to remove the child from her mother's arms.

Delaira was fighting the creatures before one of them pulled Lara's small body away and dropped her onto the hard ground. The other creature pointed a device at Delaira's head, a short flash burst out, and Delaira collapsed next to the body of her daughter. The creature that had dropped Lara bent over and picked up Delaira's unconscious body and tossed her over its shoulder.

Gracie stared at the tiny body of the little girl who barely an hour ago was giggling at Mohan. It was Earth all over again. Gracie knew she couldn't let it happen again.

She pulled the laser pistol out of Mohan's hand, walked up behind the Alluthans, and aimed it at the back of the creature holding Delaira. She fired two short blasts into the heads of each one of them, watching as they collapsed.

Her virus was working. Their body shields were down, which meant the shields protecting their fighter ships would be down soon. Gracie walked over to where Delaira lay. She knelt down and felt a faint pulse. Standing, she turned to look at Mohan, whose eyes were frantically searching the dusty darkness looking for additional creatures.

Gracie knew what she needed to do. The virus would barely touch the mother ship. The only way to stop it was to be on board and upload a virus directly into its systems.

"Stay with Delaira," Gracie said quietly to Mohan, not looking at her.

"Gracie?" Mohan whispered as she touched her arm. "Where are you going? What are you planning?"

Gracie turned and looked at Mohan. "I can stop them," Gracie said. "I can stop this from happening again… to your world, to other Delairas," Gracie said, stepping away.

"I cannot let you go, Gracie Jones," Mohan said determinedly. "I will not let you."

Gracie turned and smiled sadly at Mohan. "You have to," Gracie said, taking another step away before she started jogging after the other creatures.

"Gracie!" Mohan called out frantically behind her. Gracie raced through the narrow opening of the corridor the other creatures went through. Turning, she fired the laser pistol up at the ceiling, blocking Mohan from following her. "Why, Gracie? Why must you do this?"

Gracie choked back a cough as the dust began to settle. "It was my destiny to be here. I have to stop them from harming any more worlds. Maybe this is why I lived," Gracie said, wanting to reach out and touch her friend one last time, but afraid if she did she wouldn't be able to leave. "Mohan, tell Kordon... tell Kordon I'm sorry and that I love him."

"Gracie!" Mohan whispered frantically, trying to pull the rocks away from the entrance. "Gracie!" She cried out again, watching as Gracie's tiny frame disappeared into the darkness.

* * *

Kordon cursed when he felt the first explosion. He called out to the *Conqueror* to find out what was going on. A group of unknown fighters had appeared as if out of nowhere. The *Conqueror* was taking heavy fire. The starboard engine was offline.

Fighters were being deployed, but their energy bursts could not penetrate the shields around the enemy fighter ships. Bran was transferring power to the shields. Visuals from the fighters stated enemy ships were landing on the small moon. Quan, Douglen, and Kordon could feel the explosions farther off.

"I need to find my wife and daughter," Douglen said, pulling open a cabinet to reveal a multitude of weapons.

He tossed several to Kordon and to Quan. "Let's go."

Douglen was a former mercenary who'd decided to settle after meeting Delaira during one of his commissions. Both had found love and peace within the mining community, and he would be damned if he'd let anything destroy it.

Moving through the dark corridors with the ease of experience, he was able to take maintenance tunnels to bypass some of the tunnels that were blocked. Pushing against one of the doors, he came out into a tunnel not far from where Delaira had been when they last communicated.

"This was where Delaira said they were at last check-in," Douglen choked out as smoke and dust thickened the air.

Kordon nodded. "Check each section. Bran says the attacking force has some type of shield protecting them."

Quan turned as another explosion rocked the mining colony. "Lead the way," he said grimly to Douglen. He wanted to find Mohan and Gracie.

The three men formed a triangle, Douglen in the center as he knew the tunnels, with Kordon flanking his left side and Quan his right. Each man moved silently. Douglen held up his hand. He motioned there were two targets coming toward them.

Each man moved into a crevice and waited. When it was clear it was the attacking creatures and not some of the miners, Douglen opened fire with his laser rifle. The burst glowed brightly as they flashed over the shields protecting the creatures. The creatures kept advancing, pulling up their own weapons. They moved side by side, seemingly unconcerned with the fact they were being fired upon.

Kordon gritted his teeth as he fired shot after shot, just to watch them flare harmlessly in front of the creatures. He didn't even flinch when one of the blasts from the creature's laser fire ripped through his uniform, cutting a deep groove through his thigh, while another shot cut a path along his shoulder. Pain blossomed, then faded as he pushed it away.

"Shit!" Douglen said as he went down on one knee.

"How bad?" Quan called out, firing blast after blast as he moved across the corridor to cover Douglen.

"Through the calf," Douglen bit out.

"We are just sitting targets here. We have no defense against them unless maybe hand-to-hand," Douglen said as he continued firing at the creatures getting closer and closer to them.

One creature leaned over a boulder blocking half the corridor. Kordon watched as he pulled his arm back and slammed his fist into it. He did it four times before the boulder cracked into pieces. The damn thing must have weighed five hundred pounds or more.

"Shit!" Quan said. "Hand-to-hand is out."

Kordon growled in frustration as the two enemy targets walked through the remains of the boulder. There was nothing stopping the Alluthans from killing all three of them now.

Pulling his laser pistol up, he stepped into the corridor and walked toward the two creatures firing round after round. It was the height of insult that they did not even bother to return his fire. It was almost like they were enjoying the fact they could kill them at any time.

They were within a few feet of Kordon when he raised his laser pistol at one of their heads with a curse. "Arrogant bastards! Zion warriors do not die without a fight," Kordon said as he pulled the trigger again.

Kordon waited for the creature to finally respond to his presence. He didn't know who was more surprised, him or the creature, when it jerked back a step before collapsing. Half of the creature's head was missing. Kordon didn't wait for the other creature's response. He turned and fired.

Quan came up behind Kordon with a grin on his dirty face. "Why didn't you do that in the first place?"

Kordon stared down at the two creatures, frowning for a moment as his mind raced through all the possible reasons the enemy's shields had failed. Every one of the reasons pointed to one person— Gracie.

"Gracie," Kordon said, his head jerking up to look down the corridor. "It was Gracie."

With an oath, Kordon began moving down the corridor more rapidly. His stomach began to twist at the thought of her being in danger. She had better have found a place to hide, or he was going to whip her ass.

Kordon turned when Douglen called out for him to go to the right. Kordon raised his laser rifle, firing at the creatures in the corridor ahead of him without stopping. Quan was firing as well. None of the men slowed down. They simply jumped over the remains and kept moving.

Douglen called out the next corridor should open into a small cavern used as a market. Kordon reached the entrance to it and stopped, pressing back against the wall to see if it was clear.

Overturned carts, shattered barrels, and trade goods littered the floor. Quan pressed against the wall across from Kordon and scanned the area. Douglen leaned back against the wall next to Kordon and grimaced. The wound in his leg burned, and blood still trickled from it. He muttered a curse and ripped the sleeve off his shirt and tied it around the wound.

A slight sound to the left caused all the men to freeze. It was so soft, they almost missed it. Kordon nodded to Quan to move to the right while he would go around to the left. Kordon motioned for Douglen to hold back and cover them. Douglen nodded, pulling his laser rifle up.

Kordon skirted the edge of the cavern, moving slowly along the wall. He stepped over a small pile of broken dishes, being careful not to step on any. He had the laser rifle pressed tight against his shoulder, moving carefully back and forth as he scanned the area. Quan motioned he was going around a stall. Kordon gave a brief nod and continued around the back of another one.

The noise came again… a soft whimper that was cut short. Kordon came around the side of the stall at the same time as Quan came around the one across from him. There was an overturned cart with a sheet of colored cloth over it. Quan mimicked pulling it off and raised three fingers. Kordon nodded and moved into position.

On the count of three, Quan jerked the cloth off suddenly, and Kordon swung around pointing the laser rifle downward. On the ground under the cart was a young woman with tears running down her face as she rocked back and forth. Beside her were the bodies of Delaira and Lara.

Quan cursed out loud. "Douglen!" he called out quietly.

Kordon knelt next to Delaira and pressed his fingers against her throat. He felt the steady beat of her pulse. Next, he pressed against the tiny throat of Lara. It took a moment, but he finally detected a faint pulse.

Douglen came around the cart. When he saw his wife and infant daughter lying motionless a choked cry of grief escaped him. He moved closer, collapsing down onto his knees next to them.

"They live," Kordon said, looking around. Where were Gracie and Mohan?

Kordon turned his hard eyes to the young woman rocking back and forth. "There were two other women with her. They were not from your community. Where are they?" Kordon asked coldly.

Quan was moving around the area overturning carts and looking in stalls. He was calling out loudly for Mohan to answer him. When he received no answer, he roared out in rage, stomping back toward them.

"Where are the two females who were with Delaira?" Quan snarled out, reaching down to grip the woman by her arms.

The young woman cried out and moved back, shaking her head. "The one that looked like a cat told me to stay with Delaira and Lara. She said to stay here—that someone would come to help us. I don't know where she went," the young woman sobbed.

Douglen leaned down over Lara, pulling her tiny body against his broad chest. He closed his eyes a moment as if he was focusing deep inside himself. When he opened them, Lara's multi-colored eyes stared back at him and a small grin twisted her lips.

"Delaira put Lara into a sleep to keep her quiet," Douglen said, gently brushing a shaking hand over his daughter's hair.

Douglen looked at the young woman sobbing quietly. "Mia, there were two women. Which way did they go?" Douglen asked quietly but in a tone that told Mia she had to answer him.

Mia looked up at Douglen as if in a daze. "There was only one. The… the one that looked like a cat. She said something about going after a Gracie. She told me to tell Kordon, Gracie was trying to stop the attackers. She was going to their ship. Then she left me. She left me hidden and told me to watch over Delaira and Lara."

Chapter 10

Kordon stood aboard the *Conqueror*, looking out through the front viewport. In reality he didn't see anything. Shortly after the shields on the ground force of the invading Alluthans' failed, the shields on their fighters began failing.

Two supply ships lifted off and were able to escape, but all the others were destroyed before they ever left the small moon. Bran was doing a sweep of the surrounding space, looking for energy signatures from the supply shuttles, but it appeared that whatever type of shield they used blocked it from appearing on the *Conqueror's* scanners.

A thorough sweep of the mining dome showed extensive damage. Eighteen men, ten women, and four children were killed during the invasion. Forty others were wounded. Gracie and Mohan were not among any of the groups: survivors, wounded, or dead. That left just one other option... they were among the missing. The creatures had captured four women, six counting Gracie and Mohan. Quan stood beside Kordon silently. The only way of knowing the effect of their findings on him was the muscle clenching and unclenching in his jaw.

"Sir! I'm receiving a cryptic message from a signature source belonging to the Alluthans," one of the communications officers called out.

Kordon and Quan both swung around. "Patch it through to my office," Kordon gritted out harshly.

* * *

Kordon quickly entered the password and a scrambled holovid came on. A message flashed briefly. It was a question written in an ancient language.

Whose touch? The message flashed.

"Gracie's," Kordon murmured. The minute he said Gracie's name the image cleared.

Kordon's throat tightened as he took in the dirt- and bloodstained face of his life mate. Her vivid green eyes stared back at him sadly, but with a quiet determination. It appeared she was inside one of the alien's supply ships.

"This is Gracie. Kordon, I hope you get this message," Kordon watched as Gracie drew in a deep breath. "I... There is a computer in my bag in our room. It has a copy of everything about the Alluthans that I compiled back on Earth.

"I left the information with Adam just in case it was needed, but Mohan told me it was never found. I am guessing it was destroyed in the battle. It will help your people decipher their language. It also contains ways to deactivate their shields. I guess them being solitary creatures is a good thing as they don't know I know their systems."

Gracie blew a strand of hair out of her eyes and paused for a moment as she programmed something on the console. "Anyway, I've programmed a signal you should be able to follow to the mother ship. I was able to take one of the supply ships." Gracie let out a dry, bitter laugh.

"I swear I will not die in one of these damn things if I can help it! On the computer is information about the way the Alluthans function. They are half organic, half robot. This is why they need replacement parts. Their minds are synced with each other. If you cut off the head, the rest will die. Their head is the mother ship. I don't know if I can do what I did before, but I am going to try to upload a virus that will shut them down."

Gracie's eyes filled with tears, but none fell as she continued. "I am also going to upload a self-destruct program. Kordon, I believe this is why I didn't die the first time. I-I think fate knew I wasn't done. If you get this message I want you to know I love you," Gracie said. Gracie's throat worked up and down before she finished. "This is Gracie's Touch saying... good-bye."

Kordon stared at the stilled image of Gracie on the screen. His fists were clenched so tightly his fingers were numb. The blank mask of his face hid the devastation her words wrought inside him. Quan stood with his back to Kordon. His shoulders hunched, and his head was bowed. Neither man spoke as they each played out their own private nightmares.

"Kordon," Bran's said as he entered Kordon's office. Cooraan was right behind him. "We've got a signal."

Kordon stood up as a cold rage filled him. This was not good-bye. He would not let Gracie sacrifice herself again. He would not let her face this alone.

* * *

"Gracie has information on her computer in our living quarters that she says will help us. Cooraan, it is on the floor next to our bed. Get it and get the information deciphered immediately. I know Mohan set up a program to translate between Gracie's language and Confederation Standard. Cooraan, I also want you to go over the programming she has that will deactivate those bastards' shields. I want every last one of them dead," Kordon said coldly before turning to Bran.

Cooraan gave a quick nod and left.

"Bran, I want you to follow those bastards so close we can smell what they ate. Do not destroy any ship, especially supply ships, without my expressed permission. Disable them if you have to but do not destroy. My life mate and Quan's are on one of them. I will bring Gracie and Mohan home."

Bran nodded grimly. "I'll work with Cooraan on the programming. Maybe we can modify our own shields."

Kordon nodded before turning to look at Quan, who was staring back at him with grim determination. "We have our mates to get back. Let's get to work."

* * *

Gracie shivered when she saw the huge dark shape of the mother ship. A sense of déjà vu swept through her, causing goose bumps to form on her arms. She let the automatic pilot program take over and watched as it followed the other supply ship through the open door in the side of the huge ship. The inside of the ship was huge!

Beyond huge, really, Gracie thought in dismay.

What looked like thousands of fighters were docked in stacking formation as far as the eye could see. Gracie shivered again as she let her eyes take in everything. Lights flashed along several walls. They looked like some type of lifts.

Gracie watched as the first supply ship docked in one of the empty ports. Her ship moved in slowly next to it and she heard the locks engage. The lights in the supply ship dimmed and an arm came out to clamp onto the side.

Gracie's shivering turned to quakes at the strange groaning sounds emitted by the metal reminded her of the sounds from an old haunted house she went through one Halloween. She half expected to see ghosts and goblins coming out.

Gracie peeked through the front viewport as a platform lowered on the supply ship next to her. Two creatures moved down the platform and paused, turning back to wait. Gracie gasped as she saw two women from the mining colony being shoved down the ramp. A moment later, two other women were pushed out.

She bit her lip as she watched them huddle together as the two creatures began prodding them to move. Her gaze swung back to the opening when two more creatures came to the opening. They held a struggling female between them.

Gracie's eyes widened with horror as she saw Mohan hiss at one of the creatures. The creature pressed the same device she saw them use on Delaira against Mohan's head. A moment later, Mohan collapsed, unconscious.

Gracie wrung her hands together, trying to decide what to do. She couldn't let her friend or the other women be used as breeders or die. There had to be something she could do.

Gracie stood up and began searching the supply ship. There had to be a portable computer somewhere on it. She tore open storage compartments, pulling out cartons and opening them up randomly. There were parts, what looked like some type of freeze-dried food packages, and other equipment she didn't even try to figure out.

She moved to another cabinet and tore it open. Space suits like what the creatures had worn in the domed city and what they were now wearing on the other supply ship. At the top of the cabinet was a portable tablet. Gracie's hands trembled as she pulled it down.

Gracie quickly powered it on. She would need to leave the supply ship soon or the creatures might get suspicious. She looked up at the suits hanging in the closet and thought about the plan forming in her mind.

It was never going to work. True, she wasn't much smaller than the creatures, but—it couldn't possibly work, could it? Not giving herself a chance to consider the consequences, she set the portable tablet down, pulled one of the suits out, and began dressing.

The prisoners are about to get a new guard, Gracie thought with determination.

Gracie moved slowly down the platform, breathing deeply behind the helmet. She could hear the voices giving different commands. It was confusing at first as it seemed to come from so many at one time. It was difficult to filter every conversation.

She turned, following the same path she saw the other creatures taking. She fought to keep her breath even as several creatures moved toward her. She was afraid her knees would give out from shaking so hard. Forcing herself to continue forward as if she belonged there, she was amazed they couldn't see her shaking. She couldn't help the breath of relief that swooshed out of her when the creatures passed her as if she wasn't even there.

Gracie continued down the platform before stepping into the shadows near a thick row of metal tubing. She pulled the portable tablet up. Gracie quickly opened a backdoor into the computer system, creating a virtual ghost. This allowed her to piggyback onto existing programs, making her almost invisible.

She sent out feelers for the ship's schematics. Almost instantly, a map of the ship appeared on her screen. Gracie filtered for holding cell or females. A series of code rolled faster than her eyes could follow before it stopped, and a map showing a long series of cells showed. Level 824, Section 228, Cells 18-21.

Gracie drew in a shaking breath as she counted the number of women—twenty-two. There were twenty-two women being held in the cells. Gracie closed her eyes. She needed to get them off the ship. She could program one of the supply ships to get them off. If Kordon got her message, he would know to look for the signal she programmed in and would be following them.

She opened her eyes and looked at the map again. She would need to go down. She drew in a deep breath and straightened her shoulders before saying a small prayer to any god out there that might be listening to give her the strength and protection to do what needed to be done.

Chapter 11

Kordon looked over the modifications on the shields Bran and Cooraan made. The data found on Gracie's computer astonished all the men. Her attention to detail, her annotations, and her modifications and programming skills pulled a respect from the Zion warriors rarely found outside their own people.

Kordon was learning more about who Gracie really was, and his love and respect for her grew. Among the data Cooraan found was Gracie's personal diary. He translated it for Kordon.

Cooraan reluctantly admitted he read the entries. He apologized to Kordon for invading his life mate's private thoughts, explaining he was not sure what it was until he began reading it.

Kordon was unable to be too upset after watching the huge warrior actually blush as he murmured he had been unable to stop reading it once he started as he had to know what happened next. Cooraan swore he would never mention to anyone about what he had read. It was the look in Cooraan's eyes that finally got to Kordon, and he had to ask him what was bothering him.

"Your life mate is a unique and incredible female," Cooraan responded. "I have never heard of one so strong and determined. There was much fear, but she never gave up. Once you read it you will understand. I-I can only hope to find a life mate such as her," Cooraan said. "Your Gracie is very special."

Kordon's jaw clenched at Cooraan's softly spoken words. "Yes, she is," Kordon said before turning to the console.

"We will bring her home safely. I swear this on my own life. I will do whatever it takes to help you bring her home," Cooraan said fiercely before turning to leave.

Kordon stared blankly at the screen for a few moments before taking a deep breath and opening the file containing Gracie's diary. Soon, he was lost in her world over eight hundred Earth years ago. The first sentence tightened the pain in his chest around his heart as he became one with the frightened little girl who cowered in the dark subway tunnels in a long-ago city.

Today is June 14, 2015. My name is Gracie Jones. I am 12 years old and all alone now. It all started yesterday when we were having dinner. Mom and Dad were talking to me and Violet about a new project mom was working on when the explosions started. Dad ran to the window to see what was happening. Mom pulled me and Violet under the table because stuff from the ceiling was falling down. When dad came back, he looked real scared...

Kordon read entry after entry, lost in Gracie's retelling. He learned that she got separated from her sister and parents when they were fleeing from their neighborhood. The Alluthans were destroying house after house, forcing the residents out into the streets where they began rounding them up.

During the confusion, Gracie fell and rolled under a car so she wouldn't get trampled. She saw her parents and sister being taken. She huddled there for hours not moving. Once darkness fell, she returned to what was left of her home. She was able to get a few clothing items, her laptop, and some other items which she stuffed into her school backpack.

She ran when she saw fighters flying low over the neighborhood. She ran and hid throughout the night until she finally made her way down into the subway access a few miles from her home. There were a few people hiding there. By morning, the Alluthan warriors were searching the subway systems.

Gracie ran up the tracks. She crawled under an overhang and discovered a covered stairwell. Following it down, she found herself in an old abandoned section of the subway. It was there that Adam, Adrian, Mark, and Chance found her almost six months later, barely alive.

She was painfully thin as finding food had become harder and harder without venturing further afield. She wrote about how she had spent most of her time playing on the computer, trying to find out any information she could about the creatures who took her family. She made notes of the sounds of their language and began piecing it together like a puzzle.

Both her parents were linguists who used to play games with her and her sister, making up languages or using ancient languages to create messages. Gracie was determined to find her family again. When Adam first found her, she was hiding in an old maintenance room behind an old plaid couch. Gracie wrote about how scared she was of the huge man.

It was Chance who finally talked her out with his quiet looks, gentle eyes, and sense of humor. He finally convinced Gracie they would not harm her. That was the first night in six months that she actually ate until she was full.

Kordon read of the following years of struggle. The five became known as the Freedom Five. Gracie began giving daily updates and messages of encouragement to survivors and those fighting against the Alluthans. She also became instrumental in deciphering their language and breaking into their computer systems, giving the rebel groups a continuing edge.

Throughout the diary, she mentioned her growing love for Chance and her belief he would never see her as a woman. She talked about her heartache at finding him in a passionate embrace with a woman from another rebel group. She had been so heartbroken she had left the safety of the tunnels.

She was wounded and captured when an Alluthan warrior found her hiding in an old building two days later. If not for Mark and Adam, she would have been imprisoned. They were able to kill the Alluthan by electrocuting him. They carried Gracie back to the tunnels, but it took months for her to regain her strength.

Kordon finally got to Gracie's last days on Earth. She was able to finally break through the programming codes and take over one of the supply ships. When she discovered a way to bring the shields down, it was a turning point. The problem was that in order to bring down all the shields at the same time, she needed to be on the mother ship to launch her virus to prevent the Alluthans from counteracting it. Since Gracie was the only one to know how to interpret their programming, she was the one who had to go.

Kordon's fists clenched as he read about Gracie's regret that her night with Chance was not to be. She knew deep down, she would never see him again, but hoped to have that one last memory to take with her. Her last entry talked about her shame of being afraid to die alone and her regret she would never know what happened to her friends and family. Her diary ended abruptly after that.

The door to his office open, and Quan looked at Kordon. "We have a visual on the mother ship," Quan said grimly. "It is a huge bastard."

Kordon stood up and pressed the console to close Gracie's diary. He would not let her die, and if he had anything to say about it, she would never be alone again. It was time to claim his life mate.

* * *

Gracie was breathing almost normally by the time she made it to the level holding the women. She found if she just listened in and did not react in any way she was ignored. She mimicked the movements of the other creatures. She was only stopped once and a message flashed in across the vision portion of her helmet requesting assistance in moving some equipment. Fortunately, it was small containers that were relatively light. Once the task was completed, the creature giving her the order turned and disappeared as if she didn't even exist.

Gracie moved down the corridor, stopping in front of a set of doors. She stood there for a moment wondering if some special code was needed when a scan displayed asking her to input her identification. Gracie almost panicked until she realized the inside of her helmet contained an identification code. Gracie punched the code in, and the doors slid open. Gracie took a step inside and moved toward the console. Only one Alluthan stood at the console. Gracie moved forward and stood to one side.

"Request permission for recharging," the Alluthan asked in a disembodied voice. "Permission has been granted. Replacement is in position."

Gracie stood still as the Alluthan turned to her. "Replacement 233-9095 is in position. Transfer locking codes complete."

She hoped there was nothing else expected of her. She watched on the screen inside her helmet as a series of codes popped up. Using the movement of her eye, she created a file and saved the codes.

Her eye moved rapidly over a series of characters giving the Alluthan acknowledgment of receipt of the codes. The Alluthan seemed satisfied as it turned and moved to the exit. Once Gracie was alone, she let her breath out and held up her trembling hand. She so sucked at espionage. She would make a really, really lousy spy, she decided.

Gracie turned to the console and located the cells containing the women. Pulling the codes up, she discovered the security codes needed to unlock them were the ones transferred to her. The biggest trial was going to be figuring out how to get twenty-two women up several levels, onto the supply ship, and out of the mother ship without being discovered. Right now, she was drawing a definite blank.

Gracie moved down the corridor and entered the first locking code. The doors slid open, and Gracie moved quickly down the corridor looking for the number of the first set of cells. She rounded a corner and skidded to a stop in front of cell block 18.

Inside was a small group of women huddled together toward the back of the cell. Gracie didn't recognize any of them. She tried talking through the helmet, but everything came out muffled. Pulling the helmet off, Gracie took a deep breath before grinning. *Maybe I wouldn't be so bad a spy*, she thought as the women gasped in surprise.

"Hey! I'm Gracie," Gracie said in English before grimacing and repeating it more slowly in Confederation Standard. "I'm going to get you out of here."

One of the older women, probably a few years older than Gracie, slowly approached the bars of the cell. "Who… who are you?"

"Gracie," Gracie rolled her eyes. Like that told her anything. "Just follow me."

"Are there others with you?" another woman said, coming forward.

Gracie bit her lip and shook her head. "Not yet, but there will be. We need to get the others out and get to one of the supply ships," Gracie said quietly while entering the unlocking code for the cell.

Gracie didn't wait to see if the other women followed her. She would do what she could. The first thing was to get everyone out. Next she would look for any weapons. She only had the small laser pistol she got from Mohan. Next she would upload her viruses. Next ... Gracie groaned ... she needed to focus on one thing at a time.

"Gracie Jones?" a soft voice called out.

"Mohan?" Gracie said excitedly as she moved to the next cell.

Mohan reached through the narrow bars and touched Gracie's cheek. "You are safe. I was so scared when I could not find you."

"Are you okay? What are you doing here? How did they capture you?" Gracie asked as she punched in the codes to open the cell holding her friend.

Mohan nodded her head. "I tried to follow you. One of the creatures took me by surprise. I tried to run, but the other ones cut me off," Mohan pulled Gracie into her arms and gave her a big hug. "Does Kordon know where you are?"

Gracie pulled back and looked into her friend's eyes. "I hope so. I programmed a message and sent it to him. I also set up a repeating signal, kind of like a tracking signal," Gracie said. "I still need to upload a virus, find some weapons for us, and commandeer a supply ship to get us out of this sardine can."

Mohan chuckled. "I like your language. It is funny," Mohan said. "If anyone can get us out of here, Gracie, you can."

The older woman who'd first talked to Gracie moved forward. "My name is Kacie. I don't know who you are, but if you can get me a weapon I'm pretty damn good with one. I can also pilot a ship if the one you get us isn't too different from the ones I'm used to. All I know is, I'm ready to get out of here." Several of the other women murmured in agreement.

Gracie smiled at Kacie before turning to the other women. "I've fought these creatures before. I need to disable their shields and shut down their systems. I promise to do everything I can to get you home."

"Tell us what we can do, Gracie," Mohan said.

"Mohan, get on the console and see if you can contact the *Conqueror*." Gracie turned as another woman approached.

"I can program just about anything if you get me into their systems," a slender girl of about twenty said.

"My name is Mouse. If you can find some weapons, Beyra and I can get them," another girl with short, curly brown hair and a huge grin said. "We are good at acquisitioning items." The other girl giggled and nodded.

Gracie turned as one woman after another mentioned things they could do to help. Several volunteered to find additional suits similar to what Gracie was wearing. Gracie was overwhelmed as the enthusiasm spread among the women, and their optimism flared an answering call inside her.

For the first time, she felt hope. She felt it blossoming and unfolding like the petals of a rose seeking the sunlight. Kordon's face flashed through her mind, and a grin spread across her face as she looked at Mohan.

"It's time to kick some alien butt and let them know they messed with the wrong women!" Gracie said with determination.

"This is the 'fuck you' part?" Mohan asked with a grin. "I believe that was the word you were screaming when I first saw you."

Gracie nodded and grinned back. "This is the 'fuck you' part."

The next two hours were spent locked down in the detention cells. Gracie tapped into the console. She showed Ladara, the young girl who knew programming, how to get into the system and explained the difference in the program files.

She uploaded several viruses, nodding in excitement as Ladara made some suggestions for modifying it to spread more rapidly. She called it a flash burn. Gracie made Ladara promise to show her how she did it when they got back home.

In the meantime, Gracie worked on uploading the viruses to disable the shields. Mohan was sending messages to the *Conqueror* using a seldom-used frequency with the hope of it not being intercepted.

Mouse and Beyra were dragging weapons back every ten to fifteen minutes. Gracie didn't even bother to ask how or where they found them. Soon enough suits and weapons were piled up to make Gracie feel they had a fighting chance.

"I'm programming each of the helmets to translate the Alluthan language to Confederation Standard. It won't translate everything but enough hopefully to give each of you a chance if we get separated to figure out where you are."

Gracie pulled up a holo-map of the ship. All the women gathered around her. "The *Conqueror* should be in range soon if they got my message. We need to get to this level. This is where the supply ships are docked. I found one that is fueled. I can keep control of the supply ship as the rest of the ship begins to shut down through a bypass code in the virus I created. It is going to be a tight fit, but all of us should be able to make it.

"Most of the Alluthans seem to travel in packs of three to five. I thought we would leave in small groups—three groups of three and two groups of five, and one group of four. We will leave at two-minute intervals so we can keep each other in sight.

"The scary part will be when we need to separate for the lifts. Hopefully, there won't be any problems. If there is—" Gracie looked at each of the women carefully. "—then we will deal with it. Everyone goes home. Everyone. Now, get suited up and check your weapons." Each woman nodded in grim determination.

Mohan called out from behind Gracie. "Gracie, I have contact with the *Conqueror*."

Gracie walked over and smiled back at Mohan. Pulling the headset on, Gracie said, "This is Gracie reaching out to the *Conqueror*. Do you hear me?"

Chapter 12

Mohan's husky voice nearly brought Quan to his knees when he heard it. It was only the fear in her voice that brought out the warrior in him. He could feel the fierce protectiveness of the Zion male wanting to protect his life mate rise inside him.

"Mohan, are you injured?" Quan asked in a tight voice.

"No," Mohan responded as Gracie handed her the headset. "Gracie has a plan to get us off the mother ship. Quan…" Mohan's voice faltered for a moment before she continued. "If anything should happen…"

Quan growled in a low, dangerous tone. "Nothing will happen to you. You do whatever you need to do to remain safe, Mohan. I am coming for you."

Mohan's soft, trembling breath came over the system. "I know you will. But, if anything should happen, I want you to know I love you," Mohan said quietly. "I am proud to be called your life mate."

Quan clenched his fists at her soft words. "I'm coming for you, Mohan. You be ready for me."

"I will be. Gracie will tell you what the plans are," Mohan said.

Quan heard Mohan call to Gracie. He immediately patched through to Kordon. "Kordon, Gracie is on the comlink."

* * *

Kordon was reviewing some of the modifications Cooraan and Bran had finished when Quan contacted him. Quan's voice actually shook for a moment before he cleared his throat. A communication signal was received from Mohan. She and Gracie were aboard the Alluthan mother ship along with twenty-one other women. They needed assistance.

Kordon stopped for a moment to steel himself for the sound of Gracie's soft voice. The moment he heard it, he swore when he got her back in his arms, she was never going to leave them again. Kordon forced his voice to remain controlled when he answered Gracie's call.

"I hear you, Gracie. We have a visual on the mother ship," Kordon said around the lump in his throat.

Gracie closed her eyes as Kordon's deep voice washed over her—calming her. "I have uploaded the viruses and have already noticed several of their systems are beginning to shut down. We are going to work our way down to the level containing the supply ships. I set up the same repeating signal so you will know it is us.

"I've also set the mother ship for self-destruct. Be prepared to get out of here fast because when it goes, there are going to be some major fireworks," Gracie paused to draw in a deep breath before continuing. "I love you, Kordon. I want to come home to you."

Kordon's jaw clenched tightly at her softly spoken words. "Bran and Cooraan were able to modify our own weapons and shields based on the information you had on your computer. We will begin firing to draw attention away from you and the other women. Get out of there safely, Gracie.

"A group of our fighters will intercept you and cover the supply ship until you are safely aboard the *Conqueror*. We will begin firing on your mark." Kordon paused. "And Gracie, we are going to talk about this when it is over," Kordon added tightly. "I'm going to whip your ass for this little stunt."

Gracie giggled at Kordon's veiled threat. She knew deep down he would never hurt her and that he was not really mad at her. "Promises… promises."

"I love you, Gracie," Kordon said quietly. "Get out of there safely and come to me."

* * *

Gracie finished uploading the last of her false leads. She was flooding the Alluthans' computer system with false programming to make it more difficult to find where her viruses were. She bit her lip, worried that they would be able to stop them. Gracie set the supply ship she'd chosen on standby. It would activate only on her command.

Gracie started when she felt a hand on her shoulder. Turning, she saw Mohan dressed in one of the Alluthan suits Mouse and Beyra stole. "We are ready. I will lead the first team out."

Gracie nodded. "I'll go with the last one. I set up the map to show in everyone's helmet. If you get stopped, whatever is being said will transfer to my helmet and I will respond. I thought it would be best since I understand their language."

Mohan reached around Gracie and hugged her tightly for just a moment before pulling back. "Let us go home," Mohan said, looking deeply into Gracie's eyes. She must have felt content with what she saw, because she pulled her helmet on and moved to the doors of the detention cells.

Gracie watched as her friend walked out with the first two groups of five women. Kacie nodded once to Gracie before following with her group. Two minutes later, Mouse and Beyra flashed a mischievous grin to Gracie and left with their groups. Now, there were only Gracie and the other three women.

Ladara looked at Gracie. "It is time," she said quietly.

So far, none of the small groups had been stopped. Gracie nodded and looked one more time at the programs she had running on the small portable tablet. *So far, so good,* Gracie thought with a sigh of relief.

Gracie was about to slip her helmet on when the doors to the detention cell slid open. Two Alluthans were entering. They stopped for a moment, looking back and forth between the three women dressed as Alluthans and Gracie, who was standing there in a uniform but no helmet.

Ladara raised her arm and fired on them. Both dropped when a huge hole appeared in each of their chests. She walked up to both of them and fired into each helmet at close range. Turning, Ladara looked with concern at Gracie.

"I don't know if they were able to send out anything," Ladara whispered as she pulled her helmet off.

Gracie turned to the portable tablet and grimaced. A signal had been sent. She looked up at Ladara. She would be damned if she got this far only to be stopped. The signal was sent but not complete. They would have to move quickly.

"Move now. Walk slowly," Gracie said, pulling her helmet on and sending out a warning to the others before she sent the command for Kordon to begin firing. They would need all the distractions they could get.

Ladara and the other two women quickly moved out of the detention cell, with Gracie right behind them. Gracie sent a message to Ladara warning her that a group of Alluthans was approaching.

Let me do the communicating. If it gets hairy, get out fast. I'll cover you. Gracie sent the message across the screen in Ladara's helmet.

We all go home. You said that. We are not afraid to fight or die. Ladara returned firmly, letting Gracie know they would not abandon her.

Gracie blinked back tears. She would never be alone again, she realized. Gracie was about to answer when she saw a flash of communication across her helmet. Four Alluthans approached the small group. Gracie moved forward so she was in front. Each of the women behind her moved slightly to one side so they were spread out enough to fire without hitting Gracie, but still looked like they were part of a group with her leading them.

233-9095 maintain position for incoming orders, one of the Alluthans approaching them flashed as it stepped forward.

Gracie immediately froze and waited. *Request incoming orders,* Gracie responded.

233-9095 orders received. Disruption in detention cells Level 824, Section 228, Cells 18-21. Request additional information, the Alluthan stated.

Replacements in position. Permission for recharge. Replacements currently analyzing equipment failure. Resolution estimated in 5.8286 units, Gracie replied, making up the number and holding her breath to see if they would buy it.

The Alluthan stood still for a moment before a response flashed across Gracie's screen. *Permission for recharge granted. Proceed.*

Gracie moved past the Alluthans, walking at a steady pace even though everything inside her was screaming for her to run like hell. They were almost to the lifts when the first shudder against the mammoth ship knocked Gracie into Ladara. Turning as one, the four women opened fire on the Alluthans behind them just as the lift opened. The battle had begun.

* * *

Kordon's face was grim as he ordered the *Conqueror* to begin firing. They were working systematically on taking the engines offline on the huge mother ship and causing specific damage. He ordered any fighters leaving the great ship to be destroyed. Any other ship they were to disable unless it was sending the specified signal Gracie would be sending out.

Kordon fought against the urge to climb into one of the fighters himself. Everything inside him wanted to be there to protect Gracie, but his place as Grand Admiral was on the *Conqueror*.

Instead, he requested Quan and Cooraan to be there. Both were excellent pilots and would not hesitate to give their lives for Mohan or Gracie. Bran was monitoring the shields, weapons, and engines. Kordon requested Toolas to be prepared with an emergency medical team in the landing bays.

Kordon's mind ran through all possible scenarios at amazing speed, adjusting as reports came in. "Fire at will. Take out all laser cannons. T-force, take out any fighters that come out. Quan, be ready with your squadron to protect the supply ship. It will be coming out hot and heavy," Kordon said coldly.

The men and women aboard the *Conqueror* were the best of the Confederation military. Kordon had reviewed each member wanting to be on his crew before accepting them. He picked each of them based on their skills, loyalty, and ability to work fluidly under pressure. As the flagship of the Confederation military, he made sure it was lethal.

Kordon listened in as reports came over his comlink. The modifications Bran and Cooraan made based on the data from Gracie gave them an edge. The shields were holding on their fighters, and they were cutting through the Alluthans' defenses. The *Conqueror's* laser cannons destroyed the forward and aft laser cannons on the mother ship and continued to inflict devastating damage.

Fighters continued to pour out of the mother ship at an amazing speed and huge numbers. The Confederation was greatly outnumbered, but with the modifications to their shields and weapons, they continued to press forward.

"Quan, any sign of a supply ship yet?" Kordon asked calmly into the comlink.

"Negative," Quan replied tersely. "Nothing but fighters pouring out of the mother ship as yet. Have you heard from Gracie or Mohan?"

"Negative," Kordon replied heavily.

Kordon frowned as he saw the mother ship turning. "The mother ship appears to be trying to retreat. Take out the engines now! I want that damn thing dead."

Kordon's blood ran cold at the thought of the women not being able to get off the mother ship before it self-destructed. He refused to think of Gracie dying. She had been through too much to die now. Those damned creatures were never going to touch Gracie's life again if he could help it.

"Kordon, a supply ship has left the mother ship," Cooraan said calmly. "I am picking up Gracie's signal."

"Bring them in," Kordon said tersely in response.

"Affirmative," Quan replied.

Kordon watched as bright flashes lit up the background of space. Pieces of destroyed fighters bounced off their shields. The Alluthans were attempting to flee, but already Kordon could see lights flickering on and off throughout the huge mother ship. Kordon's eyes followed the movement as a tight formation of Confederation fighters surrounded an Alluthan supply ship moving steadily toward the *Conqueror*.

Pressing his comlink, Kordon informed the landing bay officer he wanted to know the minute the supply ship was safely on board. After receiving confirmation of his order, he waited impatiently. Once the supply ship was safe, he would give the order to fire without restraint.

"Sir, the supply ship is docked, and the females are secure," the landing bay officer informed him.

"See that the females Gracie and Mohan are escorted to the bridge immediately," Kordon replied.

"Bran, take that bitch out," Kordon said coldly.

"I thought you would never ask," Bran replied as the *Conqueror* lit up with laser cannon fire. Huge flashes began flaring all over the mother ship. The remaining fighters began trying to return to the mother ship as it continued to turn away.

Kordon gave the order for the *Conqueror* fighters to return to ship. Gracie said the self-destruct on the mother ship would automatically begin when the supply ship was safely outside the ship. He would have less than five minutes to get the *Conqueror* a safe distance away.

"All fighters are safely docked and secure," the landing bay officer informed him.

"Bran, get us out of here," Kordon said sharply, calculating they had less than three minutes left.

"Quan, do you have a visual on Mohan and Gracie?" Kordon asked as his gut twisted.

"Cooraan said he saw Mohan briefly. Toolas is looking over the females to make sure they are not injured," Quan said tensely. "I haven't heard anything about Gracie yet. Many of the females still have the Alluthan suits on. I am heading that way now."

* * *

Mohan turned when she heard her name called out loudly in the landing bay. Toolas was just finishing checking her over, even though she had reassured her she was fine. Seeing Quan, Mohan gave a cry of joy and pushed past the other women and men standing in a tight circle. Quan's arms closed around her, and he buried his face into her neck, breathing deeply as he drew in her scent.

"Never again, do you hear me! Never again will I let you be in such danger," Quan said harshly as he crushed his lips to Mohan's softer ones. "By the gods, I love you, Mohan," Quan groaned out.

Mohan lifted a shaky hand and touched Quan's cheek. "Gracie is not with us," she said with a slight hiccup as she fought back a sob. "She remained on the mother ship."

Quan's nostrils flared as he jerked back with a muttered curse. "Shit! Kordon!" Quan practically yelled into the comlink. "Gracie isn't with the females." Quan gripped Mohan's hand tightly in his own and started running toward the corridor leading to the lifts.

* * *

Kordon jerked as if shot when Quan's voice came over the comlink. What did he mean Gracie wasn't with the other females? She'd promised she would be. She'd said she was coming home. Kordon barked out for Bran to change course and redirect the *Conqueror* back to the mother ship.

They were already a good distance from it. Kordon called out to one of the helmsmen to get him a visual of the mother ship on the front viewport. He could feel the *Conqueror* beginning the turn when a huge flash followed by a series of explosions rocked the mother ship, tearing it apart right before his eyes.

"Brace for shockwave impact," Bran called out as alarms flared throughout the *Conqueror*.

Kordon stood still as wave after wave hit the *Conqueror*. He reached out a hand and gripped the back of the commander's chair for support as the *Conqueror* shuddered. His eyes remained glued to the Alluthan mother ship as she slowly broke apart into billions of pieces.

Chapter 13

Gracie and the other three women were almost to the supply ship when a group of Alluthan warriors approached them. Gracie stopped and waited. They had made it down almost halfway when the lift stopped and opened.

Gracie looked at the screen and watched as the lift programming shut down and a warning of possible intruders flashed across her helmet. The bodies on Level 824 had been found. Gracie barely bit back a scream of frustration. She was really getting tired of these creatures screwing up her life. A message flashed for 233-9095 to halt.

Gracie quickly motioned for the other women to continue. Ladara tried to send a message refusing, but Gracie quickly told her over a hundred Alluthan warriors were gathering on the level.

We won't leave you, Lardara argued.

You have to. The other women don't deserve to die as well. Go. I have an idea. Here is the start sequence for the supply ship. Get to the Conqueror. *Tell them to blast the hell out of this ship*, Gracie responded. *Trust me. Just tell Kordon I expect him to come find me again.*

Ladara paused for a moment before continuing past the Alluthans with the other two women like nothing was wrong. Once past them, though, she turned and looked at Gracie for a moment before heading down a set of steps. Gracie watched as Ladara and the two women disappeared before overriding the lift command and letting Ladara know to get to the one on the next level.

233-9095 remove helmet for analysis. The Alluthan ordered.

Gracie looked at the group. There were five of them in total, with more on the way. She could really use a good distraction right now. There were a few shudders from where the *Conqueror* was attacking, but she needed a full-scale assault right about now. Gracie desperately searched for some excuse, but finally decided she was just shit-out-of-luck. Reaching up, Gracie slowly turned the helmet and pulled it off with a wry grin on her face.

"Mmm... hi?" Gracie said as she let the helmet slip from her fingers to fall to the metal floor. At the same time she palmed the small laser pistol she'd taken from Mohan. "Yippee-ki-yay," she murmured as she brought the pistol up and began firing.

Gracie was able to take two of the Alluthans out before they realized their shields were not working. She scrambled behind a beam as the other three began firing. Gracie covered her head and tried to make herself as small as possible behind the beam as the other three Alluthans continued to fire at her as they began walking toward her.

Gracie bit her lip. This was it. She was pissed as hell because she didn't want to die. She wanted to get back to Kordon. Gracie let her head fall back against the metal beam for a minute before she took a deep breath and braced herself.

Turning, she rolled out from behind the beam, firing as she went. If there was one thing she did know how to do, it was how to fire a gun. All four of the guys made sure she was an excellent marksman.

Gracie hit two of the creatures squarely in the chest and neck. She continued rolling even as she felt a hot burn, followed by an explosion of pain in her right shoulder and lower leg. There was only one Alluthan left, and it had adjusted its aim to follow Gracie's roll on the floor.

Gracie's arm shook, and she lost control of the pistol as her arm went numb. She continued rolling until she came up against the other side of the corridor. She quickly pulled herself into a sitting position behind the metal beam and leaned back as pain ricocheted through her. Gracie pulled her right arm against her, feeling the blood soaking the sleeve.

Her lower leg also felt like it was on fire. Gracie watched as the Alluthan continued forward, no longer firing. She knew what would have happened now if she hadn't already set the mother ship for self-destruct. The Alluthan would not kill her because she was a female of breeding age. She would be used as an incubator until she could no longer produce, then be discarded.

"Go to hell, you sorry-ass motherfucker. I took your kind down once before, and I've done it again," Gracie said in English with a bitter laugh as it stopped in front of her.

Gracie tilted her head backward and looked up into the reflective surface of the Alluthan. She refused to let the pain radiating through her take her to the darkness of unconsciousness. She was going to be awake when those bastards bit the dust.

"Go ahead, make my day," Gracie said with a grimace as another Alluthan came to stand next to the first one.

Gracie pushed back as the Alluthan who'd shot her pulled her to her feet. She swayed as she tried not to put too much pressure on her wounded leg. The Alluthan turned to the second one, and she knew they were communicating. But it wouldn't matter. They were lucky if they had eight minutes left on the countdown to "D-day."

Gracie refused to look over her shoulder at the Alluthans. She let her mind go blank of everything but Kordon. He was the only thing that mattered now. He was the one she loved. She was glad she had met him and had been able to spend at least a little time with him.

Gracie started when she heard the sound of a laser pistol discharging behind her. She waited for the pain of being shot to pierce her again but nothing came. She almost jumped out of her skin when the Alluthan who came up to her put a gentle arm around her waist.

"We need to get out of here fast," Ladara said.

Gracie stared at Ladara in stunned silence for a moment before she turned and began limping toward the lift. Ladara leaned down and picked up Gracie's helmet, laser pistol, and portable tablet. She helped

Gracie put on her helmet before handing her the laser pistol in her left hand.

You didn't leave me, Gracie sent to Ladara's helmet.

No, you said everyone is getting off, and you were not there. The others went to the supply ship. Mohan has taken off, and they are heading out of the mother ship. I am hoping you can do your magic again and get us out of here, Ladara signaled as she helped Gracie into the lift.

Gracie leaned back against the back wall of the lift and nodded tiredly. The pain was fading to numbness now. Gracie braced herself as she felt the huge ship shudder. The supply ship must have made it through and was clear because she could feel the increasing vibrations as the ship was hit.

We have five minutes before the mother ship explodes, Gracie said as a particularly hard hit almost knocked her off her feet. It would have if Ladara hadn't reached out to hold onto her.

Both women looked up when the lights on the lift flickered, then faded. The lift slowed to a stop. They were stranded. Gracie looked up at the level and groaned. *Damn Murphy's Law,* she thought. Only she could get trapped on the level where all the fighters were and every freaking Alluthan warrior was bound to be!

You have got to be kidding me. Gracie groaned out loud.

Ladara looked puzzled for a moment. *What is it?*

The fighter deck level. All the friggin' Alluthans on this stupid ship are probably here. We need to open the doors manually, Gracie sent tiredly as her shoulders drooped. *Was it too much to ask for one little bitty break?* Gracie wondered despondently.

Ladara worked at pulling the lever inside the lift, and the doors slowly opened. Yep, every frigging warrior was there. Only they seemed to be flying into the ship instead of out of it. Perhaps, in all the confusion... Gracie wondered in hope.

Get us to the closest fighter, Gracie sent across Ladara's helmet.

But... Ladara started in surprise. *We are taking a fighter?* She asked hesitantly.

You're damn right we're taking a fighter. In all the confusion they won't know who is coming and who is going. We have about three minutes to get going. Gracie said with determination, trying to ignore the pain, loss of blood, and numbness threatening to overtake her.

Gracie and Ladara moved as one toward the closest fighter. None of the Alluthans even turned to question them. Many of the Alluthans were moving toward an exit further down the platform.

Gracie held on to the side of the fighter as Ladara climbed up first. Ladara reached down and held out her hand to help Gracie up. It was awkward, but Gracie was thankful for the help. She had to jump from one step to another and could only use her one hand.

Blood from her arm and leg marred the side of the fighter as Gracie leaned against it. She was breathing heavily by the time she got to the opened top. Ladara slid into the back seat while Gracie fell into the front with an inelegant groan. She used her good arm to pull her leg around.

Ladara, can you strap me in while I get us up and out of here? Gracie asked faintly as she shivered. *Great,* she thought. *Now I decide to go into shock. Murphy, you son of a bitch. I am really, really beginning to hate your sorry ass.*

Ladara quickly strapped Gracie in just as Gracie pulled the lever up and set the course into the console. Thank God the Alluthans still used the same programming. The fighter rose swiftly as Gracie punched in the commands.

Ripping off the helmet, Gracie took a deep breath as the fighter moved swiftly through the huge mother ship. There would be no stopping them now… at least not with them still alive.

She programmed in the signal hoping beyond hope that the *Conqueror* would pick it up. It would really suck to get out of the mother ship before it exploded only to find herself blown up by one of the *Conqueror's* fighters or the ship itself.

"Gracie, do you think this thing can go any faster?" Ladara asked nervously. "You said we only had a few minutes to get out before this ship exploded. I would really, really like to not be in it when it does."

Gracie laughed hoarsely. "You and me both," Gracie responded and pushed a series of buttons increasing the speed of the fighter. "Hang on!" Gracie gritted out between clenched teeth as she weaved in and out between incoming fighters.

Ladara gasped as she saw the huge doors beginning to close. "Gracie, faster," Ladara said urgently from behind her.

"Keep your shorts on. I'm doing the best I can without getting us killed," Gracie muttered as she jerked on the control stick. "This is just like playing video games back home," Gracie joked halfheartedly.

Gracie pulled up and increased speed. Behind her, she could hear Ladara talking to herself: *We aren't going to make it. We aren't going to make it.* Gracie was determined they were going to not only make it out of the ship, but that she was going to make it back into Kordon's bed… and never leave it again.

Gracie turned the fighter on its side and scraped through the closing doors with just feet to spare. "Elvis, listen to the fat lady. She is singing her heart out!" Gracie crowed as she pushed the fighter to even greater speed now that she was clear of the mother ship.

Everything seemed to slow down as one minute they were speeding away and the next a percussion hit the fighter from behind as the mother ship exploded. Gracie and Ladara were pushed forward by the force, and the power on the fighter flickered on and off as it was pushed forward.

Gracie's last thought was, *You probably can feel a tree fall in a forest even if you can't hear it. God,* she thought as darkness descended, *Murphy really is on my shit list now.*

Chapter 14

Kordon looked over the reports being sent to him. There was minimal damage overall to the *Conqueror* from the shock waves. There were a few injuries to some crew members, mostly bruises, but a few broken bones and concussions.

Bran and Cooraan were working on the damages to some of their systems, including minor damage to the engine's main core which had been knocked off-line, preventing them from going into light speed. It had been almost twelve hours since the battle, and it would take another fourteen before the *Conqueror* was ready to travel.

Thirty-eight fighters were destroyed. Kordon felt the weight of each death on his soul. The fighters were primary Zion warriors, and he'd known all of them personally. Their deaths were a cause for celebration for they would be accepted into the next life. It was the Zion way. They would be reborn again as warriors, for they died in battle.

Kordon stood up and walked over to the viewport. He could still see debris from the mother ship in the distance. Some of the metal seemed to reflect from the lights of the *Conqueror* when it struck them.

He bowed his head in anguish. He did not even know Gracie's beliefs. In all the archives and in her personal diary, she never mentioned if she believed in being reborn after her death. He should have asked her.

There was so much he should have asked her. He didn't know her favorite color or what her favorite foods were. He didn't know if she would want to live on the *Conqueror* or if she would be content to live on his home world of Zion in his home there.

Kordon closed his eyes as grief and pain surged through him, unlike anything he ever felt before. He clenched his fists and pressed them against the clear material protecting the viewport.

He felt like his heart was being torn out of his body as the grief swelled up inside him until he felt like he was going to explode from it. Was this how Gracie felt when she found out everything she knew and everyone she loved was gone? If so, no wonder she tried to end her life. The pain and grief was unbearable.

Kordon didn't react when the door to his office slid open silently. He knew he wasn't alone, but he no longer cared who needed him. He needed time to get control of his emotions before he faced his crew. This was one time when he knew without a doubt he would not be able to keep the cold, indifferent mask on his face.

"Sir," Mohan said quietly from behind him. "Sir. I am getting a signal. It is very faint, but I believe it is from Gracie."

Kordon turned slowly and looked at Mohan, who stood before him. She was wearing the same dirty clothes from when she was taken on the domed moon. Her eyes were red from crying, and her fur seemed dull. Quan stood next to her with his arm around her waist. From the way her body leaned into him, it was probably the only thing keeping her upright.

"Patch it through to my office," Kordon said wearily.

Mohan nodded before turning. As the door slid open, she turned again to look briefly over her shoulder. "She wanted to live. She wanted to come back to you. If it is possible, she will have done so."

Kordon nodded briefly, dismissing Mohan. He knew the damage the *Conqueror* received was minimal from the shock waves as the mother ship exploded, but it was still damaged. He was under no illusion as to the type of damage a ship the size of the Alluthan supply ship or a fighter would have received. The shockwave would have torn it apart.

Kordon pulled the signal coming through onto his console. He leaned back for a minute and listened. It took a moment for him to finally narrow in on it. At first, he thought it could have been just a distortion the *Conqueror* was picking from debris still hitting its shields.

Leaning forward, he pressed several commands, increasing the volume and filtering the signal. It took several adjustments before he heard a faint voice through all the static and other noises.

"This is Gracie reaching out to the *Conqueror*. Can you hear me? Please! Kordon, I need you to come for me. This is Gracie reaching out to the *Conqueror*. Kordon, if you hear this, Ladara and I are in an Alluthan fighter. The power has failed. Life support is at a minimum. We are using the power from the suits to help keep us alive. Please, help us." The signal was fading. "I can't use any more of the power in my suit. I only have about fifteen, maybe twenty minutes left. Kordon, please help us. This is Gracie. I love you, Kordon. Good-bye." The last words were said with a faint sob.

Kordon surged out of his chair, practically running for the door. Once on the bridge, he began issuing orders. Kordon told Mohan to send out a return signal letting Gracie know he was coming for her. Kordon looked at Quan, who was already nodding his head and following him. Bran met them down in the landing bay.

"I have the sensors set for maximum. If there are any life forms alive, it will pick it up," Bran said as he handed Kordon a flight suit.

Cooraan was already suited up and climbing into one of the huge transport ships. It was large enough to transport and retrieve any of their fighters and was designed for rescue missions such as this. Quan would take one of their fighters and scan the area, and Kordon would take another. Once they found Gracie, Cooraan would come in and scoop her up— fighter and all.

"We have ten, maybe fifteen minutes to find her. I want her brought home alive," Kordon said fiercely as he climbed up into the cockpit of one of the fighters.

"I'll be scanning from the *Conqueror*," Bran assured him as he moved back behind the protective shield.

Kordon went out first, followed closely by Quan and Cooraan. He set the scanner and moved quickly until he was in the debris field left over from the mother ship. He cursed loudly when he saw the amount of debris floating like ghosts in the inky blackness of space.

"Nothing yet," Quan's voice came out over the comlink. "I'll take the starboard side. Cooraan, you better take the outer rim. There are a lot of pieces floating out here."

"Thanks for letting me know something I couldn't see for myself," Cooraan responded sarcastically.

"Bran, do you have anything?" Kordon asked tersely.

"Nothing yet... hold on." Bran's voice faded. "I'm sending you the following coordinates. I'm picking up a faint signal."

* * *

Kordon watched as the information came over his screen. He touched the pad and moved toward the coordinates Bran gave him. A part of him felt the faint stirrings of hope while another part dreaded not finding what he was hoping for. As he bypassed a piece of debris twice the size of his fighter, his scanner suddenly lit up.

He gingerly maneuvered his fighter around it. In front of him was an intact Alluthan fighter. He could barely make out the two figures in the cockpit. He brought his fighter as close as he safely could and fired the towline.

The magnetic clamps connected to the front of the fighter. The figure in the front turned as it connected and looked out the viewport. A small hand came up and splayed across the clear protective surface for just a moment before it disappeared, and the head of the figure slumped forward.

"Cooraan, get your ass in here. I have them, but they are in bad shape," Kordon growled into the comlink.

"Right behind you, Kordon. Keep them steady while I get the lock on them," Cooraan said as he pulled the larger transport ship up behind the fighter. "Release your towline."

Kordon pressed the release and watched as it floated briefly before it started to retract back into the fighter. Cooraan had the hooks into the wings of the Alluthan fighter, and Kordon watched in grim silence as it was pulled into the holding bay. Once it was in, Cooraan would fill the bay with oxygen.

Kordon waited impatiently until the heavy doors of the transport finally sealed, and Cooraan came on to inform him he was pulling out.

It seemed an eternity until they were able to safely get out of the minefield of debris. It was as slow coming out as it was going in, but to Kordon it seemed as if time itself stood still. He quickly maneuvered his fighter back to the *Conqueror* landing bay once he was clear.

"Get Toolas in the landing bay with an emergency medical team immediately," Kordon growled to the landing bay officer. "Tell her to expect the worse."

Kordon bit back an expletive. He knew what the smears on the side of the fighter were. He had seen them often enough in his battles. One of the women was injured—and badly. His fear escalated when he saw the speed at which Cooraan was coming in. He wouldn't do this unless his sensors inside were indicating an emergency.

Chapter 15

Gracie let her head fall back simply because she no longer had the strength to hold it up. She was freezing, could hardly breath as the oxygen levels were dropping dramatically, and weak from blood lost. The tears in her suit were hindering the suit's ability to keep her warm. Ladara raised a weak hand and laid it on Gracie's shoulder when Mohan's faint voice urgently repeated that help was on the way.

You did it, Gracie, Ladara sent the message across the screen from behind her. *You brought everyone home like you said you would.*

Gracie was too tired to respond. One slow tear coursed down her cheek when she heard Mohan's voice. Kordon would know she had tried to come back to him. She only had a few more minutes of power in the damaged suit.

She put the helmet back on to help retain heat and to use the power of the suit to patch into the fighter. It was a huge drain on it, but it was the only way she could get the communications back online long enough to send out an SOS. But it came at a price. It drained her suit and its life-support capabilities.

Gracie, your suit level is low. I can see it on the screen in my helmet. You must patch into mine. We will share until they get here, Ladara sent in alarm.

Not... yet, Gracie sent weakly. *I have a little time. Ten minutes, maybe more if I use shallow breaths. I don't want to drain you as well.*

Ladara leaned forward and placed her hand on Gracie's uninjured shoulder. *You must promise to connect with me before you run out. If you do not, I will try,* Ladara sent across Gracie's helmet.

Gracie let her head move in a weak nod of agreement. She just needed to hang on for a little while longer. Shivers shook her body as it attempted to keep warm. Every violent shake sent waves of pain through her as her injured arm and leg protested the movement. Luckily, she thought as her vision became fuzzy, it seemed like the bleeding had stopped, or at least slowed down.

What seemed like hours later, Gracie's head jerked when she felt a thump on the outside of the fighter. She was down to less than two minutes of air, and the helmet was flashing a warning.

Gracie turned her head slowly and looked out through the clear viewport window of the fighter. About twenty-five feet away was one of the *Conqueror's* fighters. Gracie couldn't make out for sure who was in the pilot's seat, but everything in her body was screaming it was Kordon. He had come for her.

Gracie weakly raised her uninjured arm and splayed her hand on the window to let him know she knew he was near. That last bit of effort was more than her body could handle. Gracie's vision went dark, and she slumped forward as the last of her oxygen ran out.

* * *

Dreams were often a strange and wonderful thing, Gracie thought vaguely as she drifted in a warm cocoon of darkness. Flashes of light, strange and familiar voices, strong arms, a deep voice threatening to whip her ass if she gave up floated through Gracie's mind as she drifted between wakefulness, life, and death. *Perhaps death wasn't so bad,* Gracie thought. A deep growl and firm hands on her face told her she must have said that aloud.

"Death is not better. Do you hear me, Gracie? Death is not an option. You will fight. You will live," Kordon growled hoarsely.

Gracie could feel his hot breath against her cheek as he leaned close to her ear. She couldn't seem to get any more words out, so she just squeezed the hand holding her uninjured one. She would fight. This one last time, she would fight. Then she was going to sleep for a very, very long time.

A frown creased her forehead. Why was she so tired? The thought faded as fingers gently caressed her forehead until the frown was gone. The touch felt so good Gracie couldn't help but try to lean into it.

"Admiral, I need to get her to medical as soon as possible," a light feminine voice said. "I have her stable for now, but she needs additional healing that I cannot do here."

Kordon nodded and reluctantly released Gracie's hand as the medical staff began moving Gracie out of the triage area set up in the landing bay. Kordon stiffened when Gracie made a slight whimpering sound at the loss of his touch. One of the other medical staff was checking Ladara over to make sure she wasn't hurt.

Kordon paused when he felt the light touch on his arm. Turning, he looked at Ladara. "She is an extraordinary woman. I hope she will be all right."

Kordon nodded briefly. "She will be. See that this woman is given quarters, food, and fresh clothing," Kordon ordered the medical technician before he turned to leave.

"Bran, you have the bridge. I will be in medical should you need me. Send me the reports on the ship as soon as it is done and plan a course for Paulus," Kordon ordered as the lift opened, and he stepped in.

"We should be finished in another ten hours. I'll get the reports to you immediately. I also have the data collected from the Alluthan mother ship that we were able to download before it exploded. If not for Gracie's understanding of their programming, we wouldn't have gotten so much.

"I am still analyzing their weapons and engineering. Cooraan sent Toolas the information on their organic DNA, and he is reviewing the robotic part of them. We will get you the preliminary report as soon as we can," Bran said as the lift opened onto the level containing the medical unit.

Kordon nodded. His mind was not on the *Conqueror* or even the Alluthans any longer. It was focused solely on Gracie. He knew he needn't worry about the *Conqueror*. They could run the warship without him for a little while. That was why he'd chosen the crew he had.

* * *

Three days later, Gracie's brain finally decided it'd had enough sleep and was ready to wake up. She had been conscious part of the time over the past couple of days, but she just didn't have the strength to respond. It was like her body had said enough was enough, and it was going to do what it wanted for a little while.

She heard Mohan's soft voice and felt the soft fur from her hands as she brushed over Gracie's face or hands when she touched her. In the background, she knew Kordon was there. He never left her except to take care of his personal needs. He always returned within what seemed like minutes.

She heard other people coming in and out asking Kordon questions or him giving orders, but he was always near enough that she could feel the warmth of his skin against hers. She liked it when he talked to her. He told her about growing up on Zion and how beautiful it was. He told her about his home there, and how he was going to take her there after she woke up. He said his favorite color was green now because of her eyes.

Her lips actually twitched at that. She never would have realized the tough exterior of the warrior was a cover for a romantic interior. He was always touching her, either her face or her hands or her hair. It didn't matter. She loved it and would unconsciously move toward it, seeking more.

Gracie forced her eyes to crack open just a little so she could look out from under her eyelashes. The room was dim, but she could see the glow from the portable tablet in Kordon's lap. He was talking with Bran and Cooraan.

"We should reach Paulus by tomorrow afternoon. The council has requested a full report as soon as possible," Bran was saying.

He was leaning up against the wall near the door. Cooraan was sitting in a chair across from Kordon with his legs stretched out in front of him. Both men appeared relaxed, but Gracie could tell something was wrong.

"What is it?" Kordon asked with a frown.

He had already given a detailed report to the council on the Alluthans. The data they had collected, along with the information from Gracie, would be turned over to the appropriate divisions for further analysis. He would make the expected appearance and leave with Gracie for Zion as soon as possible.

Bran cleared his throat before replying. "You know I have some resources inside the council's inner circle, don't you?"

Kordon's eyes narrowed. Yes, he did know. He had his own resources, but had not had time to review any of the reports sent to him with everything going on. From Bran's tone, though, he thought he better make the time before tomorrow.

"Go on," Kordon said tightly.

Bran ran a hand across the back of his neck and stood up away from the wall. The conversation had Gracie's attention now, and her brain quickly assessed what he could possibly say. She was somewhat fascinated by the behavior of the other two men as she never expected to see either of them uncomfortable. They always seemed so in control when she saw them.

"My resource says the human councilman has met with some of the other councilmen in secret. He is not even letting any of his aides in and has been very closemouthed since he found out about Gracie," Bran was saying.

Gracie's ears perked up when she heard her name mentioned. Why would they be having private meetings? Gracie knew enough about politics to know it was never good when they started doing that. She remained still hoping to learn more.

"What do you think it is about?" Kordon asked in a low, dangerous voice.

Bran held up his hand. "I'm just relaying what I am being told. I think you need to watch your and Gracie's back. I have a bad feeling about this. I never did like the slimy son of a bitch. He was always too smooth."

Kordon nodded and looked at Gracie. He started when he saw her watching him intently. A slow smile curved her lips.

"You were just getting to the good part," she whispered out huskily. "I wanted to know more."

Cooraan grinned as he stood up. "It is good to have you back with us, Gracie Jones."

"You scared all of us, and that is not an easy task for a Zion warrior," Bran teased as he took a step closer to Gracie.

Gracie turned her head and looked at the two huge men standing over her. "Thank you. I know you helped rescue me. I can never repay your kindness for all you've done to help me," Gracie whispered.

Both men shifted uneasily. If the room hadn't been so dim, Gracie would have giggled at seeing both of the men actually blush a little. Bran cleared his throat and shifted from one foot to the other again before stepping up to the bed and brushing a quick kiss across Gracie's forehead.

"I would do it again in a heartbeat for you, Gracie Jones," Bran said before stepping back and addressing Kordon who was still gazing at Gracie. "I'll get back to the bridge. Just watch your backs tomorrow. Quan, Cooraan, and I will also be there to help in case you need anything."

Kordon turned and looked at his friend and nodded. "Thank you."

Cooraan reached out a hand and touched Gracie's cheek softly before bending over and giving her a kiss. "You are one lucky and amazing woman, Gracie Jones."

Gracie smiled up at Cooraan as he stood up. God, he was huge! "No thanks to Murphy!" She replied with a soft giggle.

Cooraan just grinned back and nodded to Kordon. They had a lot of work to do before they reached Paulus. If Bran had a bad feeling something was going to go down, Cooraan was more than willing to be prepared. He didn't trust the human councilman any more than he could breathe in a vacuum.

Kordon watched as both men left before turning his attention back to Gracie. She was staring at him with huge, dark green eyes filled with emotion. He gently bent over and pulled her into his arms, burying his face in her neck.

Gracie's arms wrapped as tightly around his neck as she could in her still-weakened state. "I was so afraid," she whispered hoarsely.

A shudder ran through Kordon at her softly spoken words. "When you are strong again, I believe I told you I was going to whip your ass for doing such a dangerous thing and scaring me so badly," Kordon murmured teasingly against her neck.

Gracie giggled and pulled back enough so she could rest her forehead against his. "Do you promise?" she whispered.

Kordon groaned as the image made his cock swell with need. "I'll do more than promise," he said with a muffled groan. "I need to get you healed as soon as possible. I need to feel you wrapped around me."

Gracie let her left hand slide down between them until she could feel the hard length pressed against the front of Kordon's uniform. She ran her fingers along the front and sighed. She was ready to get her strength back too.

"I can feel how much you need me," Gracie said as a smile lit up her face. "How long have I been out? What happened? How did you find us?" A worried frown marred her face for a moment. "Is Ladara okay?"

Kordon let out a chuckle as Gracie started firing questions at him. Relief flowed through him. She would be all right. He would do everything in his power to make sure she was safe and well cared for from now on.

"You have been unconscious for the past three and a half days. Mohan refused to rest until you were found. She knew you wanted to come home and insisted on trying to help find you. How she was able to intercept your signal, I will never know. I don't think I would have even noticed it, but she did. When I heard your voice…"

Kordon stopped and took a deep breath before continuing. "When I heard your voice it was as if the gods had blessed me with a gift beyond imagining. Bran adjusted the sensors to scan for the slightest life form. You can imagine how difficult it was to locate one small fighter amongst the remains of the mother ship. We were almost too late," Kordon whispered as his eyes darkened with the memory.

Gracie reached up and touched Kordon's cheek. "But, you weren't."

Kordon shook his head. "I found you, and Cooraan was able to pull the fighter into the transport ship, but by then your oxygen was depleted. Ladders was not in much better shape. Your body was in the beginning stages of hypothermia, you were in shock from blood loss and your wounds, and out of oxygen.

"Cooraan picked up your failing respirations on his scanner. He proved what an accomplished pilot he was. The landing bay officer never saw a transport enter and land so quickly without crashing.

"Luckily, Toolas was prepared for the worst. I was able to get you out, and Toolas immediately began working on you. Ladara was still conscious, barely. She told me what happened after you sent her and the other women off. I owe her a life debt for saving you," Kordon said as he gently pushed Gracie's thick, strawberry blondee hair away from her face so he could press a kiss into her forehead.

"You were supposed to tell me when she woke," Toolas's gentle rebuke came from across the room.

Gracie leaned back and grinned at the healer. "It's my fault. I wanted to know what happened while I was out of it."

Toolas laughed. "I'll tell you exactly what happened. The Admiral has not left your side the entire time and has been running the *Conqueror* from my medical unit," she said good-naturedly.

Gracie flushed as she looked worriedly from Toolas to Kordon. "I'm sorry. I hate being such a bother. You should have kicked him out."

Kordon growled at that, and Toolas burst out laughing. "Actually, it is nice seeing so many of the crew without having to be treating them. I've enjoyed the company. Overall, this is a rather healthy bunch, and unless they get hurt it tends to be very quiet and lonely here. Besides, I don't think there is anything that would have been able to peel the Admiral from your side until he knew for certain you were going to be fine."

Kordon sent a scowl at Toolas but didn't deny it. "You tend to forget everything you have done for the people of the Confederation of Planets. Your skills and your willingness to fight the Alluthans saved thousands, if not more, lives once again… including the Earth, which is a part of the Confederation now," Kordon's deep voice said firmly.

Toolas smiled and nodded in agreement. "Admiral, if you don't mind, I would like to examine Gracie now that she is awake. Perhaps you would like to take this chance to get cleaned up. I would like for Gracie to eat when I am done. If you like, I can order something for you as well," Toolas said in her firmest voice.

Kordon reluctantly released Gracie and stood up, still holding her hand in his. He forced himself to pull away with a nod. He knew Toolas wanted to give Gracie a chance to talk to another woman.

Toolas was concerned after everything that had happened since they found Gracie that she might be beyond mentally exhausted and wanted to make sure she wasn't suffering from the depression that had taken hold of her before. Toolas gently explained that physical and mental exhaustion combined with Gracie's injuries and her learning recently of the death of everyone she knew might be too much for her mentally.

"I will return shortly," Kordon said, brushing his hand over Gracie's hair.

Gracie smiled and nodded in return. "I know. I don't plan on going anywhere … at least not yet," she whispered and turned her head so she could brush a kiss into his palm.

Kordon gazed into Gracie's eyes for a moment more, wanting to memorize the beauty of them before he looked at Toolas. "I'll be back," he said fiercely.

Gracie couldn't help the laugh that escaped at his words. In his deep voice with the slight accent it reminded her of a character in a movie. Just the thought of how strong and fierce Kordon could be made Gracie realize she had her own "Terminator." Only she knew just what a softy he was underneath the layers.

Chapter 16

Toolas asked Gracie a million and one questions before helping her up and into the bathroom. Gracie decided she could happily spend the next year enjoying the warm spray of mist as it surrounded her. She washed her hair, which was growing like crazy.

Before the crash, she always kept it short as it was easier to manage, but for the past three years it was just as easy to pull it up and back or braid it. Now it hung down to her shoulder blades in thick waves of blonde with strands of auburn threaded through it.

Gracie's eyes softened as she remembered her older sister always wishing she had the red highlights. A smile curved her lips as she remembered she and Violet using a red permanent marker once to color it. Her dad had been horrified when he saw his oldest daughter's hair. Her mom just laughed and said it would eventually wash out, although all the permanent markers in the house disappeared after that.

Gracie made a mental note to look up information on what happened to her family. Mohan said Chance and Violet married and had children. She was sad she'd missed seeing her sister, but a part of her wondered if the fates knew she was not meant for Chance.

Gracie gasped as calloused hands slid around her waist to draw her back against a strong, warm body. She had been so lost in thought she didn't hear Kordon come into the bathing stall. A shiver ran down her as his hands moved in slow, deliberate circles along her hips toward her belly.

"I thought you were going to your living quarters to get cleaned up?" Gracie asked huskily as she pressed back against Kordon's naked form with a moan of need.

Kordon leaned down and pressed a kiss against Gracie's bare shoulder. "I made it halfway there and couldn't stand being away from you," he murmured as he ran his tongue along the curve between her shoulder and neck.

Gracie arched her neck sideways to give him better access. "Kordon, I want you," she whispered desperately.

Kordon groaned hotly against her as her ass pushed back against his throbbing cock. He wasn't lying when he said he couldn't stay away from her. He'd made it up to the level where his living quarters were and promptly commanded the lift to return him to medical.

Toolas took one look at his face and shook her head. With a word of warning not to tire Gracie out, she promptly left, ordering the room sealed in quarantine until Kordon overrode the command. No one would be disturbing them. She made sure several dishes of food were left on the low table Kordon had been using to work at, knowing they would be hungry later.

"I'm going to love you, Gracie. Forever," Kordon said as he turned Gracie around in his arms and captured her lips with his own.

Gracie wrapped her arms around Kordon's neck as he kissed her fiercely, her lips parting when he ran his tongue along her lower lip in an invitation to let him in. A low moan escaped her as he slipped inside. She battled her tongue with his in a feverish attempt to get closer. Pressing her breasts against his chest, she groaned loudly at the feel of her tight nipples against his skin.

Kordon broke the kiss and pulled back just far enough to look down into Gracie's eyes. "Are you in pain from your wounds? Toolas said the healing accelerator has healed most of the damage, but I need to know I will not hurt you," Kordon said in concern.

Gracie wanted to say the only pain she was having had nothing to do with the wounds she'd received. Her pussy was pulsing with need, and her breasts and skin were so sensitive she wanted to scream with frustration.

Gracie reached up and answered Kordon by pulling his head back down until her lips claimed his while her other hand wrapped tightly around his throbbing cock.

Kordon moaned again at the feel of Gracie's hand wrapped tightly around him. His hips moved of their own accord as she began stroking him slowly up and down. He pulled away and turned, pulling Gracie up his body until her legs were wrapped around his waist and her back was pressed against the back of the bathing stall. He lined up his thick cock with her hot channel and slowly began pushing into her.

His head dropped down for a moment as the sweet torment of her wrapping around him took his breath away. He could feel every inch of his cock getting caressed by her silky smooth flesh. The bands on his cock seemed to swell in an attempt to make sure he was locked to her so tight they could never be parted.

"Kordon!" Gracie gasped as she felt the bands swell and the ridges on the end of his cock rub her sensitive vaginal wall. "Oh... oh!" Gracie pushed down, impaling herself on Kordon's thick cock.

Kordon gritted his teeth tightly as he slid even farther into Gracie. "By the Gods, Gracie," he moaned deeply. "You are so slick and hot."

Gracie giggled as she nipped Kordon's chin. "You like that? Let's see if you like this," she murmured before she rose up slightly and let her weight drop her back down.

She couldn't go too far as the first band on his cock was swelling, preventing him from pulling all the way out. She could feel it moving in her as she moved. Both of them groaned loudly.

Kordon bit back a curse and held Gracie's hips as he began moving his hips back and forth with increasing speed and force. Gracie's voice caught on a sob as the pressure inside her built. She was so close to shattering. Kordon seemed to understand how close she was because he moved one of his hands up to pinch the taut nipple of her right breast.

Gracie pulled back with a sharp cry as she exploded at the combination of pleasure and pain.

The orgasm washed over her in waves of burning heat. Gracie could feel her body actually shaking from the force of it. Kordon's fingers dug into her hips as he pushed up forcibly one more time, then he let out a long, loud groan.

Gracie felt the hot waves of his seed washing deep inside of her as the first band released. Kordon groaned as he pulled out after a few moments. The second band was already swelling and would have locked them together if he had stayed inside her any longer. Gracie let her legs drop down to the floor, but Kordon continued to hold her up so she wouldn't end up a puddle on the bathing-stall floor.

"I want to take you from behind," Kordon said as he let the mist from the bathing stall clean them.

Before Gracie could say anything, she found herself wrapped in his strong arms. Kordon gave the command for the mist to turn off. He stepped out of the bathing stall and set Gracie down gently while he reached for a drying cloth and gently dried her. He paid close attention to every part of her body. It felt like he was trying to memorize her.

He carefully dried her hair and combed it out until it lay in a slick wave down her back. Shivers racked Gracie as he followed the drying cloth with his mouth. Gracie moaned at the feel of his warm lips on her face, neck, and shoulders.

Gracie turned into him when he worked his way down to her breasts. Her nipples were hard and swollen. She couldn't look away as he took one of the sensitive tips into his mouth, sucking on it.

Gracie threaded her fingers through his short hair, letting her nails scrape along his scalp. She held his head in place as she pressed her breast against his lips, wanting more. When one became too sensitive, she pulled it out of his mouth with a slight pop and offered her other nipple for his attention. With each tug, she could feel her pussy heat up and moisture slick her folds as he nipped, pulled, and licked.

"That feels so good," Gracie moaned, watching as he rolled the swollen nipple over his tongue.

"I want to see my son or daughter here. I want to watch him suckle from you," Kordon said fiercely, looking up into Gracie's eyes. "I want to give you my child, Gracie."

Gracie felt her womb clench at the thought of having Kordon's child feeding from her. Holding the tiny image of their love against her while Kordon watched. It was a dream she'd never thought possible. Gracie didn't even realize she was nodding her head in silent agreement.

Kordon smiled as he let his lips move down to Gracie's flat belly. "I want to see you rounded with my child. You will be so beautiful I will not be able to keep my hands off you. I will have to mount you from behind as you swell, and I will hold both you and our child close," Kordon said, looking wickedly up at Gracie as he felt her shiver.

"And, I will taste you every opportunity I can," Kordon added huskily, moving farther down Gracie's body until she felt his hot breath against her mound.

"Kordon," Gracie choked out as the vision of him tasting her caused her pussy to heat up even further. "I need you," she cried out.

Kordon let his fingers slide across Gracie's slick folds before he pulled them out and licked them while looking up at Gracie. He groaned as the sweet taste of her flooded him, causing his already hard cock to jerk in expectation.

Kordon quickly finished drying Gracie's legs and stood, sweeping her off her feet into his arms. Turning with determination, he moved toward the narrow bed. He cursed, wishing he had taken her to their living quarters where the bed was much larger, but there was no way he would make it.

Laying Gracie so she was draped across the bed, Kordon pulled her legs up over his shoulders. He buried his face in her swollen mound, holding her still as she cried out when his hot mouth covered her sensitive core. When she would have fought him, he snarled a warning at her. Gracie's fists gripped the sheets tightly as she pressed against the unforgiving mouth determined to taste every inch of her.

Kordon's brain was focused only on bringing pleasure to Gracie while tasting every inch of her sweet pussy. He pulled her slick, swollen folds back so he had access to the hidden nub. He liked how the soft, blonde curls wrapped around it in an attempt to hide it. He would have to see if she would mind if he removed the soft curls later to compare, but for now, he liked the feel of them against his mouth.

He could feel the pressure building inside of Gracie. Determined to have her come again, he pulled the nub gently between his teeth while pushing two of his fingers deep into her slick pussy, pumping them as he sucked. The combination was too much for Gracie, who bowed from the force of her orgasm and wrapped her thighs against Kordon's head to keep him from moving.

Kordon drank Gracie's sweet essence before pulling her legs apart and turning her over so her upper body was draped across the bed but her lower half was off. Kordon bent over Gracie and pushed his cock into her swollen pussy. He could feel the spasms still gripping her from her orgasm and groaned loudly as it seemed to pull his cock deeper. He felt the other three bands swell immediately and knew he would not be able to leave her until he was totally sated.

He slipped his arms under her and held her tightly while he began pumping madly into her. Each band rubbed up and down inside her as he pushed and pulled with such force it pressed her breasts into the bed. Kordon slid his hands down until her breasts were captured in the palms of his hands. He pulled on her nipples as he pumped her.

"Kordon," Gracie gasped as she felt him hitting her womb. "What are you doing to me?"

Kordon gritted his teeth as he felt the pressure in the second band on his cock swell painfully before he felt the release as he pushed deep into Gracie, holding them both still for a moment before he started again.

"You are mine, Gracie. For now and always." Kordon breathed out harshly as he pushed into her over and over. "I have already stated my intentions to claim you." Kordon groaned as the third band released in a powerful burst, spilling his seed deep into Gracie.

Gracie gasped as she felt the warmth inside her. She never knew a woman could feel so much of the man when he was buried in her like this. Gracie tried to push up off the bed, but Kordon ran his hand down her spine until his palm was between her shoulder blades.

"Stay like this." He groaned deeply. "I am not done. I have never been this swollen before, and it is difficult to hold back," he gritted out.

"What did you mean by your intentions to claim me?" Gracie groaned out as she felt the pull of Kordon as he began moving again.

She would be lucky if she could walk after this. Gracie stretched out, gripping the far side of the bed with her hands and spreading her legs further apart. She had no idea the position caused her ass to raise up and gave Kordon a better view of watching his cock disappearing into her. Gracie jumped when she felt his hard hands grip her ass in a bruising hold, and he spread her cheeks.

"By the Gods, Gracie, I can't get enough of you," Kordon whispered out hoarsely as he pumped into her faster and faster.

The sight was so erotic and the feeling so sensual he exploded into her as her body suddenly clamped down on his. Their cries mingled and twisted together, becoming one just as their bodies were. Kordon collapsed over Gracie's body protectively, caging her within his arms as he breathed deeply trying to catch his breath.

Kordon pressed a kiss to Gracie's damp skin, moaning as her body responded to the touch of his lips by milking more of his hot seed from his cock. He had never felt so sated or weak as he did now. His cock was still fused to Gracie as if it was determined she take everything he had inside him and more, to make sure she would accept the child he wanted to give her.

"Kordon?" Gracie asked suddenly sleepy again.

"Yes, Gracie Jones," Kordon replied softly, continuing to press kisses into her shoulder and neck.

"What did you mean when you said you put in your intentions to claim me? I'm not some dog or car or anything, you know," Gracie said, sighing as her body relaxed in satisfaction.

Kordon chuckled. "I am not sure what a dog or a car is, but you are mine. A Zion Warrior lets his council of elders know of his intentions to claim a female. He normally also informs the female's family. Since you do not have a family that we know of, I simply informed my clan's council. My father is one of the members of the council and was very pleased with my choice."

"Mmm, well, where I come from the guy asks the girl, and if she says yes, then they get together. I guess in a way they claim each other. Because I can tell you one thing, if you don't ask me..." Gracie lifted her head just enough to look over her shoulder into Kordon's eyes. "... then it's not going to happen."

Kordon chuckled at Gracie's stubborn declaration. She might not admit it, but she had already given him her answer. He would not be in the least bit surprised if he had not quickened her with his seed.

Her ability to not be intimidated by him also impressed him. He could not remember having a female who didn't do everything she could to please him. Gracie looked at him as if she was his equal. Kordon gently pulled out of Gracie as he finally felt his cock soften enough. He pressed a gentle kiss to her shoulder as she moaned at his withdrawal. Kordon gently picked her up and took her back into the bathing stall.

"Isn't this where we started?" Gracie asked as she leaned heavily against him.

Kordon couldn't contain his laugh. "Yes, I believe it is. But, I will restrain myself this time. You need food and rest. I promised Toolas I would not tire you out too much. If I don't feed you and let you get some rest, she will ban me from the medical unit," Kordon said as he gently washed her.

Gracie let her fingers follow the pattern of symbols running down the side of his body. Kordon groaned as her fingers traced the pattern on his hip. He reached down and grabbed her hand, pressing it against his hot flesh. His cock was beginning to swell again. Kordon gave a dry chuckle. This was unprecedented even for a Zion Warrior. Four orgasms with the intensity of the ones he'd just had, normally required at least a few hours before he would be ready to go again.

"Gracie, stop. I need to get some food into you. You were already too thin before. Toolas has been giving you supplements, but it is not the same. You need to be fed. I swore when I first saw you that I would feed you until you were nice and plump," Kordon said as he grabbed her other hand which was trying to join the first.

Gracie looked up at Kordon in disbelief. "You want me fat?"

Kordon flushed. "You could never be fat. But I would not object to you being a little rounder. Especially…" Kordon whispered against the palm of the hand he pulled to his lips. "… If it is with my child."

Gracie shivered as she felt Kordon touch his tongue to the center of her palm. "Okay. But, there will be no claiming B.S. unless you ask me first," Gracie insisted sleepily.

Chapter 17

Gracie insisted she be allowed to move back into Kordon's living quarters that night. They spent the rest of the evening eating, talking, touching, and sleeping. Gracie still couldn't believe all the questions Kordon threw at her.

"What is your favorite color?" Kordon asked while feeding her.

Gracie rolled her eyes, remembering how he insisted on feeding her every bit of the food he ordered. She finally gave up and just let him. If it made him happy, then who was she to argue. She leaned back against the pillows he stacked behind her and opened her mouth for another piece of fruit.

"Dark blue," Gracie replied, licking the juice from her lips.

Kordon's eyes followed Gracie's tongue. "Why?" he asked in a distracted voice.

"Because I love your eyes. I've never seen such dark blue eyes before, and yours are beautiful," Gracie said, leaning forward and dropping a kiss on his nose.

Kordon picked up another piece of fruit and fought back a groan as Gracie licked it before snapping it out of his fingers with her tiny white teeth. "How would you feel about living on Zion?"

Gracie frowned. "I'm not sure. If I had a choice of living there with you, then I'm okay with it. But, if you expect me to stay there while you are on the *Conqueror*, it isn't going to happen. I go where you go," Gracie said firmly as she opened for another piece of fruit.

"Do you have family there?" Gracie asked suddenly. "You said your father was on the council, didn't you? Do you think your folks will be okay with you choosing me?"

Kordon hated the sudden look of fear that came into Gracie's eyes. "They will love you as I do. My mother will guide you in the ways of my people. Gracie, they will respect you as the warrior you are. This is a great honor and not given lightly. Tales of your skills and bravery are already being told on Zion. Many of the crewmen aboard the *Conqueror* are from Zion, and they saw what you did."

Gracie just nodded after that. They talked about what happened after she boarded the mother ship, how the other women came together to fight, along with many other subjects until Gracie finally fell into an exhausted, dreamless sleep in Kordon's arms. Kordon stayed awake holding Gracie tight against him for over an hour before he was satisfied she was in a deep sleep.

Rolling out of bed, he glanced once more at Gracie's sleeping figure before he moved into his living quarters. He opened the reports from his resources within the council and began reading. The more he read the darker his expression grew.

He now understood what the human councilman was planning. He would kill the arrogant bastard first. He might even kill the councilman just for having the gall to think he could get away with his ludicrous plans. Kordon finished reading the report thoroughly before he called for Bran, Quan, and Cooraan to join him in his quarters.

Kordon walked quietly into the room and pulled on a pair of pants. He didn't bother with a shirt. He stood over Gracie's still figure, smiling down at the way she was spread out over the bed in utter abandon.

Her hair was spread across both their pillows, she had one arm tossed out as if she was looking for him and the other lay curled under her chin. She had one leg bent and the other thrown out so the tips of her toes peeked out from under the covers.

Her dark lashes lay like beautiful crescents on her cheeks, and her lips were parted as she softly snored. He didn't like the dark shadows under her eyes, but that would change. His father was pressuring him to become a member of the High Council on Zion. He could easily commute between his home and the capital city on Zion when needed. It would give him more time with Gracie and would make it easier to protect her.

Kordon turned when he heard the chime at the door indicating the men had arrived. Leaning over he brushed a soft kiss across Gracie's forehead before turning and leaving the room. He ordered the door to close behind him so they did not disturb her.

Quan raised his eyebrows in surprise. Kordon must be upset if he was willing to pull himself away from his life mate long enough to meet with them. He looked like the warriors of old. The thin braid of hair with his family's beads and colors braided into it swung behind him as he walked over to pour himself a drink. He indicated for the other men to help themselves. Quan moved silently over and poured a glass of the amber liquid before moving back toward the couch.

"So, what is important enough to pull you away from your mate's bed at this time of night?" Quan asked before swallowing half the contents of the glass.

"The human councilman, Proctor," Kordon said darkly. "He will be lucky if I don't kill him tomorrow when we meet."

Bran nodded and Cooraan grinned. "I never did like that slimy *blasnit*," Cooraan said. "Is it an assassination or just outright murder?"

Kordon turned and looked at the men who he knew would stand behind him. "He plans to claim Gracie as his own," Kordon said coldly.

Bran grimaced while Quan jerked upright. Cooraan let out a low growl of anger. All three men were very protective of the little human female who sacrificed so much for others. None of them would stand by and let her be used for the political purpose of some overly pompous ass trying to get reelected to the council.

Bran spoke first. "What do you intend to do?" he asked.

"I've already petitioned my clan council for permission to claim Gracie as mine. They unanimously agreed. As far as I am concerned, she is my mate. The paperwork the Confederation requires is a mere formality I will do to appease them, but I could care less about their requirements," Kordon said before swallowing the contents of his drink in one swig.

Quan chuckled. "Need I remind you that as the Grand Admiral who is neck-deep in the Confederation bureaucracy, it might have an impact on your position if you don't complete the necessary paperwork."

"Not to mention killing one of the councilmen," Cooraan said before adding hastily. "Not that I don't agree with you."

Kordon studied each man for a moment before he replied. "I am resigning my position. I will be joining the High Council on Zion. I am taking Gracie to my home there," Kordon said quietly.

Quan grinned widely. "Hope you like neighbors. I am taking Mohan there after I take her to see her parents. She has this idea I need to ask her father's permission to claim her."

Bran looked back and forth between the two men with a grin. "The High Council will be getting a good man," Bran said to Kordon before turning to Quan with a smirk. "It is the Zion custom to ask the female's family for permission, if you haven't forgotten. What are you going to do if her father turns you down?"

Quan grinned. "Kill him, of course."

Cooraan growled softly. "That will really endear you to Mohan."

Quan chuckled and shook his head. "I have already gotten permission from both her parents and our clan council. I am merely taking her home to please her. She wishes to have both her parents bless our union as is the custom of her people. She is also worried about if I can handle having them as part of my family now. I guess her brothers are known to be a little wild."

"It will help Gracie to have someone she knows living close to us. I welcome you as a neighbor and as a friend," Kordon said with feeling.

Bran cleared his throat. "Now that we have that cleared up, what are you planning to do about the councilman's attempt to claim Gracie?" Bran asked before adding, "... Besides killing him, of course."

Kordon looked grimly at the men before he began outlining his plans. All three men listened intently, nodding and giving suggestions. They would do whatever was necessary to keep Gracie safe and happy, even if it meant killing someone to do it.

Chapter 18

Gracie nervously adjusted the material of her black, form fitting jacket again as she followed Kordon off the transport ship. They'd left the *Conqueror* a half hour before, after Toolas gave Gracie the all clear. Kordon insisted Toolas examine Gracie once more before he would take her off the warship. Gracie gave in gracefully as she considered she'd won the first battle of wills for that day.

The morning, or rather late afternoon on Paulus—Gracie was still having trouble with time since it was hard to tell on board the *Conqueror*—began enjoyably enough. Kordon woke Gracie up with his kisses. He made love to her so gently she felt like crying afterward. She had never felt so loved before.

Afterward, they bathed each other, which led to another round of lovemaking. Gracie bit back a giggle as she remembered Kordon leaning back against the bathing stall with his head thrown back.

"You are going to kill me!" he growled, trying to control the waves washing through him as the last orgasm racked his body.

"But just think, what a wonderful way to die," Gracie said, licking her lips as she rose off her shaking knees.

Gracie leaned heavily against Kordon as he wrapped his arms around her and held her tight. A fierce protectiveness washed over him as he felt her delicate weight pressing against his. *How was it possible for someone who felt so fragile to be so strong?* Kordon thought tenderly. He moved one hand up to hold Gracie's head against his chest while the other remained wrapped around her waist.

"I want you to wear the ceremonial dress of the women from Zion. All females on Zion wear dresses," Kordon said gruffly.

Gracie pulled back to stare up into Kordon's dark blue eyes. She shook her head. "Thanks, but no, thanks. I haven't worn a dress since I was about two. I never did like them. My mom finally gave up trying to make me wear them since I always wore shorts or pants under them anyway," Gracie said with a grimace.

Dresses were horrible. If they were too long, you got tangled up in them. If they were too short, everything hung out when you bent over. A girl couldn't run, climb, crawl, or anything else very easily in them either. Since all of those seemed to have been a part of Gracie's life for so long, she never gave dresses a thought. Nope, pants, shorts, or capris were the way to go.

Kordon frowned down at Gracie. "Nevertheless, you will wear what I tell you. I had Mohan replicate one of my clan's designs in your size. She delivered it late last night."

Gracie's eyes gleamed with amusement. "If my mom couldn't get me in one, you might as well give up. I don't wear dresses, end of discussion. If you want me to wear a pantsuit, okay. Shorts... great. Jeans, you'll be my hero forever. But dresses..." Gracie chuckled. "... never."

* * *

Now as they walked toward a covered ground transport, Gracie looked at Kordon's clenched jaw and tightly pressed lips through her lashes. He was not very happy with her right now. Gracie ran her hand down the soft, black fabric of her jacket and matching pants again before she let one of her hands drop down to brush her fingers against his.

Kordon glanced down, his gaze softening when he saw the worried look in her own dark green one. "Did your parents ever mention that you are extremely stubborn?" he murmured.

Gracie let a small smile curve her lips. "All the time," she whispered back. "Thank you... for everything."

Kordon nodded once more before he moved to walk in front of her. She knew what the men were doing. Adam, Adrian, Mark, and Chance used to do it whenever she had to leave the tunnels. Only this time it was Quan, Cooraan, Bran, and Kordon.

They effectively formed a tight, protective circle around her smaller form. Kordon was in front with Bran to her right, Cooraan to her left, and Quan to her rear. Mohan followed a short distance behind Quan.

Kordon explained he'd been ordered to bring Gracie to the Confederation of Planet's council chambers the moment they were on the planet. He explained the Council wished to meet Gracie and thank her personally for destroying the Alluthan mother ship and rescuing the women who were taken.

Gracie didn't want to go, but Kordon was insistent. There was something he wasn't telling her. She could feel it deep down. That was how she finally won the battle about the dress. She agreed to compromise with him. She would go before the Council if she could wear pants. She joked about how much easier it would be to run if she needed to escape them.

Kordon had stood still for a moment as if contemplating the fact she might actually have to run before nodding his head in agreement. Now, as a shiver ran down her spine, she couldn't help but feel like she was walking to her sentencing instead of to a welcoming.

Kordon entered the transport first, followed by Gracie. The others moved to fill the seats across from them. Gracie smiled as Mohan took the seat next to her. Gracie threaded her fingers through Mohan's and squeezed it. Mohan turned and smiled encouragingly at Gracie.

"Much has changed in your life in a short time. I want you to know I feel privileged to know you, Gracie Jones. I am fortunate to call you my friend," Mohan said in English.

Gracie smiled up at Mohan. "I'm the one who is fortunate, Mohan. I consider you my sister. In some ways, you remind me a lot of Violet. I wish I knew what happened to them," Gracie responded.

Mohan looked surprised at first, then sheepish. "I have been doing more research. I should have sent you the translated copies of my father's archive that I have. I can tell you briefly about your family and friends. There was much documentation after the battles about them… and you."

Gracie's breath caught for a moment before she released it. She felt Kordon's hand clasp her other hand, and he gave her an encouraging squeeze. Kordon nodded to Mohan to continue when she looked at him for guidance.

"Tell her what you can before we get to the Council Chambers. I will make sure she gets the details once we arrive on Zion," Kordon said quietly.

Gracie realized Kordon's grasp of English was improving daily. She forgot he was learning her language as she spoke in Confederation Standard all the time. Gracie smiled her thanks to Kordon before turning her attention on Mohan.

"Please, tell me what you know," Gracie begged.

"I told you Chance and your sister, Violet, mated and had three children. Their descendants still rule on Earth, along with the descendents of Adam, Adrian, and the one called Mark. Each of them also found mates.

"The High Council on Earth is made up of a representative from each region. There are no longer what you call 'countries' on Earth. After the Alluthan war, the population of Earth was down to a little over a hundred million. It was decided a High Council would be formed so the remaining population could be as one. A standard language was decided on and rebuilding began.

"Adam became the first Chancellor of the Council. He ruled for many years before stepping down. He mated with a female rebel leader from Japan. Their union created four children, two boys and two girls.

"Adrian was on the Council as well and spent much time working with the one you call Mark on developing the technology they recovered from the Alluthans for Earth. It was through their work that Earth's space travel became more prominent during the twenty-second century. Adrian mated with a freedom fighter from the area known as France, while Mark mated with an American doctor. Each had three children, two boys and a girl," Mohan said.

"From what I have read in the archives, each of them was very happy in their unions and very successful in working to rebuild your world.

"One thing you should know, Gracie. They all missed you very much. Your sacrifice made you a legend among the people of Earth. There are statues of you in every city on the planet, and your words of hope, love, and strength helped form the new constitution that is still guiding the planet today."

Gracie blushed at first, then paled as the weight of what Mohan was saying pressed down on her. When she gave her messages every day on Gracie's Touch, she'd done it not for herself but for the millions of others. She wanted them to know there was someone out there fighting for them who wouldn't give up, no matter what. She never expected it to have such an impact. If her death had this type of impact on the Earth, she wondered vaguely what her resurrection would have. Just the thought of what could happen was enough to scare the daylights out of her.

Gracie was about to say as much when the transport slowed suddenly. She had been so interested in what Mohan was saying, she hadn't even paid attention to where they were going.

Gracie looked around, suddenly feeling the beginnings of a panic attack coming on. What would be expected of her? Was she supposed to act a certain way? Did they expect her to make some kind of grand speech? If so, they were going to be shit-out-of-luck. It would be short and simple—"Thank you, glad I could help, now leave me alone and let me finally have a life" was sounding pretty good. She might even be able to shorten it to "Thanks, see you." That sounded even better.

Kordon slid out of his side of the transport and held his hand out to Gracie. He squeezed her hand gently when he felt the small tremors moving through her fingers. He pulled her out and into his arms briefly, ignoring the stares of those standing around outside of the Confederation Council building. He was not concerned. His primary focus was on protecting Gracie and making sure she was safe.

He'd talked at length with Toolas before they left the *Conqueror*. She stressed her concerns over Gracie's mental and physical health. While Gracie stated she felt fine and didn't feel stressed out, her body was saying something else.

Toolas was concerned about Gracie being underweight. She made sure Kordon understood that while the physical wounds from the injuries she received from the Alluthans appeared to be healed, her body still needed time to finish the process.

She also reinforced that Gracie had been through a lot of trauma in a short period of time, and she might not even realize just how much until she was in a safe environment. It was Toolas's final words of disapproval that tightened Kordon's grip on Gracie.

Toolas said Gracie's hormone levels were elevated, indicating she could be pregnant. Toolas was concerned that if Gracie didn't gain weight and became too distraught, it could be a danger to both her and the embryo.

"Keep her calm, safe, and happy," Toolas had scolded him fiercely. "That young girl has been through enough."

Kordon leaned down and brushed a kiss across Gracie's lips before turning to look at the other men surrounding them. He nodded briefly. Mohan moved to stand in the center of the group, next to Gracie. Quan leaned down as she moved to pass him and whispered in her delicate ear.

"Remember, if things get difficult, get Gracie and yourself out of there and to the back of the building. Kordon's brother, Saffron, will be waiting with a transport. He will take you both to Kordon's home on Zion, where we will meet up with you," Quan said quietly.

Mohan looked deeply into Quan's dark eyes for a moment before nodding. "Be careful," she responded, quietly letting her hand slide against his cheek briefly.

Gracie looked suspiciously at Mohan. "What is going on?" she asked under her breath.

"Just be ready to go with me if things get bad, Gracie Jones," Mohan whispered back. "There is something going on, but we are not sure what it is. It is better to be prepared."

Gracie frowned at Kordon's back. Why didn't he say he suspected something earlier? Gracie let out a low growl of frustration. He was just as bad as the guys used to be. She was really going to have to let him know she might look defenseless, but she was a lot stronger than he knew.

Gracie could feel her blood beginning to boil. If any of those councilmen thought she was going to be some pushover, then she would set them straight. She finally had her man, had kicked some serious ass—twice—and was over eight hundred years old, dammit. She was ready to do what she wanted!

Gracie threw her shoulders back, making sure every inch of her five-foot-four frame was standing tall and proud. *Bring it on,* Gracie thought with another low growl, which brought a chuckle from Cooraan who glanced at her with a mischievous grin.

"Just leave some for us," he leaned over and whispered as they moved up the pristine white steps of the huge building.

Gracie flashed him an answering grin before turning her eyes to look at the building she was about to enter. A set of four huge black pillars cast in a type of stone offset the dozens of white steps leading up to a set of twelve-foot doors. Even the doors looked intimidating with the huge carvings of warriors, warships, planets, and suns.

Gracie took the steps slowly, wanting to see the whole thing. There were statues of different creatures around the top of the building and great creatures of all types and sizes looking down on those coming up the steps. Gracie shivered when it looked like a couple of the creatures actually moved.

"They did," Mohan whispered. "They are the sentinels. They guard the Council Chamber at all times."

Gracie's eyes widened as she watched the huge gray creatures as they moved. They looked like they were carved out of stone, much like the ancient gargoyles on the buildings in New York. Only these guys looked a lot meaner. Their claws curled around the polished stone above their heads and were the size of carving knives. They had long, narrow snouts and rows of teeth.

One of the creatures stretched out and jumped to another spot on the building. Gracie gasped as she saw it's long, leathery-looking wings spread out for a moment. She would have tripped if not for Cooraan's hand reaching out at the last minute and steadying her.

When they got too high up the steps to see the creatures any longer without trying to walk with her head bent all the way back, Gracie focused on the next new discovery. Smaller, deadly looking insects moved along the vines cut into the stone. Gracie kept her distance from them as they made a humming sound of warning with their wings beating so fast she couldn't see them moving.

"What are those?" Gracie asked wide-eyed.

"*Blasnits*," Mohan said. "Nasty little creatures, but very effective killers. They swarm their victims, eating them from the inside out. Once they become bloated they leave a slimy trail behind them of the undigested remains. These have been genetically altered to remain on the pillars unless they are needed."

Gracie shivered in horror. What if some poor mother brought her kids here, and they started messing with them? What a horrible way to die. Two other aliens dressed in some type of uniform and carrying swords as well as laser pistols opened the doors for them.

It seemed like the sound of their boots echoed forever along the cold stone as they walked toward the opened doors. Gracie wondered halfheartedly if this was how Marie Antoinette felt when she was being escorted out of the palace to be beheaded.

"I don't think I like this. Why are we doing this again?" Gracie asked nervously as their small group walked through into a dimly lit corridor.

Large carvings, paintings, and tapestries lined the walls. The ceiling looked like it was over fifty feet high with curved domes lit with scenes from what looked like different worlds. Gracie imagined if it was a museum it would be pretty neat—if you liked the cold, dark, and scary stuff. Personally, she'd had enough of that on the Alluthan mother ship. She was ready for brightly lit, cheerful, and open right about now.

Gracie moved closer to Kordon and tucked her fingers up under his jacket so she was holding onto his waistband. She didn't care what it looked like or what anyone thought. She needed to touch him.

Kordon paused a moment and looked over his shoulder with a reassuring smile. "The Council Chambers are not quite as bad. Several of the new council members have insisted on it being remodeled," Kordon said when he saw the frightened look in Gracie's eyes. "I will not let anything harm you."

Gracie nodded. "This place makes a haunted house look like Candy Land. Is it just me or is this place really depressing?"

Bran bit back a chuckle as did the other three men. "It is meant to intimidate any who enter into agreeing with the council," he said.

"Not in this bloody lifetime," Gracie growled out in understanding. "I've been to the pits of hell and survived. This is going to be a walk in the park compared to some of the places I've been," she said with bravado.

Kordon's eyes flashed in anger at the memory. "We are prepared. Just follow Mohan if she tells you to. She knows what to do."

Gracie frowned up at Kordon. "Yeah, that is something else we need to talk about when this show is over with." Gracie pinched Kordon lightly. "No more withholding information from me. I can't fight if I don't know what is going on."

Kordon turned so quickly he caught Gracie off guard. Grasping her face between his hands, he tilted her head backward, forcing her to look into his deep blue eyes. Kordon didn't say anything for a moment. Gracie stood still when she realized he was trying to get his emotions under control before he spoke.

Kordon took several deep breaths before he felt able to speak calmly. "I will protect you, Gracie. I do not want you to ever have to fight again. Twice I have almost lost you. Twice I have felt an emotion so devastating, so paralyzing that it nearly brought me to my knees. I have never known fear until I met you. It is not an emotion I like. I will protect you and our child with my life, Gracie Jones-Jefe. I have claimed you as mine, and I always protect what is mine."

Gracie opened her mouth, but nothing came out. Kordon took advantage of her stunned silence to take her savagely in a kiss that proclaimed to all who she was to him. Gracie melted as Kordon's strong arms moved down her arms and wrapped around her. Her arms moved upward to wind around his neck in a desperate acceptance of his possession. She was determined to do a little claiming of her own.

Kordon pulled away almost as abruptly as he had pulled her into his arms. It took a moment for Gracie to realize Quan was standing in front of them, blocking several guards from approaching them. Gracie's face flushed with heat, and she lowered her eyes.

She couldn't believe she had totally tuned everyone and everything out the moment Kordon had touched her. Gracie glanced up at Kordon to see if he was as affected as she was. If she had not been so in tune with him she would have missed the slight tightening of his jaw and the muscle ticking in it rapidly. To anyone else who might see him, his face was as cold as the stone statues lining the outside of the building.

"Grand Admiral, the council has requested that you and the female be escorted into the Council Chambers," one of the guards said.

Two other guards moved aside to allow them to pass. When Bran and Cooraan moved, three additional guards moved forward and placed their swords in front of them. Bran, Cooraan, and Quan all growled in a low, dangerous tone. Quan moved Mohan back behind him gently as he took a threatening step forward.

"The Council requested you come alone with the female," the guard said, ignoring the threatening growls of the other Zion warriors.

Kordon's eyes remained cold. "Very well," he replied stiffly.

Bran started to protest, but a slight signal from Kordon froze the protest on his lips. With a curt nod, the men stepped back. Mohan moved up behind Gracie and gently laid her palm against her back.

"Stay safe, Gracie Jones. We will be close if you need us," Mohan said quietly in English.

Gracie started slightly when she felt Mohan pressing the small laser pistol into the back of the waistband of her pants. "I will. You said the back door, right?" Gracie murmured with a wary smile.

Mohan chuckled. "Yes," Mohan replied before melting back behind Quan again with a small nod of her head.

"We will wait for you outside," Bran snarled out as the three guards moved closer to them.

Kordon held his hand out for Gracie. He tightened his fingers around her delicate ones and gave them a gentle squeeze. With a nod to the others, he turned and followed the head guard through the newly opened set of doors farther down the corridor.

Chapter 19

Gracie held tightly to Kordon's hand and walked as straight and tall as she could. She had never felt so small as she did right then. Between Kordon and the guards, she really was the runt of this litter, she thought dryly. She let her eyes scan the room as they entered.

The Chamber wasn't very large. There were thirteen people seated behind a large, curved bench about three feet higher than floor level. Kordon walked confidently down the center, letting his fingers slip from Gracie's as they entered the room.

Gracie understood he wanted to keep his hands free in case he needed them. Gracie slowed so she was just a couple of feet behind and to the right of Kordon. She wanted to make sure she had room as well. If things got ugly, she wanted to be ready for the worst.

Gracie looked at each council member. Over half of them were from species she hadn't yet met. She recognized the human councilman right off. She barely hid her laugh under a fake cough as she stared at him. He was your typical politician. Gracie would have thought they might have evolved a little over the past eight hundred years, but if the puffy hair, fake smile, and greedy gleam in his eyes were anything to go by, the evolutionary bug missed him.

Gracie watched in disgust as the councilman leaned forward, running his eyes up and down her like she was a prize thoroughbred waiting to be snapped up. She could feel her blood beginning to boil. She really hoped the little prick gave her an excuse to take him down a notch or two. She was so focused on what she would like to say to the slimeball that she almost ran into Kordon's back when he stopped in front of the panel of councilmen and women.

Kordon stood perfectly still. He didn't bow or even acknowledge any of them. Gracie took her cue from him and remained perfectly still even though she really wanted to just scream at them to get whatever they wanted to say said, so she and Kordon could get the hell out there.

Finally, one of the women stood up. She was beautiful in an unusual way. She was very tall and slim with light bluish skin. Her hair was a darker blue and hung almost to her knees. She moved very gracefully. She looked Kordon in the eye before tilting her head to one side and giving a small nod of welcome.

"Welcome, Grand Admiral. On behalf of the Planetary Council, I would like to extend our appreciation for the *Conqueror's* victory over the alien invaders," the woman said.

"Councilwoman Burrol," Kordon said coldly. "My reports detailed the events. While the *Conqueror* was indeed helpful in defeating the attacks by the Alluthans, credit for the actual victory should go to Gracie Jones."

Burrol smiled gently at Gracie, who was trying to act like she stood in front of a council of aliens every day. From the look in the woman's eyes, Gracie had a feeling she wasn't doing a good job of acting. It took every ounce of strength Gracie had not to turn tail and run when all eyes moved to her.

"Gracie Jones, please step forward," Councilwoman Burrol said quietly.

Gracie hesitated a moment, looking to Kordon for guidance before she took a tentative step forward. "Councilwoman Burrol," Gracie said, inclining her head just as the woman had to Kordon.

* * *

Kordon forced his fists not to clench as Gracie stepped forward and nodded. He kept his eyes forward, but all his senses were focused on the guards stationed throughout the chamber. There were twice as many as were normally in the room.

Kordon had been before the council hundreds of times. Never before had the doors been sealed and locked or the clear shield activated when he was there alone.

Something was definitely going on. Kordon wanted to take Gracie and leave. He knew of the emergency exit for the councilmen should an invading force gain entrance to the chambers. He knew every inch of the layout for the Council's Chambers. He planned to use it if things took a turn for the worse.

Kordon forced his focus back on Gracie. He was so proud of her. She truly was a mate for a warrior. She was as fierce and stood as tall as any Zion warrior before a battle.

"You speak Confederation Standard?" Councilwoman Burrol said in surprise.

"Yes, ma'am. Mohan and Kordon have been teaching me," Gracie replied steadily. "May I be so bold as to ask why I am here? I am still recovering from my wounds and am tired. No offense, but I would like to return with Kordon to either the *Conqueror* or head on to Zion. I am so ready for a vacation."

The Earth councilman rose at Gracie's question. "My dear Gracie Jones. I cannot express my happiness at the discovery that you survived so much tragedy. You must be devastated at finding yourself so far from home and away from all those you loved and knew. Then to find yourself at the mercy of such huge, overwhelming aliens as the Zion warriors and facing the Alluthans again—you must be overwhelmed," the Earth councilman gushed on in a smooth, honeyed voice.

Gracie looked at the councilman in humor. Did he really think she was buying his load of bullshit? If so, she had a bridge in Brooklyn he could buy. Shaking her head, she smiled sweetly before replying.

"On the contrary, sir, I could not be more impressed with the reception and care I've received from the *Grand Admiral* and the crew of the *Conqueror*," Gracie said with an emphasis on the Grand Admiral.

The Earth's councilman's smile faded as he looked with disdain at Kordon. "Yes, well, he was only doing what he was ordered to do," he said smoothly before turning his smile on Gracie again.

"My name is Altren Proctor. As the representative for Earth, I am more than happy to welcome you into my protection. I have already contacted your family back on Earth and informed them you are under my protection now, and that I would be responsible for your safe return back to Earth where a welcoming celebration is being prepared.

"I know all of this must be confusing to you, and I will do everything in my power to make it as easy for you as possible. The people of Earth are ecstatic about learning that the Mother of Freedom is actually alive. I do have to say you look absolutely breathtaking, my dear. I feel honored that you will be under my protection. I am sure we can get to know each other much better on the long trip back to Earth."

Gracie clenched her fists tightly by her sides. Kordon moved a step forward, but Gracie put her hand out to stop him. The guy must think she was a fool not to hear all the little emphases and innuendos he was dishing out in his little speech.

"He's mine," she hissed under her breath in English.

Kordon looked down at Gracie for a moment before he nodded and took a half step back. He was very curious as to what she planned to do. His plan was to kill the councilman, grab Gracie, and escape out the back. Now he wondered if Gracie would save him the trouble of killing the man. She had the same look in her eyes as she had earlier when he told her she was going to wear a dress.

"Listen, Al. I really appreciate the offer, but I've had a better one. I'm going with Kordon. You see, I've claimed the huge, overwhelming alien as mine. While I also appreciate that you've contacted my sister's descendants, I don't know them from jack shit.

"In case you can't count, it's been eight hundred-plus years, so I think all my immediate family is gone. As for placing me under your protection, might I remind you I was the one who saved Earth's ass from the Alluthans—not once, but twice. I think that places you more under my protection than the other way around," Gracie paused and looked closely at each and every councilman and woman to let them know she was seriously pissed.

"I've been almost blown up twice, shot, crashed on a deserted moon for three years, and found out I am over eight hundred years old. I don't need nor do I want anyone trying to tell me what to do with my life or how I should live it.

"I am taking my mate and going to Zion to live peacefully and quietly, and if you or any other bozo tries to stop me I am going to kick your ass so hard it will be coming out of your head. Do you understand the words coming out of my mouth?" Gracie snarled up at the councilman who had turned pale and sat down in stunned silence.

There was a moment of stunned silence as Gracie let her words sink in. Turning, she placed both hands against Kordon's cheeks and pulled him down to kiss him hard. She wanted everyone in that room to know she was the one doing the claiming. It was her decision. Gracie broke the kiss when she heard Councilwoman Burrol softly clearing her throat.

Gracie turned but didn't step away from Kordon. Instead, she grabbed his hands and pulled them around her waist. Kordon pulled her back against his hard form, holding her possessively against him.

"I apologize for the confusion, Gracie Jones. It appears the council was given incorrect information about your mental and physical health and desires." Councilwoman Burrol, as well as several other members of the council flashed an irritated glance at Proctor.

"It is obvious you are in good health and are more than competent to make your own decisions. A request for claiming is normally made by the male of the species. In honor of the great sacrifices you have made to not only your planet, but to the Confederation of Planets your petition to claim Grand Admiral Kordon Jefe as your mate is approved by the council by a vote of twelve in favor, with one opposed. May great happiness follow you, Gracie Jones.

"Now, for your petition, Grand Admiral. It is with great sadness and reserve that the Council accepts your resignation. Your suggestion for your replacement will be taken under consideration.

"On a personal note, I am happy that you will be on the High Council of Zion. Your leadership and expertise, along with your knowledge of the

Confederation and the partnership the Confederation has with the Zion people will be greatly appreciated.

"Your final duties as Grand Admiral will be to see that the information on the Alluthans are given to the correct divisions for review and analysis. May great happiness follow you as well, Kordon Jefe," Councilwoman Burrol said as she bowed her head in respect.

Kordon watched as each of the councilmen and women, with the exception of Proctor, stood and bowed to him. Gracie looked up and grinned at Kordon before she pulled away and bowed her head as well. Kordon felt emotion tighten his chest at not only Gracie's show of respect, but at her open claim on him as her mate. Kordon looked at each of the councilmen and women, bowing to them in return.

It was only when he got to Proctor that his eyes narrowed. Pure hatred poured from Proctor's eyes as he glared down at Kordon. It was the look he turned on Gracie that had Kordon reaching for his laser pistol. The look of determination and lust was enough to make Kordon want to kill the man right there. It was only Councilwoman Burrol's sharp tone breaking Proctor's possessive glare on Gracie that saved his life.

* * *

Saffron stood up from where he was leaning against a nondescript transport. He had a huge grin on his face as he saw his older brother round the corner of the building. His eyes widened when they landed on Gracie.

He knew about his brother's petition to claim an Earth woman. His father and mother were skeptical at first. Of the few dealings the Zion warriors had with Earthlings, none had been positive. Most of the men were weak and easy to intimidate.

The women were better, but only because they were easy on the eye and fun to fuck. While that was their good quality, the bad more than made up for it. Most Earth women Saffron met were whiny and weak. They could also get really strange when they thought he should feel something more for them than as a good lay.

Now, as the little thing next to his brother walked toward him, he couldn't help but wonder where his brother's brain was at. Sure, she was cute. But a good fuck would break her in half. She was a tiny thing with barely any meat on her bones.

This couldn't be the warrior woman who'd fought off thousands of half organic/half robotic creatures and blew up their mother ship. She looked like a good wind would knock her over. Hell, he would be afraid just touching her would break her.

"I see you made it out of the council chambers without the sentinels after you. Did the other council members want to be rid of the Earthling so bad they didn't care that you killed him in front of them?" Saffron chuckled good-naturedly as Kordon approached.

"Gracie!" Mohan rushed forward to wrap her arms around Gracie tightly. "I was so worried. Quan said Kordon knew of a way out of the chambers, but when you never came I feared the worse."

Gracie laughed as she hugged her friend back. "It was so cool. All the councilmen and women except for this one prick bowed to Kordon and told him good luck."

Kordon shook his head as he pulled Gracie closer to him. Quan, Bran, and Cooraan approached silently from behind him. All three men looked both surprised and worried. Kordon looked at them with a slight frown over Gracie's head and shook his in a brief message to convey all was not good. Gracie was oblivious to the silent message. She was just relieved to finally be out of the spooky building.

"So, what happened?" Saffron asked with a bemused smile at Gracie, who was rubbing her head against Kordon's chest. His brother was just as bad as he leaned over to brush a kiss to the top of her head. "I was under the impression there would be blood, some fighting, and a little bit of chasing followed by an escape."

"There would have been if not for Gracie," Kordon said with a shake of his head. "She was magnificent."

Gracie blushed as all eyes turned to her. "Well, that jerk made me mad with his holier-than-thou 'you need protection' bullcrap. He would have probably pissed his pants if he saw an Alluthan walking toward him."

Kordon chuckled. "Proctor convinced the other council members that Gracie was too fragile in mind

and body to understand everything that happened to
her. He declared he had her family's permission to
claim her and protect her."

Mohan leaned back into Quan's arms. "So, what
did you do, Gracie?" she asked.

"I told him to take a hike!" Gracie declared
fiercely.

"She told him she was over eight hundred years
old and didn't answer to anyone. She also stated that
she was claiming me," Kordon said with a huge grin.

Saffron choked on the drink he had just taken a
swig of. "What! A female cannot claim a Zion warrior.
You are considered one of the best warriors on Zion.
No female can claim you. Especially when you
consider your rank among our people and the clan
that you come from."

Gracie turned on Saffron so fast he took a step
back. "Well, I did, and the council says he's mine, so
back off! I'm not giving him up," Gracie growled,
clenching her fists tightly.

Kordon grabbed Gracie around the waist and
pulled her up against his body. "Calm down, little
one. I accept your claim on me. My clan has already
accepted my—your claim on me. I am yours," Kordon
looked fiercely at Saffron. "You will not insult my
mate, brother. She has been through more than you
could possibly imagine."

Bran nodded his head in agreement. "She blew up
the Alluthan mother ship."

"She brought down all their shields when they
were attacking us," Quan said.

"She gave us enough information on them to not only decipher their language but also their programming and technology," Cooraan added.

"And she survived on a deserted moon all alone for three years," Mohan finished off proudly.

Saffron looked at Gracie again through new eyes. He could see her fierce determination, her love and protectiveness for his brother, and her fear of not being accepted by him. But what he really saw was the strength and honor she brought out in those who were known for being the fiercest, strongest warriors on Zion.

"I see the same look in your eyes that I see in my mother's when she looks at our father. I am honored to call you my sister, little warrior," Saffron said quietly.

Gracie pulled away and took a hesitant step toward Saffron. He found himself unable to stand being the cause of her look of uncertainty. Saffron opened his arms and Gracie flew into them, giving him a huge hug.

"Thank you," Gracie whispered into his chest.

Saffron looked at his brother in hopeless wonder. "Does she have this effect on all the males she meets?"

"The desire to protect and care for her?" Quan asked.

"The desire to see her smile and laugh?" Bran asked.

"The desire to bundle her up and take her home and…?" Cooraan asked with a mischievous grin at Kordon.

Kordon growled at all four men. He quickly pulled Gracie out of his younger brother's arms and back into his. "The desire to please her?" Kordon asked as he brushed a kiss across her mouth.

"The desire to feed her?" Gracie asked hopefully. "Because I have to tell you, being scared shitless can make a girl really, really hungry."

Quan grabbed Mohan and gave her a huge kiss. "Sounds good to me. I'm hungry too."

Mohan's fur changed colors vividly as Quan's double meaning drew laughs from all the men. She turned and bared her teeth at Quan, who quickly took a step back with his hands thrown up in the air in surrender. Gracie just sighed. She would need sharper teeth before that trick would work on Kordon.

Chapter 20

The group climbed into the transport. Saffron soon was in the air above the capital city. Gracie had to admit Paulus was beautiful. It reminded her a little of the ancient Roman cities she used to read about. The buildings were large, white, and opulent.

It was growing dark and lights were beginning to glitter throughout the city. Saffron must have been very familiar with it as he flew through several narrow corridors, missing most of the congestion, before landing in a back alley.

"This place is small but it has great food," Saffron said, powering down the transport.

Gracie groaned as her stomach rumbled. "As long as it doesn't try to eat me first, I'm happy."

Kordon laughed as he helped Gracie out of the transport. Wrapping his arm around her waist, he led the way through a back entrance. Gracie didn't say anything. She figured he knew what he was doing.

A small, rotund man with four arms came forward to greet them. Saffron said something in a language Gracie didn't understand, and the man nodded vigorously. Turning, the small round figure moved quickly down a hallway before turning into a room.

"You will have complete privacy," the man said briskly. "I will wait on you myself."

Saffron nodded. "Thank you, Brut."

Gracie moved to sit on a set of cushions on the floor that were situated around a low table. Kordon moved in next to her, pulling her close. Gracie squeaked when the cushions moved around both her and Kordon's body, expanding until it supported them comfortably.

"Wow!" Gracie said in awe as she touched the cushion. "I could have really used this in both my alcove back in the tunnels and on the supply ship. My bed and the seats on the supply ship weren't nearly this comfortable."

Saffron looked at Gracie again as if he was curious about something, but wasn't sure about asking her about it. He nodded as Brut set down a tray with drinks on it. Kordon said something to him, and the little man's face lit up with pleasure as he glanced at Gracie. Within minutes, another tray was set down in front of her.

Kordon reached out and poured the cool liquid into a tall glass before handing it to Gracie. "You might enjoy this. It is a mixture of fruits. It is not too sweet and is very refreshing."

Saffron leaned over and picked up one of the appetizers that Brut delivered. "What really happened in the Council Chambers?" he asked, before sitting back again.

Kordon looked sharply at Gracie before turning his attention to his brother. "Nothing to worry about."

Gracie picked up one of the appetizers and sniffed it before taking a small bite. "You might as well spit it out. I'm just going to be pissed at you if you keep hiding things," Gracie said before she stuffed the rest of the appetizer into her mouth.

Cooraan laughed at Kordon's resigned look. "I don't think you are going to be able to hide anything from your little warrior, Kordon."

Gracie nodded as she picked up three more of the appetizers and set them on the plate in front of her. "If he tries, I'll just hack into his computer system and figure it out anyway. Then, I can plan payback," she added with a grin at Cooraan.

Bran, Quan, and Mohan laughed at Kordon's groan. "Tell us," Bran said, sipping his wine.

"I don't trust Proctor. He wants Gracie. I am not sure why yet, but he will not give up so easily," Kordon said quietly.

Bran nodded. "My resources have told me there are some major changes going on in the Earth Council. Proctor is making a bid to become the Supreme Chancellor. I suspect he feels if he has the Mother of Freedom at his side he would be unbeatable. It doesn't hurt that the Mother of Freedom is young, beautiful, and is known all over the planet."

Gracie's hand stopped in midair as she was about to eat another appetizer. She looked at all the men who were staring at her. Setting the appetizer down on the plate in front of her, she stared down at the plate, not seeing anything for a moment.

"I don't want to go back to Earth," Gracie said quietly, not wanting to look at anyone at the moment. "I don't belong there any longer."

Kordon reached for Gracie's hand. He frowned when he saw the quiver in it she was trying to hide.

"You belong with me. You will not return to Earth unless you wish to."

Gracie looked up into Kordon's eyes. "Everything I knew, everyone I loved is gone. I don't want..." Gracie's throat tightened as memories flooded her.

It may have been eight hundred years for everyone else, but for her it had only been three. Her memories were still too sharp and fresh to ignore. To go back and actually see everything gone was more than she could handle at the moment. Maybe in a few years she would be able to deal with it after she found her own place in this new world but... not now.

"Do not fret. You will not go back unless that is what you desire," Kordon said, pulling Gracie to his chest.

Gracie turned her face into Kordon, drawing his comforting scent into her as she blinked back tears. She merely absorbed his quiet strength into her as she let the memories wash over her. She pulled away with a self-conscious chuckle, muttering an apology to the others.

"I don't know why I feel so emotional," Gracie laughed as she brushed a tear away.

"I do," Kordon said with a huge grin on his face again. "Toolas said she believes you are with child."

Gracie's head jerked up as all the men, and even Mohan, laughed and started congratulating Kordon and her. She stared in wonder at Kordon. She was really, really going to have to talk to him about keeping information from her.

Gracie let her hand drop down protectively over her flat stomach and laughed in amazement. Toolas thought she was pregnant. She and Kordon were going to be parents? Gracie smiled up at Kordon when he turned and gave her a hard kiss.

"I protect what is mine, Gracie. I claim you and our child. I have claimed you from the first time I heard your voice. The sound of your voice reached out and touched a part deep inside me I never knew existed. I love you, Gracie Jones-Jefe," Kordon said quietly so only Gracie could hear him.

"I love you too, Kordon. Forever," Gracie whispered as she leaned up and gave him a gentle kiss on the lips.

The rest of the evening passed quickly. Brut brought in tray after tray of food. Gracie ate so much she complained she was just going to curl up right there and sleep.

The men drank and talked while Gracie and Mohan made plans for where they were going to live, when Mohan was going to have kids so they could all grow up together, and what they would need to do before the baby was born. Gracie hadn't laughed so much or felt so happy since before the invasion of Earth. She looked around the small group who were more family than friends and decided maybe, just maybe, she would have to send a wedding invitation to Murphy.

* * *

The next two months flew by. They all returned to the *Conqueror* to finish up their duties, with the exception of Saffron who returned to Zion. Bran was appointed the new Grand Admiral of the Confederation military based on Kordon's recommendation.

Quan was returning to Zion with Mohan in a few months. He would work with his brothers in their transport business. Cooraan was going to remain on board the *Conqueror* with Bran. Gracie and Mohan spent time with the new communications officer, showing him the changes in programming they'd developed.

There was still a concern there might be more Alluthan mother ships out there. Gracie explained how they were solitary-type ships unless a large amount of resources were available. Bran and Cooraan were sharing the adaptations to the shields and weapons systems so all the Confederation of Planets' warships were upgraded.

The biggest changes were beginning to show on Gracie. She was now sporting a small bump in the front of her uniform. In the back of her mind was still the fear of Proctor trying something, but it was moving further and further into the past the longer she was aboard the *Conqueror* and nothing happened.

Kordon watched as Gracie laughed at something Mohan said. She was positively glowing. He felt his cock jerk at the thought of making love to her again. He loved holding her, touching her, and sliding his hands over the slight swell of her stomach. She had gained weight over the past couple of months, and her breasts were getting plumper as her pregnancy advanced.

They were leaving tomorrow for Zion. Both of his parents were anxious to meet Gracie. His mother was overjoyed at finally having a daughter. Kordon was the oldest of four sons. His mother often mourned the fact she had no daughters to spoil.

As he was the only one with a mate, Gracie would be swept under her wing. Kordon listened with half an ear to what Quan was saying. He and Mohan were also leaving tomorrow, but they were heading for Ta'nee to see Mohan's parents.

"You need to keep your eyes and ears open. Proctor has disappeared. After what happened with Gracie on the council, he was replaced," Quan was saying.

Kordon jerked his attention around. "What have you heard?" he asked in a low tone, not wanting Gracie to suspect anything.

Quan shrugged. "Not much. I heard he was royally pissed at you. His only hope for redemption is if he can get his slimy hands on Gracie. There is more power and prestige in being the Supreme Chancellor of Earth than merely a councilman of the Confederation. He can set policies and will have more power."

"I don't want Gracie to know. She should be safe once we are on Zion. Proctor would be a fool to try anything on a planet filled with warriors," Kordon said in cold anger.

Quan gave Kordon a brief nod before excusing himself. Kordon walked over to where Gracie was sitting with Mohan and the new communications officer. Bending down, he brushed a kiss across Gracie's lips.

"I have some reports to finish. I will see you later in our living quarters," Kordon said quietly.

Gracie grinned up at him. "Okay. We should be done in a little while."

Gracie watched with longing as Kordon turned to leave. *Damn, but the man has a great ass,* she thought with a sigh.

Mohan chuckled as she watched the longing in Gracie's eyes. "He has changed so much since he met you."

Gracie looked around curiously. "What do you mean?"

"He was always known for being cold and reserved. Even that night we shared together on Cumin, he never showed any emotion," Mohan said without thinking.

Gracie froze. "What do you mean 'the night you shared together'? Are you saying you've slept with Kordon?" Gracie asked tightly.

Mohan looked up from what she was doing and flushed, the soft fur on her face changing colors. "It was nothing."

"You and Kordon? You two slept together? Gracie asked again.

"Gracie, I did not mean to upset you," Mohan said anxiously. "The Ta'nee are a very sexual species. I am only half-Ta'nee and can fight the need. Unfortunately, sometimes it is too much. I had been drinking more than normal. I didn't even know it was Kordon until eight months later when he brought me aboard the *Conqueror* as his communications officer. He was very clear it would never happen again," Mohan said fretfully. She reached out to touch Gracie, but stopped when Gracie pulled away.

Gracie stood up abruptly. "I-I need to be alone for a little while," Gracie said before turning away.

Mohan stood up in distress. She wanted to follow Gracie, but was unsure of what to do. She no longer thought of Kordon in any way. Her love and desire was only for Quan. She should have realized Gracie would have been upset. She remembered reading about how the ancient Earthlings felt about their mates. Some Earthlings still followed the old customs. Mohan let out a small cry of distress knowing she had hurt her friend deeply.

Chapter 21

Gracie sat looking out the viewport in one of the rooms designated for relaxation. There were consoles for viewing or contacting family, portable tablets for reading or watching holovids, and chairs designed for just relaxing.

Gracie sat doing none of that. She had no family, she didn't feel like reading or watching a movie, and she was too busy crying to relax. She and Murphy were having a pity party, and she just wanted to be left alone. It wasn't as good as the one she'd had on the moon, but it was coming in a close second.

Picking up another tissue she'd replicated, she wiped her eyes and blew her nose. Why did it seem just when everything was going good, Murphy came along to throw a car at it. *Of course,* Gracie thought as new tears flowed down her cheeks. With her luck, Murphy was probably laughing his ass off at her for being so stupid.

She leaned her head back and closed her eyes, wanting to just forget about everything. The combination of crying, being pregnant, and the quietness of the room soon lured her into a restless sleep.

That was where Kordon found her two hours later. He grimaced at the signs of tears still wetting Gracie's cheeks in her sleep. There were dark shadows under her eyes again, and her face was slightly red and puffy from all the crying she had done.

When Mohan sought him out to tell him about what happened, it took a moment for him to understand. Mohan haltingly explained the ancient beliefs of the Earthlings. Once she was finished she was wringing her hands together and crying.

She was afraid Gracie would never forgive her. She read accounts of that happening frequently in some of the old literature from Earth. She called them romance stories. She said if the woman felt betrayed, she would not have anything to do with the male or the female, even if the female was related, ever again.

Kordon assured Mohan that Gracie would forgive them both. It had happened before they even knew she was alive. Mohan was so beside herself, Kordon finally called for Quan to take her back to their living quarters and comfort her.

Now, as he gazed down on Gracie as she cried in her sleep, he wondered. Every few breaths, a little sob would escape. It tore him up to see her like this. He had sworn to protect her. So far, he felt like he was doing a poor job of it.

Bending down, he gently lifted her into his arms. He bit back a curse when she stiffened for a moment before relaxing and turning her face into his chest. He tightened his arms around her and carried her back to their living quarters. She had fallen into a deeper sleep as he carried her.

He laid her gently down on their bed and silently removed her shoes and clothing before removing his own. Kordon crawled into the bed and pulled Gracie up against his warm body, holding her tightly. Gracie moaned and stirred restlessly like she wanted to pull away, but Kordon held her tight, rubbing his hand up and down her back until she gave a soft hiccup and settled back down.

* * *

Gracie woke the next morning feeling like her head was filled with cotton. She lay on her side trying to remember how she'd made it back to her and Kordon's living quarters. For the life of her, she couldn't remember anything after she closed her eyes. She frowned as she remembered sitting in a chair in one of the off-duty rooms.

Her eyes filled with tears as she remembered why she had gone there in the first place. Gracie sniffed as her nose itched from trying not to cry again.

"Shush, my little warrior," Kordon said, wrapping an arm around Gracie and trying to pull her back against him.

Gracie stiffened and tried to move away from him, but Kordon just tightened his arm. "Let me go," she sniffed.

"Never, my Gracie," Kordon said as he pressed a kiss into her shoulder. "I never meant to hurt you. Please do not cry," Kordon whispered.

"I hate you!" Gracie sniffed again.

"I know. I am just a terrible mate," Kordon replied, pressing another kiss into her neck.

"I really, really do," Gracie whispered.

"I know," Kordon whispered back as he pulled her over onto her back. He kissed a stray tear from her cheek. "But I love you very, very much, my Gracie."

Gracie looked up into Kordon's eyes with such a look of betrayal, Kordon began to hate himself. "If I had known, I never would have—" Gracie began before she was cut off by Kordon's lips on hers.

Gracie resisted at first, but Kordon persisted. He was determined to show her that she was his world. She was the only thing that mattered. Gracie tried to turn her head to one side, but Kordon slid his hands up to hold her head still while moving his body over hers to cage her under him.

"Gracie, please," Kordon groaned. "You are the only one for me. Surely, you know that. You claimed me," Kordon said with a slight grin. "I have never been claimed before."

"Never?" Gracie asked, sniffing loudly.

Kordon shook his head solemnly. "Never. And I have never claimed another."

"Never, never?" Gracie asked, searching Kordon's dark, blue eyes.

"Never, never," Kordon replied groaning as he felt Gracie moving restlessly under him.

"Kordon?" Gracie asked.

"Yes?" Kordon groaned again as he ran his lips along her neck.

"I need to go pee," Gracie giggled. "It seems the bigger the baby gets, the more I have to go."

Kordon bit back a chuckle of resignation. Shaking his head, he moaned as he pulled away from her and sat up. "You are going to kill me, Gracie."

Gracie sat up and brushed a kiss across Kordon's lips, before replying. "If you ever look at another woman, including Mohan, I probably will."

Kordon fell back against the bed laughing as Gracie scrambled out and headed toward the bathroom. He leaned back, enjoying the view of her ass before giving up with a loud growl and following her. They could make love in the bathing stall.

* * *

Several hours later, Gracie was hugging a tearful Mohan and promising they were still best friends. It took a while, but both men finally just pulled the women apart and loaded them into their respective transports. Saffron grinned when he saw Kordon carrying a protesting Gracie on board.

"Being difficult?" Saffron asked as Kordon strapped Gracie into the seat behind him.

"You have no idea," Kordon said, ducking his head as Gracie swung at it.

Saffron just laughed as he received permission for take-off. "Better you than me, brother.

Gracie leaned forward just enough to thump Saffron on the back of his head. "I heard that, you rat."

Kordon laughed as Saffron begged forgiveness. Soon, he would have Gracie in his home. He already made plans to have his parents, namely his mother, come and spend time with them. He wanted Gracie to feel at home on his world.

He also worried about her. Toolas told him it was important for Gracie to get plenty of rest during her pregnancy. She was worried about Gracie being so tired. She also reminded Kordon that Gracie was much smaller than he, and the baby appeared to be growing rapidly. She recommended Gracie seeing a healer as soon as possible. Kordon had already spoken to his mother about finding one close to their home.

The journey to Zion would take two days. There was only a small bunk that folded down on the transport for sleeping, and they would take turns. Gracie was used to sleeping in small spaces. She couldn't help but laugh when Kordon growled in frustration at realizing there was absolutely no way they could sleep together unless she was on top of him. He finally gave in when he saw Gracie's head drooping about ten hours into the flight.

Two days later, Gracie got her first look at Zion. She could feel Kordon's pride in his home world when he talked about it, but she never expected to see anything so beautiful. Huge mountains graced the horizon and large colorful birds flew overhead. Gracie turned in a circle as she walked down the platform, watching as a large flock passed overhead. She brought one hand up to shade her eyes as she looked over the green trees where they landed.

In the distance, she could see a magnificent series of waterfalls flowing off the cliffs into the ocean. The landing area was situated on a lower-level cliff. It was the size of probably a dozen or so football fields back home. Kordon and Saffron both grinned at Gracie's wide-eyed expression of awe.

"Come, we have transportation waiting for us," Kordon said, cupping Gracie's elbow in his hand.

"What about our stuff?" Gracie asked anxiously. She'd forgotten all about it.

"It will be taken care of," Kordon assured her. "I wish to show you our home."

Gracie looked up as several transports flew over. It was all so different from Earth. Or, at least the Earth she remembered. She wondered if Earth was like this now. Gracie eyes widened as she realized there were homes built into the side of the cliffs. Beautiful arched doorways with large terraces lined the cliffs.

"Where do you live?" Gracie asked, suddenly feeling a little overwhelmed.

"We live outside of the city, but not too far to commute. Our home is located along the cliffs. We will take a transport known as a glider to it. They are designed for traveling back and forth and landing in small spaces," Kordon said.

"I hate to leave, but I promised father I would take a look at some of his *kippins* tonight. A few of them have been sick, and he wants to make sure they are on the mend," Saffron said. "Gracie, welcome to Zion. May you find happiness on our world," Saffron said formally before bowing and pressing a kiss to her hand.

"Thank you, Saffron," Gracie said, giving him a hug and a kiss. "For everything."

"I will inform our parents you are home. Perhaps you can bring Gracie over for dinner after she has settled in," Saffron said. "Until later, brother."

"Until later," Kordon said with a smile. "Come, Gracie. Our transportation is over here."

Kordon led Gracie across the tarmac and through a series of paths before coming out in front of a long, silver transport. An older man hurried around and opened the door for them. Once they were seated comfortably inside, he moved around to the other side and slid in behind what looked like a console. Within minutes, they were lifting off vertically, then moving forward.

"How goes it, Josef?" Kordon asked.

He reached over to hold Gracie's hand as she looked out the windows. While the outside of the glider looked like it was solid silver, the top portion was actually clear when you were inside looking out. It was almost like a two-way mirror Gracie saw once when she was exploring one of the abandoned buildings in New York.

"Everything is well, my lord. Your living quarters have been prepared as you requested. Your personal effects should be there shortly. The staff has been informed of your new status and that you have brought home a mate. I wish you and your mate great happiness, my lord."

"My lord?" Gracie asked, turning to look briefly at Kordon before letting her gaze move back to the landscape far below them.

"I am Lord Kordon Jefe. I am a member of the High Council. As such, I review the laws, make determinations on what is best for Zion, and if necessary, act upon those decisions to enforce them,"

Kordon said. "You will be called Lady Gracie Jones-Jefe."

"Will… will we be getting married or anything?" Gracie asked hesitantly as she didn't understand the laws of Zion for such things.

"I have already petitioned to claim you to our clan council. They unanimously approved. Now that we have returned, there will be a ceremony acknowledging my claim on you," Kordon explained before hastily adding. "… And your claim on me, of course."

"Of course," Gracie said with a grin. "What is that?"

Kordon leaned over to see what Gracie was pointing at. He saw several warriors riding on some of the war beasts they used for patrolling the more mountainous regions. The war beasts were very hardy, strong, and could scale almost vertically when necessary. He raised them at one of his homes further up in the mountains.

"They are war beasts. That is the only name they have ever been called because that is what they are used for. I have several large herds. They are the safest and easiest way to get around the mountains that cover our world. They can cover terrain few other creatures could."

"What are they doing?" Gracie asked, watching as they moved single file up a path until the trees covered them.

"They are probably going on patrol. Our world is a world of warriors. All males train from a young age to be strong," Kordon explained.

Gracie shivered at the thought of young boys training to fight. She had seen enough fighting and death to last her a lifetime. Her hand went to her stomach protectively. Would their son be expected to learn to fight as well? One part of Gracie felt it would be a good thing while the other part argued that fighting should never be the answer.

She let her finger move to the scar on her shoulder. Closing her eyes, she felt the slight raised pucker of skin where Toolas couldn't quite heal it without leaving the scar. Regret and sorrow swept through her as she realized that there would always be a need for warriors.

Gracie's eyes opened when she felt Kordon's hand on her cheek. "You are unwell?" he asked, concerned.

Gracie smiled back and pressed a soft kiss into his palm. "I'm fine. Just a little nervous," she replied.

Kordon's eyes softened as he gazed down at her. "If you get overwhelmed, frightened, or have any questions, you must let me know. I will always be here for you. We will take this as slowly as you need to."

Gracie shook her head with a soft laugh and murmured. "And to think I thought you were going to squish me when we first met," Gracie leaned against Kordon. "I'm glad you didn't."

Kordon tightened his arm around her, pulling her into the safety of his body. "I seem to remember

squishing you later and you quite enjoying it. I know
I did," Kordon whispered in her ear.

Gracie blushed when she heard Josef smother a
chuckle. "You are so bad," she said, pressing her
burning face into his neck and kissing it.

The rest of the ride was done in silence as Gracie
took in the beauty of Kordon's world. She knew she
had a lot to learn, but as she leaned back in his arms,
she didn't feel quite so scared anymore.

Chapter 22
Cumin System: Rim-Spaceport

"You have news?" the dark-cloaked figure asked quietly.

The man sitting across from him made sure he kept the dark-cloaked figure and his guards in his view. "You have the credits?" The dim light in the back of the bar caused the deep scars along the man's forehead and cheek to look even darker.

A gloved hand dropped a bag on the table. "One hundred thousand credits. You will receive another hundred thousand on delivery of the package."

Krac looked at the cloaked figure. He knew who the man was: Altren Proctor. The man was a feeble Earthling whose greed would either get him killed or elected to the coveted position of Supreme Chancellor of Earth.

Personally, Krac could care less as long as he got the credits. He almost didn't take the job, but the idea of kidnapping the former Grand Admiral's mate from off his home planet of Zion from under his nose was too much of a temptation. He liked impossible challenges.

"You didn't tell me the female was expecting a child," Krac said, leaning back in his seat. "That will cost you extra. I don't normally take females, much less pregnant ones. You just ask for trouble when you do that."

"I don't care what you normally do. I want the female. I will take care of the child she is carrying.

You bring her to me. That is what you are being paid to do," Proctor hissed with frustration.

"Fine. Add another fifty thousand credits and I will have her to you in ten days. It will take time to get her, and take her to a safe location to transfer her to you," Krac said. "I'll give you the location where to pick her up once I have her."

Krac didn't say anything else. He simply stood up and picked up the bag, shoving it into his pocket. He walked over to the bar, wrapped his arm around one of the barmaids, giving her a huge kiss before melting into the darkness.

Proctor raised his hand, and one of his guards moved forward. "Is he marked?" Proctor asked.

"Yes, sir," the guard replied. "You will know where he is at all times."

"Very good," Proctor said rising. "I want you to tell the men to follow him. The moment he has the girl, kill him."

"Yes, sir," the guard replied before he moved back to follow.

* * *

Gracie was sick the next morning. It seemed she was not over the occasional bout of morning sickness. Kordon held her and wiped her face before helping her up. Afterward, Josef's mate, Helin, prepared her a simple breakfast and a hot tea that soothed her stomach.

"I have to go into the city to meet with some of the council. My mother is coming to welcome you and help you settle in. I hoped to put it off for a few more days, but several issues have come up that demand my attention. Josef and Helin will be here if you need anything," Kordon said tenderly.

A smile curved her lips. "I'll be okay. I think if I could survive three years alone on a moon I can handle a few hours here," Gracie said with a wave at the luxurious surroundings.

Kordon had given Gracie a brief tour of their home yesterday afternoon after they arrived. The glider landed on the balcony overlooking the cliffs and ocean on the south side.

A large courtyard complete with a fountain filled by one of the small waterfalls coming out of the rock face led to the entrance. Polished stone floors and a brightly lit foyer greeted her as she walked through. The rooms were naturally formed caverns in the cliffs. The rock was white with a mineral that would glow when hit by small shafts of light which was filtered through a mirroring system throughout the home.

Kordon told Gracie each room was connected through a series of tunnels. Some were natural while others he had excavated. Additional rooms could be added, but at this time he was happy to keep it rather small. Gracie shook her head at his idea of small. There were eighteen rooms total.

There were five bedrooms, six baths, a formal dining room, an informal dining room, the kitchen, a library, a private family area, a greeting area for guests, and his office. In addition, there were two gardens—the upper garden near the forest at the top of the cliff which was for their private use and the lower garden which they passed through before entering the house.

Gracie watched as Kordon left the house in the glider. He insisted Josef stay. "Is there anything I can get for you, my lady?" Josef asked politely.

"What? Oh, no, thank you. I'm fine. I think if it is all right with you and Helin, I'll just do some exploring. Kordon gave me a tour of his home last night, but I have to admit I was so tired I don't remember much," Gracie said with a smile.

"Might I remind you this is now your home, my lady," Josef responded. "Helin and I are most happy to be of assistance if you need us."

Gracie smiled and shook her head. "Thank you. I'll let you know."

Josef bowed and left through one of the many passageways. Gracie wondered if she should ask for a map until she was familiar with where everything was but then chuckled as she remembered how fast she had learned to navigate the subway tunnels under New York. No, she would figure it out.

* * *

Gracie spent the rest of the morning exploring each room. Beautiful carvings were etched into the walls of many passages. She loved touching them and wondering who did the delicate artwork.

By early afternoon, she found herself in the upper garden. She understood why Kordon insisted it was for his private use. A natural fence of rock wrapped around it, keeping the thicker forest from encroaching. A large, clear pool of water bubbled up out of the stone.

Gracie dipped her fingers in the clear liquid and was surprised to find it was warm. Flowers grew everywhere in all different colors, sizes, and shapes. Small- and medium-size statues of warriors, war beasts, and other animals decorated the garden.

In one corner, there was an open gazebo with a double lounge chair, a small table, and two additional chairs. Gracie was surprised when she rounded the path and saw an older woman pouring a hot liquid into two cups. There were several covered dishes set on the small table, as well.

"I was hoping you would find this spot soon," the woman's beautifully accented voice called out. "Come, you must be famished. You have been exploring for quite some time."

Gracie looked at the woman curiously as she walked toward her. "Hi, I'm Gracie. Kordon's not here right now, but he should be back later," Gracie said as she climbed the two short steps up to the gazebo.

The woman turned and smiled gently. "I know. You would not believe what I had to do to get my son out of here. I had to bribe his father into making up an excuse."

"Your son? You are Kordon's mom?" Gracie asked suddenly nervous. She ran her hand down over the front of her shirt and pants.

"Yes. I am Cora." Cora turned to look at Gracie. "And you are the tiny warrior who captured my son's heart," she said, walking up to Gracie and taking both her hands in her own. "I am very pleased to meet you, my daughter."

Gracie's eyes filled with tears as she stared up into eyes of the same dark blue as Kordon's. "He has your eyes," Gracie whispered.

Cora laughed and pulled Gracie into her arms for a big hug. "Yes, he does—and his father's temperament. Come, sit and relax. I must speak to him about keeping information from me. Kordon did not mention you were with child. He merely asked that I find a healer familiar with a human's anatomy. I must remind him that not all healers are the same."

Gracie laughed. "I know exactly what you mean. He often forgets to tell me important stuff."

"Now, tell me how you met my son and how you became known as the warrior woman. Saffron could not say enough about how beautiful you are and insisted I come to welcome you as soon as possible," Cora said.

The rest of the afternoon was spent with Cora. Gracie told her about her life back on Earth, the years alone on the moon, and how she almost killed Kordon when she met him.

Cora gave amusing tales of Kordon and his brothers growing up that had Gracie holding her sides from laughing so hard. Gracie was just saying good-bye to Cora when Kordon came home with a deep scowl on his face. Cora merely waved away his accusation of her plotting to get him away so she could keep Gracie to herself.

"I will pick you up tomorrow morning. The healer will be expecting you," Cora said mildly as she stepped into the glider that landed to take her home.

"Healer?" Kordon growled out dangerously, forgetting momentarily he had asked his mother to help find one. "What healer?"

"Your mate is expecting your child. She needs to be seen by a healer familiar with human anatomy to ensure she and the child are safe and healthy. I made the necessary arrangements this afternoon. You don't expect me not to protect my new daughter and your child, do you?" Cora looked reprovingly at her older son until he fought back a smile.

"You put Father up to this today, didn't you?" Kordon asked.

"Of course," Cora said laughing. "Now I must go pay up," she added with a twinkle in her eye.

It took a moment for Gracie to catch on, and when she did she blushed. Cora bade them good-bye and was soon gone. Kordon turned Gracie toward the entrance to their home and led her inside.

"Are you hungry? Helin left dinner in the cooler for us," Gracie said. "I told her I could warm it up for you, and she showed me how to work the warmer."

Kordon wrapped his arm around Gracie and picked her up. "The only thing I am hungry for is you. Can I eat you, Gracie Jones-Jefe?" Kordon whispered against Gracie's ear.

"Anytime you want," Gracie whispered back.

* * *

Gracie lay curled in Kordon's arms that night, watching as the second moon rose over the ocean. They had made slow, tender love before Kordon took her fast and furious.

She fell into a light sleep for about an hour before she woke again. She lay there enjoying the light breeze that blew in through the open doorway leading out onto a small balcony. It was her second night on Zion, and she felt like she had never lived anywhere else.

A small sigh escaped her as she let go of the fear and loneliness that seemed to have been a part of her life for so long. Kordon's arm tightened around her.

"What is it?" he asked sleepily.

"Nothing," Gracie whispered into the darkness of the night.

Kordon leaned up on one elbow. "Tell me about the nothing, then."

Gracie rolled over onto her back. She couldn't believe how beautiful he was. She reached up and lightly traced her fingers over the pattern of symbols across his brow before letting them run down along his cheek to his neck. Kordon grabbed her fingers as they moved further down along his shoulder.

He pressed his lips to her fingers. "Tell me," he murmured.

"I was thinking about how happy I am here. It is like my life before was just a dream, and this is my reality," Gracie whispered. "Does that sound weird?"

Kordon lay back down and pulled Gracie tightly against his warm body. "No. This is your home, I will do everything I can to make you happy here, Gracie. You are my life."

Gracie snuggled down. "You're mine, too. I love you so much," Gracie said, suddenly very tired.

"Sleep now, my little warrior. I will be going with you to the healer tomorrow," Kordon said.

Kordon ran his hand up and down Gracie's back until she relaxed and fell into a deep sleep. He lay awake for a few extra minutes making sure she was indeed asleep. Only when he was satisfied she was did he relax.

"I love you too, little warrior. I love you too," Kordon murmured as sleep overtook him.

* * *

The next day, Kordon and Cora accompanied Gracie to the healer who was very thorough in her exam. She gave Gracie a list of things she wanted her to do. Kordon snatched the list out of Gracie's hand immediately and scanned it. He asked the healer all kinds of questions Gracie had never even thought of.

The healer was a little concerned that Gracie's blood pressure was elevated, and stressed to Kordon that Gracie was to rest frequently. She also gave her a list of recommended foods, exercise, and a vitamin supplement. They made another appointment for a follow-up on her progress, as the healer wanted Gracie to return in two weeks to check her blood pressure and make sure it was where it should be.

Cora insisted on taking Gracie out to lunch and on a short tour of the markets afterward. Kordon growled in frustration when he received a message from the council and had to leave. He extracted a promise from his mother that she would make sure Gracie did not get overtired. Laughing, the two women sent Kordon on his way.

* * *

The next several days seemed to fly by. Gracie spent most mornings helping Helin in the kitchen and the afternoons in the upper-level garden. She found she loved working in the garden. She thought it might be because she'd never had much of a chance to spend time outside or to play in the dirt on Earth.

She was almost four months pregnant now, according to the healer. Gracie calculated back and determined she must have gotten pregnant the first time she and Kordon made love. A smile curved her lips at just the thought of Kordon. He was attentive to her every need and so tender with her. Helin teased her about the changes in Kordon since Gracie entered his life.

"He hardly ever smiled before and was so cold and distant. Now, I see a smile almost always on his lips except when he has to leave you," Helin said.

Gracie found out Helin had been Kordon's nursemaid when he was a child. Her mate, Josef, had served with Kordon's father and fought under his command in the early wars before Zion joined with the Confederation. When Kordon built his home, he asked Helin and Josef to watch over it. She shared tales similar to Cora's of Kordon and his brothers growing up.

"I think I'll head up to the upper garden. There are some plants I would like to transplant. Cora will not be by today. She has some meetings," Gracie said, wiping down the last of the counters.

"Go. I will bring you some refreshments up in a little while and see what you have done. I know Josef is happy you are taking over. He has never liked to garden," Helin said with a chuckle. "He is too stubborn though, to tell Kordon to hire someone else. I think it is from when he was a boy, most likely because his father was a farmer."

Gracie laughed and brushed a kiss across Helin's cheek. "Well, I am loving it. I find it to be very relaxing. I'll see you later," Gracie said, folding the towel and moving toward the stairs carved into the stone.

Gracie made her way up the staircase. She hummed an old tune as she moved toward the back of the garden near the gazebo. She had left her gardening tools there knowing she wanted to finish the small flowerbed she'd started yesterday. Climbing the small steps, she was just about to reach for the tools when a feeling she wasn't alone sent a shiver down her spine.

Gracie turned, frowning. "Josef, is that you?" Gracie called out.

"No, not Josef," Krac said, stepping out from the shadows of one of the thick plants on the left side of the gazebo.

Gracie was startled when she saw the unfamiliar face. Frowning, she said, "I don't think you are supposed to be here. If you would like to see Kordon I can get Josef to call for him."

Krac studied the tiny human female in front of him. If he admitted to having feelings, he would almost feel bad for what he was about to do. She looked far too delicate and fragile to survive, but orders were orders. Krac took a menacing step toward her, watching keenly as she stiffened.

"I am not here to see your mate, Gracie Jones. I am here for you," Krac said blandly.

Gracie turned and ran. She heard the man behind her let out a low curse before he followed. Gracie hadn't taken more than a dozen steps before she felt an arm wrap around her waist at the same time as another cut off her scream.

"I really wish you hadn't done that," the deep voice said in resignation a moment before Gracie felt darkness descend as he pressed something against the side of her neck.

Chapter 23

Kordon slammed into the council room in a rage. Within two hours of Gracie's disappearance a team of Zion warriors had been assembled. Helin had heard Gracie's short scream as she was bringing a tray up to her.

When she emerged at the top of the stairs, she found a huge male with dark gray skin holding an unconscious Gracie in his arms. Before she could alert Josef, the man had fired a dart, knocking her unconscious as well. When she woke, both Gracie and the man were gone. She cried out for Josef, who notified Kordon immediately.

"Did you find anything?" Kordon asked coldly of Saffron.

Saffron nodded. "An unknown transport left the planet an hour and a half ago. It registered as a trade ship with mechanical problems. It was docked at the port for three days prior to lifting off. The captain of the ship is registered as Captain Mannew Toc out of the Cumin System. The name checks out as being legit—only the descriptions of Captain Toc are different from the description Helin gave you."

Kordon's father looked at his eldest son. "Did you find anything at your home?" Bazteen Jefe asked quietly.

Kordon looked at his father and gave a sharp nod. "A message was left," Kordon pressed a button on the holovid to replay the message that was left on the table in the gazebo.

"Greetings, Grand Admiral. Sorry for taking your mate, but she is needed for a little while elsewhere. I can't guarantee her safety, but I will do my best to keep her and your child alive. I'll be sending you a message as to where you can find her in a few days if all goes well. You can try and kill me then, but for now, I have more important things to do," the deep voice ended.

A muscle twitched in Kordon's jaw as he fought back the overwhelming fear for Gracie and his child. "The voice was encrypted. There is no identification match. I've notified Bran. I am meeting up with the *Conqueror* in three hours," Kordon said.

"We will all be there. Gracie is my daughter, she is a Zion female, and there will be no mercy for those who took her," Bazteen said, standing and nodding to Saffron. "Call your brothers. We meet on the *Conqueror*."

Saffron nodded. "They are already on their way. Malik and Ty are in transit. Rorrak was planetside and will be here within the hour."

"Rorrak has been working undercover on an issue for the past year," Bazteen said calmly. "He may be able to give you more information."

Kordon's head jerked up at his father's words. "What aren't you telling me?" he demanded harshly.

Bazteen sighed deeply, "I did not expect for anyone to be stupid enough to attempt to take your mate from Zion, much less your home. Rorrak came to me over a year ago with concerns about changes and unrest on Earth.

"As part of the leading peace force of the Confederation, it is my duty to investigate such things. A member of the royal family there, who is a descendant of your mate's sister, approached us asking for assistance. Several attempts have been made lately on the lives of the council there, especially the Supreme Chancellor.

"Rorrak has been working to find out who is behind it. Some of our leads have pointed to former councilman Altren Proctor. Unfortunately, nothing is conclusive. He always has an alibi or is nowhere near the planet during the assassination attempts."

"You didn't think this information was worth passing on to me, knowing who Gracie is?" Kordon growled, leaning forward on the table in fury.

Bazteen looked at his older son with regret. "The other council members felt there might be a chance to draw Proctor out by using Gracie. If you'd known about it, they felt you would not agree."

Kordon sat down heavily in the chair, his face turning to stone as he stared coldly at his father. "You purposely used Gracie as bait. You purposely put her in danger even knowing she is carrying my child, your grandchild, without giving her additional protection," Kordon's voice became harder as he absorbed his father's betrayal. "Where is the pride of a Zion male who would use another's pregnant mate as bait?" Kordon asked coldly.

Beaten paled, but did not reply.

"The fate of millions, perhaps billions, rested on making that decision. It was not only our father's choice to do this. He voted against using your mate," a new voice responded to Kordon's hard question.

Kordon turned to see his younger brother standing in the doorway.

The symbols lining his face stood out against his deeply tanned skin. Rorrak was just as tall and just as broad as Kordon. He was wearing the traditional black uniform of a Zion warrior. Two long blades hung across his back and a set of laser pistols rode low on his narrow hips. His piercing blue eyes, slightly lighter than Kordon's, looked back steadily.

"Play the holovid message," Rorrak said just as coldly as Kordon.

Kordon bit back a retort. He knew his younger brother well enough to know he could be as cold a bastard as he was. Pressing the replay, the message started again. Rorrak's eyes darkened at the sound of the distorted voice.

"Do you recognize the voice?" Kordon asked, noticing Rorrak's reaction.

Rorrak shook his head. "Not the voice, but the way the words are spoken. It is Krac, he is a cold son of a bitch on a good day. If he says he will try to keep your mate alive, he will. For an assassin he has a high code of honor. One thing you don't want to do is cross him or piss him off. I can guarantee you, wherever he is, there are going to be a lot of dead bodies," Rorrak said with a resigned sigh.

Kordon cursed out loud. "I will track that bastard to the ends of the universe and gut him for what he has done."

Rorrak shook his head again. "Let's just concentrate on getting your mate back. Tell me everything you can about her and what happened in the council chambers back on Paulus. I know Krac as well as anyone can. I might be able to figure out what in the hell he is up to if I know everything."

Kordon relayed everything he knew, from the moment he first heard Gracie's voice to her disappearance earlier. By the time he finished, they were on the *Conqueror*. Bran and Cooraan met them in the landing bay.

"Your little mate seems to have a knack for attracting trouble," Bran said by way of a greeting.

Kordon nodded solemnly. "She calls it Murphy," he responded.

He remembered listening to her talk about someone named Murphy. When she whispered his name in her sleep, he had felt a wave of jealousy sweep through him. He remembered her laughing up at him and kissing him deeply before explaining about Murphy and his law. Kordon pointed out it was Murphy who technically introduced them so he couldn't be too bad.

"I think I may know where Krac is planning to take your mate," Rorrak said quietly.

Kordon's head jerked up at his brother's quiet statement. "Where?" He asked harshly.

"You said your mate was stranded on a deserted moon for three years, didn't you?" Rorrak asked.

Kordon nodded frowning. "Yes, why?"

"Krac has an unusual sense of humor for being a bastard. If he didn't plan on killing her that means he is going to want you to find her. He would know about her history as well. He would know that she knows how to survive on the moon."

Bazteen nodded. "So, he would take her somewhere she is familiar with, and where she knows how to survive until Kordon can get her."

Rorrak nodded. Bran looked at each of the men with him before barking out a command. "Let's go get your mate back."

* * *

Gracie woke slowly. Her mouth felt dry and stuffy from whatever the man used to knock her out. She realized she was in a sleek transport of some type. She moved to sit up, jerking when she felt one of her wrists chained to a metal bar. Gracie swung her feet over the side of the small bunk. It was like the one in the transport Saffron had.

Gracie pushed her hair out of her eyes with her free hand before letting it fall to her rounded belly. She felt a small flutter inside, almost like butterflies. Her breath caught for a moment before she slowly let it out. Her baby was okay.

Gracie looked around the small area. There wasn't much to see. There were some storage compartments, a small door off to the one side, and a small set of steps leading both up and down from a dark hole in the floor toward the back. Toward the front, there was a narrow corridor and a viewport showing nothing but dark space. Gracie started when a figure suddenly filled the corridor.

"You are awake," Krac said smoothly. He walked forward, pressed a panel in the wall, and pulled out a small bottle.

He walked back to Gracie and held the bottle out to her. "Drink it. You will be dehydrated from the sedative."

Gracie took the bottle gingerly and sniffed the contents suspiciously. "You didn't poison this or anything did you?" Gracie asked, looking up at Krac.

Krac stared down into Gracie's dark green eyes and chuckled. "No. I figured if I wanted to kill you I could have done that before you woke up."

Gracie blushed. "Yeah, I guess you could have done that. I guess that wasn't the smartest question to ask," Gracie said huskily before taking a deep drink.

"So," Gracie began after wiping her mouth with the back of her hand. "Will you tell me why you took me?"

Krac's eyebrow rose at Gracie's calm question. He was expecting the typical hysterical crying, followed by annoying whining, before more hysterical crying. She just sat there looking at him quietly and waited.

He leaned back across from her and studied her for a moment. "You are different than I expected, Gracie Jones," Krac said with a frown.

"Why is that?" Gracie asked, raising her own eyebrow at him.

"Most humans, especially women, would be reacting differently right about now," Krac replied with a slight smile curving one side of his mouth. That drew another frown from him. He never smiled.

"Oh," Gracie responded, continuing to look at the huge, dark silver man in front of her. "How should I be reacting?" Gracie asked puzzled.

Krac let out a small chuckle. "You know, screaming, crying, and whining. That's the typical response for females and all Earthlings."

Gracie chuckled and shook her head. "I don't know what females you've been meeting—or Earthlings, for that matter. Since none of that would help, it'd be pointless to do it. You still haven't answered my first question. Why did you take me?"

"Because someone paid me a lot of credits for you," Krac replied.

Gracie stared at Krac for a long moment before she shook her head again. "No," she stated. "There is another reason. You need me for something. I don't know what or why. But, you need me." Krac jerked up to tower over Gracie a deep scowl on his face. "Who are you? Are you really a human? I know there are some species with telepathic powers, but I am guarded against them. How do you know this?"

Gracie sat as far back as she could. "I'm Gracie Jones. Yes, I am as human as they come, and no, I do not have telepathic powers. I just guessed it. I just get the feeling something else is going on," Gracie said quietly putting a protective hand over her belly.

Krac noticed her retreat. Kneeling down, he looked into her eyes again. "I am taking you to the moon you were stranded on. I won't hurt you, but there will be others there who want you. I will do everything I can to keep you safe until your mate comes for you, but you will do everything I say, when I say, and how I say. Do you understand, Gracie Jones?"

"Jefe," Gracie nodded. "It's Gracie Jones-Jefe. I understand."

Krac felt that unfamiliar twist to his lips again. "Very good, Gracie Jones-Jefe. We will be on the moon in approximately eight hours. I am expecting a… welcoming committee."

Gracie looked at Krac and nodded. "Can I ask you something?"

Krac raised his eyebrow again. "What?"

"Can you release me? I really need to go to the bathroom. Ever since the baby started getting bigger I have to go frequently." Gracie practically begged as the water she'd just drunk, combined with the baby moving, suddenly making her have to go badly.

Krac couldn't contain the chuckle that burst from his lips. He leaned forward and unlocked the chain around Gracie's wrist and pointed to the small door. He barely had time to step back before she pushed past him and quickly opened the door with a loud sigh of relief.

Krac laughed again at her loud sigh behind the closed door. Shaking his head, he decided he would do everything in his power to make sure the strange, delicate human called Gracie Jones-Jefe was kept safe.

Chapter 24

Kordon glanced down at the report. The new modifications to the scanners and engines installed on the *Conqueror* by Bran and Cooraan gave them an advantage as they approached the moon where Rorrak felt confident Gracie had been taken. Rorrak's sources reported Proctor was aboard one of the ships orbiting the moon.

Kordon glanced up as his father and brothers entered the conference room along with Bran and Cooraan. His other two brothers were dressed ready for battle. Malik and Ty were as tall as he and Rorrak, but they had their father's darker skin and dark eyes.

"My sources say Proctor has purchased a rather large mercenary guard. There are four ships. Proctor is on the largest. If possible, we need to take him alive. There are more than just him. Someone is financing his rise to power, and we need to find out who it is.

"He is not smart enough to have masterminded the assassination attempts against the royal family. He is merely the figurehead. It is his own greed in wanting to use Gracie that is his downfall," Rorrak said as soon as everyone else was seated. "I've been working with the Earth government for the past two years on this. Proctor is working on his own with this kidnapping."

Kordon sat forward. "I don't give a damn about him. I want Gracie back safe and sound. I will kill anyone who thinks to use her," Kordon growled coldly at his brother.

Rorrak grimaced at the icy tone. He was about to respond when a message came through to Bran. He responded quietly before turning to the group.

"Several shuttles have disembarked from the ships. Three large troop transports and one smaller one. They are headed for the moon," Bran said quietly. "I've requested a squadron of fighters to launch, as well as eight large troop transports. We will come in on the far side of the moon and proceed to the coordinates we've locked onto. It's time to move."

All the men rose and moved toward the exit. Rorrak paused and placed a hand on Kordon's arm briefly stopping him. Kordon gave his brother a dark look.

"We'll get her back. I had no idea, until it was too late, she would be used," Rorrak said. "I want you to know I'm sorry."

Kordon nodded briefly before moving ahead of Rorrak. Expressing regret would never be enough if anything happened to Gracie. Kordon would kill every one of the bastards responsible if Gracie was harmed, not only for taking Gracie, but for using her as bait... even if one of those responsible was his own brother.

* * *

Gracie pushed her hair back from her damp forehead. They had been walking for what seemed like forever through the dense forest. Gracie wasn't as familiar with the area they'd landed in since it was on the outer edge of the location she had explored when she lived on the moon. Gracie realized one thing very quickly, though—she did not miss the moon at all.

She didn't say anything as they moved through the forest. After her request to go to the bathroom, Krac didn't bother with chaining her back up.

She didn't know who had been more surprised, her or Krac, when she asked him what she should call him, and he'd told her his name. She could tell he hadn't planned on telling her his real name, but it just kind of slipped out. After that, she'd discovered he wasn't such a bad guy.

Krac looked back over his shoulder at the tiny, rounded figure following him quietly. He couldn't suppress his surprise or his respect for her. She never complained or asked him a lot of questions which actually made him more curious about her.

"Is it true you are the Gracie Jones from Earth history? The one who is called the Mother of Freedom?" Krac asked quietly.

Gracie shrugged her slim shoulders. "I don't know about the Mother of Freedom, but I am the Gracie Jones from over eight hundred years ago," Gracie replied just as quietly.

"How did you end up here?" Krac stopped to look down on Gracie with a frown.

Gracie shrugged her shoulders again. "I'm not sure. Mohan said she thought the force of the explosion from the mother ship combined with being in hyperspace formed some kind of a rip in the fabric of time. I just know that until a few months ago I was stranded on an unknown moon, hoping to find a way home." Gracie added sadly, "Only to find out my home no longer exists. At least not the home I remember and knew."

Krac handed the water bottle to Gracie and waited as she took a deep drink. "Why were you not afraid of me when you first saw me?" Krac asked suddenly.

"What do you mean?" Gracie asked puzzled. She handed the water bottle back to him.

"Most species fear me. I am not... all organic," Krac said quietly searching for the right words. "I am the offspring of a human female who was bred with the Alluthan. We... are considered dangerous."

Gracie stared at the tall figure in front of her with a frown, studying his features closely. "Well, I guess you have their coloring, but that is about all from your outward appearance. The Alluthans are short guys like me." Gracie studied Krac a little closer. "You look like a human except for your coloring and maybe your eyes. You said you are not all organic. What does that mean?"

Krac looked away for a moment before he stared down into Gracie's eyes. "We are called the All-Breed. That is what they used our mothers for." Krac flexed his hands in front of him. "The embryos implanted in the females have living nano-bots in them. As the embryo grows, so too do the nano-bots. We are half organic/half bots, like the Alluthans," Krac said harshly.

Gracie studied Krac for a moment before she smiled and took a step closer to him. Laying a hand on his arm, she shook her head gently.

"You are nothing like the Alluthans, trust me on that. I have met my share of them, so I should know. You may not be all human, but that doesn't mean it's a bad thing. I've met a lot of humans, like Proctor, who are just as bad as any Alluthan. You are just different, kind of like me," Gracie insisted. "You are special."

Krac looked down at the female he'd thought he could easily use as collateral damage if necessary and realized there was no way in hell he could follow through with his plan. Tightening his jaw, he looked around the thick forest for a moment before making a decision. He pulled the pack from his back and pulled out a small communication device.

"Use this to contact your mate. If I'm not mistaken he should be here shortly. I left enough evidence for him to follow. Let him know where you are and to come get you. Take this as well. There is a rock overhang to the east. It will protect you until he gets here," Krac said, pressing the communication device into one of Gracie's palms and a laser pistol into the other one.

"What about you?" Gracie asked, confused.

Krac felt that unfamiliar twist to his lips again. Shaking his head, he reached out to touch Gracie's cheek as she looked at him with a worried expression. "Don't worry about me. I can take care of myself, little Gracie Jones-Jefe. Now go. I've got someone to kill, and I don't want to have to worry about you."

Gracie bit her lip and nodded. "Be safe, Krac," Gracie said, standing on her tiptoes so she could brush a kiss along his jaw. "You are a good man, even if you did kidnap me."

Krac touched the spot Gracie kissed briefly before shaking his head in wonder. If his life weren't so dangerous and she wasn't already taken, he would think seriously about just packing her up and taking her with him. Instead, he gave a jerky nod and took off through the forest, moving at a rapid clip. Gracie watched him go, noting he never looked back to make sure she headed to the east.

* * *

Kordon moved silently toward the man hidden in the brush. With one swift move, he slit the man's throat and moved on to his next target. Rorrak, Malik, Ty, Cooraan, and his father were doing the same. The other Zion warriors were moving in on the troop transports which had landed further away.

This group was the one guarding Proctor, who stood in the middle of a small clearing obviously waiting impatiently for someone. Kordon let out the signal his area was clear. The only ones left were the ten men standing protectively around Proctor, who suddenly stood still.

Kordon's eyes narrowed as a large male stepped confidently into the clearing. The sun reflected off his dark silver skin. Several large scars marred his face, which was frozen into a cold mask of indifference.

"Where is the package?" Proctor asked impatiently stepping forward.

Krac looked coldly at Proctor. "Where are my credits?" He asked in return.

Proctor pulled several large pouches from under his cloak. He tossed them on the ground in front of Krac. "Now, where is the package?"

Krac looked casually around the clearing noting where each man stood watching him intently. His gaze moved along the edge of the forest pausing occasionally before seeming to freeze on Kordon. Kordon stood absolutely still. He knew he was hidden, but the big bastard seemed to know exactly where he was.

"The package is safe," Krac said. Kordon could feel the hidden message all the way to his bones.

"I don't care if she is safe. I want to know where she is. I've paid you the credits you demanded. Even for the brat she is carrying. Now where is she?" Proctor spit out.

Krac tilted his head. "What do you plan to do with her?"

"Not that it is any of your damn business, but I plan to claim her," Proctor snapped out.

Krac's eyes narrowed briefly. "I don't think she is going to be too happy about that, especially with her being pregnant by her current mate," Krac drawled out in an uninterested voice.

"That's what you get for thinking. As soon as I have her, I will terminate the brat she is carrying, and with a few drugs, she will do whatever I want. By the time I return to Earth, it will be my child in her belly and my claim on her." Proctor laughed.

Krac's mouth tightened dangerously. "Are you really so fucking stupid you think her mate, a Zion warrior, will let you get away with this?"

Proctor froze as if noticing a change in Krac's voice. "It will be too late for him to do anything. Kill the bastard. He is no longer needed," Proctor said coldly, stepping back behind two of his guards as he gave the order.

Krac moved lightning fast, pulling his laser pistol and shooting the two guards. Rolling to one side, he ignored the flash of pain that struck his leg as he eliminated two more.

Proctor was screaming at the men to kill Krac at the same time as he realized the men behind him were under fire from the forest.

Turning, Proctor pulled one guard in front of him just as Kordon leveled his laser pistol at his chest. The man jerked as the shot meant for Proctor struck him instead. Proctor took off into the forest as his men pulled into a tight circle trying to return fire. Kordon fought back a curse as Proctor disappeared. He ducked for cover behind a tree as laser fire exploded all around him.

"Get Proctor! The bastard is up to something," Kordon growled out into his comlink.

"More of those bastards are pouring out of the transport," Cooraan growled back. "Bran, Gracie is on the moon. Blast the damn ships into a million pieces."

Kordon heard Bran's command to fire at will on the four ships in space. His father was ordering the troop transports to destroy the ones that had landed.

Kordon saw the silver bastard who took Gracie move into the forest out of the corner of his eye.

"He's mine," Kordon snarled out to Malik and Ty as they came up next to him. "Cover me."

Kordon took off knowing his brothers would cover his back. Firing as he wove in and out of the trees, he broke into a faster run once he was clear of the firing. He stopped to listen a few times and to check for tracks to make sure he was on the right trail before continuing after the assassin.

He jerked around when a large silver arm came out suddenly to grab him. Kordon whipped around, locking grips with the huge, silver man.

"Keep quiet," Krac whispered. "They have her. The bastard hired another assassin."

Kordon looked into the dark eyes of the man in front of him before nodding once. He opened his grip to let Krac know he understood the man was calling a truce. Krac nodded and showed four fingers.

"Damn stubborn female," Krac growled silently as he watched Proctor slap Gracie across the face. "She was supposed to hide until you came for her."

Kordon looked over in surprise at the sound of anger and frustration in Krac's voice. "You told her to contact me?"

Krac nodded. "I didn't want her to get hurt. She's... special."

Kordon felt a flash of jealousy flare at the sound of affection in the man's voice. "She is mine."

"I know. She corrected me when I called her Gracie Jones." Krac sent a twisted grin at Kordon.

"Let's kill each other later. Right now, we need to kill the bastard who just hit her. I'll take out Proctor and the two on the left. You take out the three on the right. Be careful of the one with the green skin. He is a known assassin from the Triblade system."

Kordon gave a brief nod before moving off to the right. He circled around the group silently. On the far side was a pile of rocks. He would need to work his way up them so he would have access to Gracie, who was pulled back against the them.

Sweat ran down his face as he moved. At one time he froze when he heard the assassin call out for the men with him to be quiet. It was several minutes before they started talking quietly again and he could move.

* * *

Gracie sat holding her heated cheek in the palm of one hand while the other lay protectively over her belly. She didn't say anything. She was mad as hell that she had gotten caught.

The creature who caught her may have walked on two legs, but that was the only resemblance to a human she could see. She guessed it was a male from the way it acted, but she couldn't really be sure. It had surprised her as she tried to follow Krac. She wanted to make sure he was okay.

She had set the communication device to send the signal she used before with the Alluthans. She figured Kordon would recognize it immediately. The creature who caught her had destroyed the device shortly after he captured her.

"What do you mean there is no reply from any of the ships? Surely you have your ship?" Proctor said desperately.

The creature made a series of sounds Gracie couldn't understand, but evidently Proctor did. "I'll pay you as soon as you get me to the nearest spaceport. I don't have any more credits on me. I gave them all to that other bastard," Proctor replied.

The creature made several more sounds. "Fine! Kill the other bastards or leave them here. I don't care. Just get me and the female to the nearest spaceport, and you'll have your credits," Proctor promised, waving his hands wildly.

The other men standing next to Proctor moved restlessly, keeping a wary eye on the green-skinned assassin. Gracie bit down hard on her lip as she watched all four of them drop almost as one. The green-skin assassin looked at Proctor and made a series of hissing noises.

Proctor looked at Gracie briefly before nodding. "You can do what you want with her before I take her."

Gracie wanted to scream as she watched Proctor turn toward her with a glare of hatred. "If you try anything, I'll personally cut that brat out of your stomach."

Gracie didn't say anything. She just nodded as Proctor reached down and jerked her into a standing position. She looked at the green-skinned creature as it made a disgusting sound at her and shrank back instinctively when a long tongue came out and ran over its lips.

"Move," Proctor said, pushing Gracie in front of him and holding a laser pistol to her back.

Kordon bit back a curse as he watched them begin to move out of range. He moved to follow, but a sharp sound made him freeze. He glanced over to see Krac shaking his head and pointing to the bodies of the dead men. He counted down from ten slowly and covered his head.

Kordon barely had time to duck before each of the bodies exploded, throwing bloody gore everywhere. Kordon came out from behind the rocks with a grim expression. He watched as Krac did the same.

"Bloody bastard. He likes to take a few extra with him. He kills, but his shots are filled with a time-delayed explosive so whoever comes to look at or get the body dies too," Krac said, looking with disgust around him.

"He'll have hidden his ship close by. He never travels with others," Krac said.

"What will he do?" Kordon asked following Krac as he moved through the dense forest.

"He'll more than likely kill Proctor. He knows the bastard doesn't have any more credits. He'll keep Gracie alive," Krac said moving rapidly.

Kordon moved next to him. "What aren't you telling me?" he ground out as he pushed through the brush.

Krac didn't look at Kordon. "He'll use her. She'll lose the baby. His sperm will attack it. Once he finishes with her, if she is still alive, he'll sell her to one of the illegal pleasure houses." Krac did glance at Kordon then. "I'll kill the bastard first," he said just loud enough for Kordon to hear. "You get Gracie out of the area as fast as you can."

Kordon nodded. He knew he could kill the assassin, but not without probably getting killed himself. Krac might not realize Kordon recognized the assassin as well. The species was one the Zion fought centuries ago.

Kordon used his comlink to let his father, brothers, and Cooraan know the situation. Cooraan responded that the *Conqueror* had destroyed the other ships. Their fighters were intercepting the few fighters attempting to escape. Kordon started to jerk around when another figure appeared out of the dense forest next to them.

Rorrak grinned as he jogged beside them. "Hey, Krac."

Krac lowered his weapon with a shake of his head. "You sorry-ass bastard. You are determined to get yourself killed."

Rorrak barked out a sharp laugh. "I'm not the one kidnapping my brother's mate," Rorrak responded sarcastically.

"True," Krac said before pulling up short, and raising his hand. "We're close," he whispered.

Rorrak nodded and melted into the dense shadows of the trees. Kordon did the same, moving in the opposite direction. His brother had a lot to answer for, Kordon thought grimly. But first he needed to get his mate back.

* * *

Gracie bit back a cry of pain as Proctor's fingers dug into her arm. She would never give the bastard the satisfaction of knowing he was hurting her. Gracie knew Kordon was close. She could practically feel his eyes on her. She also knew Proctor was even more dangerous now that he was desperate.

Her eyes kept flickering to the green-skinned creature walking in front of them. Whatever he was, he scared her. Gracie pulled back sharply when she saw the creature's spaceship next to a lake. She knew if she set foot in that spaceship, she was as good as dead.

Gracie kicked out at Proctor, trying to pull away as he dragged her closer. She let out a small scream when he let go of her arm and grabbed her by her hair. Gracie stumbled and fell to her knees. The sharp rocks cut through the thin material of her pants. Proctor hissed out another warning to her.

The green-skinned creature turned suddenly, moving so fast that Gracie never saw it. She vaguely heard Proctor's surprised cry before she felt herself falling backward onto the ground.

Reaching up, she could feel Proctor's fingers still tangled in her hair, but Proctor was standing several feet away from her, swaying. It took her a minute to realize his arm was missing, and blood was gushing down his side.

Gracie began screaming as she fought to get the severed arm away from her. She scrambled backward away from it in horror. The creature hissed at Proctor again before moving again. Gracie closed her eyes as Proctor's headless body collapsed. Gracie cried out as a set of arms wrapped around her.

"Hush, my little warrior. I have you," Kordon said.

Gracie's eyes flew open, and she cried out again as Kordon's face came into view. "Help me." Gracie whimpered as his face blurred. "Help me," she whispered as everything turned dark.

Chapter 25

Gracie floated in and out of consciousness. She felt herself being carried and voices fading in and out, but that was about it. Then there was blissful darkness. She felt a slight rumble and more voices a short time later before the darkness came again. Gracie burrowed into the warmth around her as it came.

"Why won't she wake up?" a deep voice asked in frustration.

"She will. She has been through a very traumatic event. I am amazed she did not shut down sooner," a soft feminine voice replied.

"The baby...?" the deep voice asked hoarsely.

"The baby is fine. From the scans, it looks like the baby is a female," the soft voice said patiently.

Gracie sighed as she let the voices wash over her. She was safe. She would wake up in a few minutes, but not yet. She was just too tired. She let a small smile curve her lips. *We are having a little girl.* Gracie thought as she let a more peaceful sleep overtake her.

* * *

Gracie turned toward the warmth tugging at her. She arched closer to it as a wave of heat washed through her. It felt so good. Gracie felt a small moan escape her throat as the delicious warmth stopped. Her hands came out searching to pull it back.

"Open your eyes and I will continue." Kordon's hot breath brushed seductively across her swollen nipple.

"If I open my eyes you better be prepared to do more than that," Gracie whispered.

Kordon looked up, watching as Gracie's delicate eyelashes fluttered for a moment before finally opening. "Hi," Gracie whispered with a small smile.

"Hello, little warrior," Kordon whispered back tenderly. "You caused those feelings again, the ones I don't like."

Gracie giggled, then held her stomach. "I've got to go the bathroom," she whispered again with a grimace.

Kordon chuckled and rolled over before sitting up. "Go, but expect company in a few minutes."

Gracie nodded as she sat up and slid off the bed. She immediately recognized they were on the *Conqueror* from the décor. She moved to the bathroom and quickly used it. Gracie brushed her teeth, then scrunched up her nose as she noticed the fading bruise on her cheek and her tangled hair.

"I look like a wild woman," she muttered quietly under her breath with distaste.

"I happen to think you look beautiful as a wild woman," Kordon said, coming up behind her and wrapping his arms tightly around her.

"How long have I been out?" Gracie asked, looking at the shadows under Kordon's eyes.

"Almost forty-eight hours," Kordon replied as he unhooked and pulled the gown off Gracie's shoulders.

"I was tired," Gracie said not wanting to remember what lead to her passing out. Blood, guts, and pregnancy did not mix.

"That is what Toolas kept telling me. We are having a little girl," Kordon said as he let his hand rest on the swell of Gracie's belly.

"I know. I heard, sort of," Gracie responded softly covering Kordon's hands with her own. Gracie turned in Kordon's arms and pressed her lips to his. "I was scared," Gracie said in a small voice.

"I was too," Kordon admitted reluctantly. "Things will be different once we are home. I have tightened security. I will never take the chance of you being taken again."

Gracie nodded. She didn't want to argue right now. She wanted to know she was alive and safe. She pulled out of Kordon's arms and turned on the bathing stall. Gracie gave Kordon an inviting smile as she slowly began removing his clothes. She let her lips follow the patterns on his skin as she pulled the material away from him.

"I missed you," she whispered against his skin.

Kordon groaned as he felt his cock beginning to swell. "I'm going to love you, Gracie… long, hard, and fiercely." He began rocking against her hand as she undid the front of his pants.

"I love it when you talk dirty," Gracie hummed against his skin.

Kordon pulled away from Gracie long enough to pull his pants off the rest of the way. Pulling her into his arms, he stepped under the spraying mist. He turned her to face the back of the stall. Pulling her arms up, he held them there for a moment while he rubbed his swollen cock along the crack of her ass.

Both of them groaned loudly when she pushed back against him.

"Stay like that," Kordon said hoarsely.

Gracie let her head fall forward as she felt Kordon's rough hands moving over her body. She could feel the slick glide of the cleansing foam as he touched every inch of her. It took everything in her to keep from begging him to stop and just fuck her. She could sense he needed to touch her and make sure every inch of her was okay.

Kordon's hands trembled slightly as he touched Gracie. He let them, and his eyes, touch every part of her. He washed her hair that was now hanging below her shoulder blades, rinsing it carefully before letting it fall over her left shoulder.

His fingers hesitated at the slight puckering scar from her wound aboard the Alluthan mother ship before he continued down her body. His hands paused again at the slight scar on her leg. He gently raised one foot and washed it before he did the same to the other. As he moved back up he let his fingers slide between the delicate line of her cheeks to touch the dark pucker of her anus. He heard Gracie's soft gasp before she relaxed. She was letting him know she trusted him unconditionally.

He continued working his way back up before he turned her around gently and told her to continue to remain still. Gracie looked into his deep, dark blue eyes and nodded. Kordon paid the same intense attention to Gracie's front as he did her back.

He gently kissed the fading bruise on her cheek before moving further down. Gracie cried out when he flicked each of her nipples before drawing them into his mouth briefly. It was just long enough to make them peak and become extremely sensitive. Gracie's eyes grew heavy as she watched him kneel in front of her.

"Our daughter," Kordon breathed out quietly as he cupped the growing swell between his large palms. "I hope she is just like you."

Gracie chuckled. "You may be regretting that wish," she teased lightly.

Kordon shook his head and pressed a kiss to her stomach. Gracie felt the slight flutter of movement as if their daughter was responding to her daddy's touch. Gracie's breath caught in a shuddering gasp as Kordon ran his fingers across her slick folds. Now, they were definitely getting somewhere, Gracie thought, panting.

"More," Gracie moaned in a low hoarse voice. "Please!"

Kordon spread the folds of Gracie's labia and buried his mouth in her sweet mound. Gracie threw her head back and grabbed his shoulders, spreading her legs further. Kordon groaned loudly when Gracie let one of her legs slide up and over his shoulder while she gripped his head tightly.

Kordon sucked and pulled on the swollen nub of Gracie's clit, loving her cries for more. He let his teeth scrape against her before burying two of his thick fingers deeply into her hot channel. He pumped in and out in time with her hips. He felt her trembling increase as her climax built to such a level that when it burst from her, she screamed. He continued to drink from her until she melted against him.

"Please…" Gracie sobbed out.

Kordon rose up, pressing a kiss that tasted like both of them against Gracie's lips. He pulled away from her long enough to wash. Commanding the mist to shut off, he swept Gracie into his arms, ignoring the towels. He was too far gone to stop.

Gracie moaned when she felt the soft sheets under her. Her legs parted automatically as Kordon lowered her down to the mattress. He rose up over her long enough to grip his throbbing cock and press it against her still-pulsing core.

With one swift push, Kordon buried himself as far as he could go inside Gracie. He felt the first band on his cock swell immediately, locking them together. Gracie came up off the mattress with a cry as she felt the ridges along the tip of his cock move along her still-pulsing vagina.

"Oh, oh, oh!" Gracie cried out as another orgasm caught her by surprise.

"Oh, Gracie," Kordon groaned out loudly as he felt her milking his cock, begging for him to come.

Kordon gritted his teeth tightly together and began moving slowly as the bands swelled and rubbed inside her. He picked up speed as Gracie began moving with him frantically. The muscles in his neck stood out as the first band released in an explosion of hot, pulsing waves.

Kordon's arms trembled from the force as his body refused to stop. He continued pumping deeply into Gracie even as waves of pleasure/pain built inside him as the next band swelled. His loud cry filled their living quarters as it expanded, then pulsed out in jets of hot come.

Gracie raised her legs up to wind them around Kordon's waist. The movement forced his cock deeper into her, and she shuddered as the bands on his cock adjusted to the new position, holding them together tightly.

She let the waves of pleasure and love flow through her like hot lava erupting from a long-dormant volcano. Wave after wave of pleasure built, then released as Kordon muttered words of love and need to her. He promised she would never have to be afraid again. He swore he would never let anyone take her away from him. He vowed he would always love her.

Gracie wrapped her arms around Kordon's shuddering body, whispering her own promises of love as he held her tightly against him. It was a long time later before the bands relaxed enough so he could have pulled out of her, but he didn't. He never wanted to be separated from her again. That was his last thought before exhaustion finally overcame him.

* * *

Ten days later, they were back on Zion. Gracie found out Kordon had grabbed her and spirited her away while Krac and Rorrak worked together to defeat the assassin. She didn't hear much about the fight, but she didn't really care. It was over. Proctor was dead, as were the men he'd hired.

Gracie received a formal invitation from Earth to visit, as well as an apology for the problems caused by Proctor. Gracie declined the first and thanked them for the second. She was quite happy to remain a distant relation.

Krac disappeared shortly after the assassin was killed, but he did send Gracie a message that if she ever got tired of Kordon to look him up. Kordon promptly swore he was going to kill the bastard. It took several hours of lovemaking to convince Kordon that it wasn't necessary.

Now, Gracie smiled at Helin and Josef as they came forward to give her a hug. Gracie ignored the twenty-plus warriors prowling the outside of their home. She would let Kordon have his way for a few months before she gently weaned him off being overprotective of her.

Cora and Bazteen were also present, much to her husband's dismay. They had completed the "claiming" ceremony aboard the *Conqueror*. Kordon refused to wait any longer. Quan and Mohan met up with them the day before, so Mohan could be Gracie's "maid-of-honor."

"I can't believe he could not wait one more day before claiming you," Cora said as she wrapped her arm around Gracie's waist.

Gracie giggled as Cora threw an irritated glance at her eldest son. "You need to take better care of her," she growled at him.

"I will, *Madue*," Kordon promised as he followed them into his and Gracie's home.

"Good. I expect to be there when your daughter is born. I have always wanted a girl to spoil," Cora said brightly.

Kordon and his father simply shook their heads. "We are already in trouble. She is pestering your brothers now to bring her more daughters," Bazteen muttered under his breath. "Your brothers are blaming you for that."

Kordon looked over at the glowing face of his mate and smiled tenderly. She and his mother were talking about what the baby was going to need. He watched them for several minutes before responding to his father's comment.

"They can blame me all they want. They are just jealous. Have you ever seen a more beautiful warrior in your life?" Kordon asked his father.

Bazteen was looking at the glowing face of his mate as she tenderly pushed back a strand of hair from Gracie's face. "No, I don't think I ever have," he said, smiling as Cora looked up at him with bright eyes.

Epilogue

"No!" the little voice said stubbornly.

"Violet Coraleen Jefe!" the deep voice growled menacingly. "You come out of there right now.

"*No!*" Violet said as her lower lip began to tremble.

"Don't cry. Please don't cry," Kordon begged as his gut twisted.

A loud sob filled the air as two-year-old Violet burst into tears at her father's stern tone. Her short strawberry blonde curls bounced as she wailed as if her little heart was broken.

"Kordon!" Two female voices called out at the same time.

"Come on, Violet. You are going to get daddy into trouble with both Mommy and *Grand-Madue*," Kordon begged his sobbing daughter. "You can wear your pants. I promise."

The dark green eyes of his mate stared up at him in a younger version, but it was still enough to make him catch his breath. "No dress? I don't like dresses!" Violet sniffed suspiciously.

"No dresses, I promise," Kordon promised in resignation.

Violet looked at her dad for a moment more before crawling out from under the table. She lifted her arms up for Kordon to pick her up. The minute his strong arms came around her, Violet wrapped her tiny arms as far as she could around his neck and gave him a big kiss on the lips.

"I love you, Daddy," Violet whispered, looking up at him as if he was her hero.

Kordon felt the familiar lump in his throat every time he held his tiny daughter. She was so much like his petite mate, he had to hold back a groan. She had him wrapped around her tiny fingers as well.

"Let's get you dressed so we can go get your baby brother," Kordon said, carrying his very naked two-year-old daughter toward the stairs.

Cora and Gracie were standing at the bottom of the steps. Cora had her arm around a very pregnant Gracie, helping her make the last one, when Gracie suddenly stopped and grimaced. Gracie looked down in resignation before looking at Cora, then turning to look at Kordon.

"Kordon, can you give Violet to your mom? I need help getting back upstairs," Gracie said as she felt the warm liquid flowing down her leg.

"But I thought you said the baby was coming? We have to get you to the..." Kordon's eyes widened as he saw the liquid pooling under Gracie.

"The baby is coming." Gracie panted. "Right now."

Kordon swayed for a moment before he thrust Violet into his mother's arms and swept Gracie up into his. He took the steps two at a time, shouldering open the door to their room. He quickly laid Gracie down on the covers, ignoring her when she cried out for something to protect the mattress. Reaching up under the dress she was wearing, he ripped her panties off just as she groaned out loud. He was glad she had listened to him for once when he had suggested she wear a dress to the hospital, since it was easier to get on and off.

"He's coming." Gracie moaned again as she clenched her teeth together to keep from screaming.

"Breathe, Gracie," Cora said gently as she brushed Gracie's hair back. "Bazteen has Violet. She is showing him what she wants to wear."

Kordon's hands shook as he saw the head of his son emerge as Gracie cried out loudly. Supporting the tiny head in the palm of his hand, he waited for the next contraction. When Gracie pushed down hard again, Kordon caught his tiny son in his hands.

Helin, who had entered the room moments earlier, quickly took the babe from his father and began cleaning his tiny nose and mouth. After a moment, a loud cry filled the air.

"Take him to her. I'll finish up here," Helin said gently, pushing the now-swaddled infant and his father toward the head of the bed.

Kordon stared in stunned disbelief at the tiny body in his hands. Everything happened so fast, he'd just reacted. He looked up at Gracie, who was staring at him with tears in her eyes. He could hear Helin in the background softly telling Gracie to push again to clear the afterbirth, and his mother getting clean linen out and the items needed to clean Gracie up. But all he had eyes for was his mate.

"You have given me so much," Kordon whispered.

Gracie held her arms out as Kordon leaned down and placed their son against her breast. Gracie bared a nipple and rubbed it gently against his tiny mouth until he latched onto it.

Leaning back, exhausted, she reached out a hand to touch Kordon's cheek, brushing her thumb across it gently. Kordon could feel the cooler air against the damp skin. He reached up and touched his cheek. It was slightly damp from his tears.

"You are the one who has given me everything I've ever wanted," Gracie said.

Kordon reached up and pressed Gracie's hand tightly against his skin. "You reached out and touched me, Gracie. The first time I heard your voice calling out to anyone who could hear you. It was Gracie's Touch that gave me the love and hope I needed," Kordon whispered brokenly. "I love you, Gracie Jones-Jefe."

Gracie smiled as she brought Kordon's hand to her breast where their tiny son nursed. "This is Gracie saying, Thank you, Murphy, for being in my life."

* * *

If you loved this story by me (S. E. Smith) please leave a review. You can also take a look at additional books and sign up for my newsletter at http://sesmithfl.com to hear about my latest releases or keep in touch using the following links:

Website: http://sesmithfl.com
Newsletter: http://sesmithfl.com/?s=newsletter
Facebook: https://www.facebook.com/se.smith.5
Twitter: https://twitter.com/sesmithfl
Pinterest: http://www.pinterest.com/sesmithfl/
Blog: http://sesmithfl.com/blog/
Forum: http://www.sesmithromance.com/forum/

Additional Books by S. E. Smith
Paranormal and Science Fiction short stories and novellas

For the Love of Tia (Dragon Lords of Valdier Book 4.1)

A Dragonlings' Easter (Dragonlings of Valdier Book 1)

A Warrior's Heart (Marastin Dow Warriors Book 1.1)

Rescuing Mattie (Lords of Kassis: Book 3.1)

Science Fiction/Paranormal Novels

<u>Cosmos' Gateway Series</u>
Tink's Neverland (Cosmo's Gateway: Book 1)
Hannah's Warrior (Cosmos' Gateway: Book 2)
Tansy's Titan (Cosmos' Gateway: Book 3)
Cosmos' Promise (Cosmos' Gateway: Book 4)
<u>Curizan Warrior</u>
Ha'ven's Song (Curizan Warrior: Book 1)
<u>Dragon Lords of Valdier</u>

Abducting Abby (Dragon Lords of Valdier: Book 1)
Capturing Cara (Dragon Lords of Valdier: Book 2)
Tracking Trisha (Dragon Lords of Valdier: Book 3)
Ambushing Ariel (Dragon Lords of Valdier: Book 4)
Cornering Carmen (Dragon Lords of Valdier: Book 5)
Paul's Pursuit (Dragon Lords of Valdier: Book 6)
Twin Dragons (Dragon Lords of Valdier: Book 7)
Lords of Kassis Series
River's Run (Lords of Kassis: Book 1)
Star's Storm (Lords of Kassis: Book 2)
Jo's Journey (Lords of Kassis: Book 3)
Magic, New Mexico Series
Touch of Frost (Magic, New Mexico Book 1)
Sarafin Warriors
Choosing Riley (Sarafin Warriors: Book 1)
The Alliance Series
Hunter's Claim (The Alliance: Book 1)
Razor's Traitorous Heart (The Alliance: Book 2)
Zion Warriors Series
Gracie's Touch (Zion Warriors: Book 1)
Krac's Firebrand (Zion Warriors: Book 2)
Paranormal and Time Travel Novels
Spirit Pass Series
Indiana Wild (Spirit Pass: Book 1)
Heaven Sent Series
Lily's Cowboys (Heaven Sent: Book 1)
Touching Rune (Heaven Sent: Book 2)

Excerpts of S. E. Smith Books

If you would like to read more S. E. Smith stories, she recommends <u>Abducting Abby</u>, the first in her Dragon Lords of Valdier Series

Or if you prefer a Paranormal or Time Travel with a twist, you can check out <u>Lily's Cowboys</u> or <u>Indiana Wild</u>...

About S. E. Smith

S. E. Smith is a *New York Times*, **USA TODAY** and **#1 International Amazon** Bestselling author who has always been a romantic and a dreamer. An avid writer, she has spent years writing, although it has usually been technical papers for college. Now, she spends her days and weekends writing and her nights dreaming up new stories. An affirmed "geek," she spends her days working on computers and other peripherals. She enjoys camping and traveling when she is not out on a date with her favorite romantic guy.

CPSIA information can be obtained at www.ICGtesting.com
Printed in the USA
LVOW01s2029070415

433627LV00033B/1534/P

9 781481 890854